I Played the Smart Pig

Smart Pig

A half-true made-up novel

MANDY GOODWIN

Copyright © 2021 by Mandy Goodwin

This paperback edition July 2021

ISBN: 978-1-8380759-9-6

For Marni Gittinger, who loved books
more than anyone I knew and dedicated
her soul to sharing that love of reading.

And for my Mom, Gloria Taylor, my heart and my hero,
who was one of the most resilient, determined
people, and to whom I owe this all.

CONTENTS

Prologue   1

1   Kittridge Street   4

2   Orange Pill   12

3   Rat Fink   23

4   Flat Tire   37

5   Principal's Office   47

6   Jewish Funerals   56

7   Audrey Friedman   67

8   Ford Mustang   78

9   Spider's Web   90

10 Leo Carrillo   103

11 Pool Party   111

12 Chatty Cathy   125

13 Common Sense   136

14   Haunted House   142

15   Yellow Canary   152

16   Henry Monowski   164

17   Orange Groves   173

18   Yellow Jacket   181

19   Oak Street   192

20   Wedding Cake   204

21   Back Seat   213

22   Broadmoor Drive   228

     Acknowledgements   239

     About the Author   240

Neglect creates mental maps used by children, and their adult selves, to survive. These maps skew their view of themselves and the world.

Bessel van der Kolk

AUDREY'S MAP

I've lived on four streets in three years.

PROLOGUE

T opa Topa. That's a Native American word for 'gopher gopher,' which are really cute little animals that like to dig holes and ruin golf courses and my neighbor's front lawn. I live on a golf course in Seattle now. Our back yard goes out onto the twelfth fairway, which looks like a big park; I play on it until the golfers come up to tee off and wave their big clubs at me like cavemen, yelling at me to "Get out of our way, kid! It's not a playground!" I get out of the way because I don't want them to yell at me some more. When they pass, playing through, I go back on because it's kind of like a playground.

In third grade, before my mom remarried and we moved to Seattle, I went to Topa Topa Elementary; that was in Ojai, which sounds like "Oh Hi" and means moon in Chumash. Chumash Indians lived on my street a long time ago, in tepees, and named everything, I guess, in the language they speak – which is called Chumash, like I said. I learned that in the World Book Encyclopedia under the O one for Ojai. We have all of them from A to Z. You can learn just about anything from the World Book Encyclopedia. If you don't know how to read, you can just look at the pictures. I do that sometimes. I don't read anything and just look at all of the pictures. The one with the human body is really neato. You can see all the

1

organs, and they have this plastic paper that you can see through; you put one page on top of the other and see the whole picture of the human body and its organs. All the organs look tangled, like a bowl of spaghetti with meat sauce.

I loved my third-grade teacher, Mrs. Rolston. She was nice, and even though we lived in California, she had an Oklahoma twang. That's what she called it anyway. She had dark, short hair that looked like scribbles, pretty blue eyes, and when she wasn't at school, she wore capris on her front porch. She lived around the corner from our tiny house on Grand Avenue, on the way up to Topa Topa, and she'd let us stop by on the weekends if we wanted to. We'd sit on her porch, and she'd give us lemonade when it was hot and ask us about our day. She said she didn't quiz us on her porch because "The weekend is for a chiiiild's imagination." I tried to imagine all sorts of things; mostly, they were nice things because my mind needed a rest.

In school, we would act out stories and build sets for our plays. We did *The Three Little Pigs*. I was one of the little pigs. I played the smart pig who had a house made out of brick. The house was actually a big cardboard box that an Amana refrigerator came in. I cut some windows and a little door in it. I painted brick and shutters on each side of the windows and even added grass to add to the hominess. When the wolf showed up and was huffing and puffing and threatening to blow my house down, I stuck my head out the window and told the wolf to go away. "Hey, big bad wolf . . . cut out!" That's what I said. It works when my mean big brother Ned says it to me. My best friend in the third grade, Grant, was playing the wolf, and I didn't really want him to beat it (only in the play). I told him that after the brick house scene so his feelings wouldn't be hurt.

Mrs. Rolston knew that I wanted to be an actress when I grew up; once, in little pig rehearsal, she told me, "Audrey, you have endowed your little pig with *verrrrrve* and I felt the . . . the . . . *urrrrrgency* of the matter and knew you felt the wolf meant business and he *could* blow things down." Verve is spunk. I have it even when I'm not playing a little pig.

My mom started doing a play at the Ojai Theatre when we first moved to Grand Avenue. The play was called *Who's Afraid of Virginia Woolf?* It wasn't about three little pigs, but about grown-ups that fight and say mean things to each other. Kind of like my mom and dad did. I'd go with her to rehearsals and watch from the peanut gallery. When I'd watch her from up there, it was like she was a movie star; she made me happy, and I admired her, and wanted to be her friend. She did a good job, acting. I would help her at home by directing her acting when her acting needed it, and she listened to me – except, she'd always skip the part with the bad words. One time at rehearsal in the theater, she forgot a few of her lines, and I told her what they were. I didn't look at the book. I had memorized them. Actually, I knew everyone's lines. I'd gone to so many rehearsals that I'd tell any actor who forgot what to say: "You say this, then you say this, then you say this."

One time, I recited a whole page and even said the bad words. I was scared my mom might be mad that I did that, blurting out the whole scene. But she wasn't. She looked proud. "Those are Albee's words, not my kid's." She smiled. Albee's the guy who wrote all the bad words and stuff that my mom didn't get mad about because I didn't write them. Albee did. One of the actors joked that if someone got sick, I could take over playing the part. I think I would have been too small to really do that. They would have had to put elevator boots on me, like gigantic Herman Munster on TV, or stilts, so I could look like a grown-up. I wasn't sure I wanted to do that. I wasn't ready to play a grown-up. I was only eight, and being a grown-up looks complicated.

As you're about to see, being a kid is complicated too . . . sometimes.

1 KITTRIDGE STREET

I HAVE TWO THUMBS FOR HITCH-HIKING AND MY MAP I DREW FROM memory in case my mom decides she doesn't like her husband and I have to remember how to get back to where I came from. My dad's still there, where I used to live. So is Mrs. Rolston and a boy named Parker – who was my best friend. A lot of bad stuff happened there, so I'm trying to leave it all behind. It's hard. I can't forget it, but I probably shouldn't talk about it 'cuz it's mostly secrets. It's the sort of stuff that you can get in big trouble for, even if you're just a kid and were minding your own business – like someone bumping into you and saying, "Hey, kid, watch where you're going!" and you didn't ask for it.

I practiced the other day reading aloud to my mom from a book she had sitting on her nightstand next to her alarm clock. My mom likes me to work on my vocabulary and spelling. When I was four, I told her I wanted to be an actress. She says actresses need to know vocabulary and spelling. She also says I like to talk a lot so I should have something to say, and I will appreciate it when I grow up. She says reading helps with that. I didn't want to go to my room and grab a book, so I read from hers. *"My innocence wasn't mine, yet, a free-for-all by others who used it for their own purpose, selfishly plundering my sense of worthiness at a very young age through their acts of betrayal; all by people I trusted, leaving me in a quiet state of anxiety and with an uncharted life ahead to try to make sense of the chaos of other people's lives, as I tried to hang onto the parts of me that didn't fit anymore, as if a picture that was never disturbed in the first place."*

I got stuck on a few big words, but my mom helped me sound them out. Some words I didn't understand, and she explained them to me. I still think a lot about what I read out loud that day. I understood a lot of it. All the words together felt like the person writing it was talking about me, like I was a broken toy or missing pieces. *I tried to hang on to the parts of me that didn't fit anymore.* It was like the writer had climbed inside of my brain and lifted my thoughts right out without me knowing. Because that stuff happened to me.

Three years earlier, Hocus pocus, abracadabra, and deja-vu all scrambled my brain in the driveway of Parker's house in 1966, where his dad's 1964 Mustang took up half the driveway. Parker was one year older than I was; seven years old, his birthday twenty-eight days before mine, he was the youngest of four boys and was three inches taller than me, back then, even with his freshly buzzed crew cut. *Peach fuzz,* I'd say as I'd quickly steal a scrub with my hand across his head. That's what I liked to call his hair after his dad took the dog clippers to it; it made him so mad when I said it. I knew how to push his buttons. I practice daily on my mean big brother, Ned, and I've gotten pretty good at teasing back – copying what they did to me.

Aunt Ru tells me that bugging my bigger brother and being a pain in the neck is "part of the territory" apparently, being the youngest. My dad did it to my Aunt Ru when they were kids. One time, he pushed her so far with teasing, she chased him around the dinner table with a knife. My dad thought it was funny. Sometimes, I think it's funny seeing Mean Ned get so steamed. I like to watch him turn red; it's neat to see a person changing colors. I guess it IS part of the territory.

I'm the baby of my family, nearly nine years younger than my mean brother. I once shared a room with my big sister, Shelly, when she turned fifteen years old, before she went away to some place I like to forget the name of. She was not happy that I shared a bed with her because sometimes I'd wet it. I'm not sure why I did. I stopped wearing diapers at one year old. I hated being wet. That's what my dad told me. I'd drop my diapers in the middle of the floor, and I learned how to potty in a regular toilet before I could speak two words at once. But Shelly wouldn't get mad at me. She'd let me move to her side of the bed and stack up against her, pulling me even closer so I wouldn't be sleeping in the pool of pee I made by accident. Shelly could be so gentle and understanding that way. She didn't make me feel ashamed. She made me feel safe.

Shelly shared a room with Lana, my biggest sister, who was a senior in high school back on Kittridge Street, until Lana wanted her own room to have her dance parties in. She stole my room which had orange walls that helped me sleep; it had a window that looked out on the back patio at the tree surrounded by gravel I'd play army men in – losing a few of the green infantry in the grass. She and her friends would shut themselves in her room, like a private tree house club, listening to rock and roll music; they'd comb their hair in the opposite direction than you're supposed to – into big rat nests that Shelly's pet rat, Ringo, would be afraid to live in. They'd use enough hairspray to kill a gazillion mosquitos, plastering their locks high like a beehive; that's what they called their hairdo – a beehive. Really, it looked more like brown or black or blond cotton candy piled on their heads. I've seen a beehive at Ma and Shorty's house. They have little square-like holes in them called honeycombs that aren't combs at all. There were no bees in their hair either. So, it was a dopey name for what they were doing. What I found peculiar about my sister and her friends was that they would put makeup on their lips called concealer that was the color of their face and that made them look like they had been in the pool too long. Once, I told Lana that I couldn't see her lips. "It's the scene, Audrey. You're too young to know," she snapped. I wasn't too young to know that it didn't look bitchin'. They looked like waterlogged, teased up weirdos, with flesh-colored lips.

We lived in Canoga Park, four blocks from the local Market Basket, off of De Soto Avenue, where Fruit Loop cereal, Bosco chocolate syrup, and Scooter Pies lived on the shelves in large groups waiting to be chosen and taken home to be devoured. If you have never had a scooter pie, well, they were out of sight. Marshmallows smashed between two delicious, mouthwatering cookies, dipped in either chocolate, vanilla, or strawberry. The box looked like the size of a Ritz cracker box. I made sure not to get them confused because they certainly did not taste the same.

Canoga Park was heaven. "Suburbia," they called it – a growing city with houses being built at warp speed as fast as the forty-five record spins when you put it on seventy-eight. The farmhouses and orange groves that we drove past in the northern valley, Van Nuys and Reseda were disappearing like ghosts hit by a flashlight. Erector set houses with ivy, lawns and pink cinder block walls were built between each home like a castle, and we would use them as our freeway, scaling the wall to go from one block to the next without having to go around.

The Valley was a wonderland with kids ruling the asphalt streets, playing until the bell rang for dinner, and ending up at a neighbor's house with tater tots and fish sticks heaping your plate – and a full glass of Coca Cola (which tasted better than milk). It didn't matter whose table you sat at; we were like extended family and looked out for one another.

El Torito, in Woodland Hills, came in first as my favorite restaurant, until it was replaced by a new place in Tarzana called McDonald's. McDonald's is a small restaurant located on the south side of Ventura Blvd that has no indoor tables but a window you order at (like frosty freeze), with its outside covered in white square tiles and tables that sit under big yellow arches. They're called the 'Golden Arches', even though they're plastic and yellow and should be at the entrance of the People Mover at Disneyland. This little restaurant the size of my sister's room makes food super-fast – as speedy as a genie blinking. *Poof!* A burger appears in a little white wrapper faster than a go-cart can leave the driveway. The food was the best I had ever tasted. That's before I had a burger and fries at the Mighty Bite. Now, that's my favorite, soon to be replaced by the tennis club's snack bar burger, which I'll get to soon enough. I can still eat a million filet-O-fish until the sea is empty and my stomach is full.

A five-minute car ride, not far from our house, they built a big mall called Topanga Plaza. A mall is a place that has stores indoors and big parking lots. It's neato. It has an ice-skating rink that we'd go to all year round. I love to ice skate. In the middle of the mall are these string things resembling wires or thick ropes that go from the ceiling to the floor with water that slowly drips down the wires. They call it a rain fountain, but, to me, it looked more like oil creeping down. It glowed like the light from the Enterprise spaceship beaming someone up; I could watch it for hours.

It was summer – and hot! The thermometer reaching almost one hundred degrees, with no breeze, and the heat covering the valley like a baby-blue electric blanket warming us up to sweaty uncomfortableness. You couldn't kick it off. There was no playing hide and seek from the sun. You had to beat it at its own game. Parker's house had a big pool in the back yard that we lived in as if we were fishes in an aquarium, and they had an even bigger front yard for slip and slide. Just the ticket to beat the heat when our dads were at work and there was nothing good on TV. Sometimes when my mom or dad wouldn't let me change the channel, I watched Walter Cronkite talking about the Vietnam War across the ocean, which was exploding like a blender with no top; army men with sticks and leaves coming out of their helmets were setting people's houses on fire with a cigarette lighter. I saw it with my own two eyes. None of the army men on tv were from Kittridge street, though. That made me feel better that our house wouldn't be next.

The set up for slip and slide was everything – childhood engineering at its finest. It needed to be top quality, like when we'd put Parker's match car racetrack together and have to balance it just right so the cars wouldn't get stuck and stop. We searched the lawn for the perfect sliding spot that had just enough of a hill to not stop us mid skid. Sliding style showed whether you were chicken or not. You didn't want to look like a bozo, gliding across the plastic water lane. You wanted to look boss. It took a lot of practice, but, by midsummer, we were fab slip and sliders. And this year would be no different; we took the time to study the lawn, as if we were Arnold Palmer finding the curve in the grass. Mostly, the hose had to reach. It took water power to fuel the fun and keep us cool.

Gabriel, their gardener, had just finished cutting the grass. This wasn't always the best idea for rolling out slip and slide because there wasn't as much cush for your tush from the grass being longer when running and making your approach. Sometimes, you'd hurt your butt or tummy, depending on what glide style you were going to attempt or if you hit the slide at all. That could happen on occasion. Sometimes, you'd slide off into the grass, wiping out. After a while of wipeouts, we soon figured out that a freshly-cut lawn made for a faster glide and we could squeeze in more, which was the purpose of wasting a bazillion gallons of water on hot summer days in the middle of suburbia – and way more fun than running through the sprinkler.

Parker and I were getting the slip and slide box out of his garage when I heard the scream. I walked to the driveway and saw Joanne Meets, who lived across the street from Parker, running to her car. She was sixteen and had just gotten her driver's license. Her brown hair was in a ponytail, and she was carrying her purse with suede tassels. As she approached her car that was parked on the street, I saw her stare across at Gabriel. He was like the lion I saw at the zoo who stared right at me, watching my every move, ready to pounce. She frantically fumbled, opening the car door of their Buick to get in. Then, she pushed the door lock down.

I remember Gabriel taking a step closer to the curb and smiling, his eyes still fixed on her like that lion. I watched as she put the shifter into gear and sped away; the tires squealed like a puppy yelping after being bitten too hard by its mean brother.

Gabriel shook his head and laughed. In his thick Mexican accent, I could hear him say, "Crazy girl." Then, he walked to his old car that looked like something from *Adam-12* that the bad guys drove. He opened the large trunk, finished putting the push mower and his rake in, and closed it with a thud. He walked to the car door, looked back at me staring at him, and spit on the ground. I think spitting is grody. I don't like spitting. Well, Gabriel climbed in his car and started the jalopy engine. It sounded like a tractor. He hit the gas and drove off. Something didn't feel right, like when the wind blows your hat off when you didn't expect it; it spooks you, and you try to grab it before it hits the pavement. I didn't understand. Did she see a bee? Did she have a rock in her shoe that hurt when she walked? Did Gabriel have a booger and it grossed her out?

I thought that Gabriel was a nice man. He would take Parker's brother, Steve, to Mexico. Sometimes, he would even stay for dinner, bringing tamales that his wife made. And he was a good gardener, knowing how to rake leaves and cut the grass just like Pam, Parker's mom, liked it. He certainly didn't know how to weed a perfect dichondra lawn like my dad, but every week he came and did his job, and that must have counted for something. It was a good reason to like Gabriel.

Listen, I'm just going to tell you right now so you are not wondering. I want you to know that Joanne didn't see a bee or a booger in Gabriel's nose. She didn't have a rock in her shoe either.

After Gabriel drove off and the stinky, grey smog from his tailpipe disappeared, I told Parker I needed to go home to get something. Really, I had to go number two, and I needed privacy. I'm like that. I cut out and headed back home, skipping down the sidewalk because it was faster than walking but easier than running – and wouldn't make me poop faster.

I skipped up the driveway past my dad's Thunderbird, and I could hear my mom's yelling coming from inside the house. I stopped skipping. I heard the front door unlatched and saw my sister, Shelly, coming through, slamming it. She stomped down the walkway and breezed right by me without saying anything, throwing her leather purse strap over her shoulder.

"Where are you going?" I yelled after.

"Far from here," she yelled back.

I turned toward the front door wondering what was on the other side; my brain wondering what I might be walking in to. Sometimes, my mom could get so angry that it was better to pretend you were the Invisible Man or Harvey or a leper. I'm not sure what would set her off. It just seemed like it came out of the blue, and her eyes would turn black and you knew she hated you. I can say "I hate you" to my mean brother or Parker, but I don't really mean it. I just have hurt feelings really. Maybe my mom didn't mean it either and had hurt feelings too.

I wasn't chancing it. I didn't want to make her madder. So, I made like a drum and beat it. I decided to poop at Parker's house.

When I came home a few hours later, my dad's clothes were laying on the front yard dichondra just outside the front door, looking like the yard had been TP'd by the Watkins Brothers (who were the neighborhood troublemakers).

I stopped in the driveway, in the middle, wondering if I should turn around and go back to Parker's. The front door flung open, and my mom stepped out onto the walkway. She spotted me on the driveway in my blue swim bottoms and no shoes, my hair still wet from swimming and slip and sliding.

"Where's Shelly? Did you see her?" my mom snapped.

"No. I was swimming at Parker's." I lied. I'd seen her in the driveway before, saying she was going far away.

"Get in this house."

Then, she looked over at the clothes on the lawn. "Your father should be home soon."

2 ORANGE PILL

S ECOND GRADE FELT LIKE A LIFE SENTENCE FOR A KID WHO WAS afraid to go home with a note from their teacher and to a mom who was unpredictable. I was told by Mrs. Travis that I was too hyperactive and needed to stay in my seat for the eighteenth time that day.

I don't think I'm hyperactive. I just think sometimes my mind is moving too fast, and I am trying to keep up like what my dad would do when he taught me to ride my bike when we lived on Kittridge Street; he would run alongside me as I weaved down the sidewalk, making sure I wouldn't crash into a tree. It was hard for him to keep up once I learned how to spin those pedals. Then one day, out of nowhere, I took off – like a speeding bullet, like Superman – leaving my dad in the dust in the middle of the sidewalk. I could hear his cheers and excitement growing fainter while I tasted freedom without training wheels.

I don't mean to be disruptive. It's a reflex – as weird as an eye twitch. That's just how my mind works. It travels at light speed, and, sometimes, I just can't focus or sit still because there is just so much going on. My restlessness came after that thing happened. That first thing, anyway – and the divorce. But that didn't change anyone's mind about how I felt about myself and the feelings I kept locked inside of me. It didn't change anything because when you're a kid everybody has a say over you except you.

Do you play twister? Well, you know how you get in that one position with your hand on green, your right foot on yellow, and your other foot on red? Basically, you look like a pretzel; it feels really uncomfortable, but that's what you spun, and there's nothing you can do about it because the other player you're playing with is all twisted up too. That's what I felt like back then after we moved to Los Angeles. Everything started to become like Twister – uncomfortable and unpredictable.

It all really started when we moved to the duplex on Detroit Street; we were in a new neighborhood and my mom made me take an orange pill every day because she said so. My mom and dad were getting the divorce, and they were still yelling and screaming – but on the phone – instead of at night when I went to bed.

I hated orange now because of that pill. My old bedroom walls were painted orange because I once liked the color and found it calming. Now, it was the color trying to take my spirit away. I once asked what the pill was for, and no one would tell me. "Why do I have to take this pill?" I asked. Silence. It was like the cat had everybody's tongue. It's an expression when you can't say anything because it's too hard to get your words out. I'm not sure why they use cats. I've never had my cat grab my tongue. Maybe they should say, "Monkey got your tongue?" – because Monkeys steal bananas.

One day, I visited my Aunt Ru and Uncle Sal's house in Culver City with my dad after he moved to his new apartment. Aunt Ru is my favorite aunt and she's my dad's sister. They live on a hill near a really busy street; it's like a freeway that has oil wells pumping on both sides, looking like dinosaurs in the distance – that I'm never to play on. Although, I have run across it a few times against my Aunt Ru waving her skinny finger at me and asking, "You wouldn't run across a freeway, would you?" Actually, I might have bolted across the 101 if Parker dared me and said he'd give me fifty cents.

I think my aunt was born with a smile on her face and with a funny sense of humor. She likes to buy my uncle stuff he doesn't need for his birthday because it's really for her. She's bought him a make-up mirror, a microwave oven, a bread maker, a blender, and a set of pots and pans – and he doesn't even cook. He doesn't mind though. Uncle Sal is an easy-going kind of cool cat who doesn't raise his voice, even if he's mad; he just likes to see my aunt happy, he says. I told her she should get him an ice cream maker for his next birthday because she could make ice cream in every flavor like *Basket and Robertson*, and she wouldn't have to buy any in the store. "Good idea, girlfriend," she told me. I didn't think it was a good idea as much as I thought it was a tasty one.

A while back, we were sitting in their kitchen at the round, white table that had coffee stains on it, and I was eating ice cream like I always did. Aunt Ru got my favorite mint chocolate chip. After my second bowl, she put it away and said I couldn't have any more. She knows kids can keep eating ice cream like dogs can keep eating dog food if you don't put it up and away. She sat down at the table, lit a cancer stick (she always has one in her hand), and exhaled the smoke – which was really thick; it was as if it were coming out of the exhaust pipe of a car with a bad engine. She's skinny, with short, permed hair and a small nose. My dad said her nose was once just as big as his but some doctor fixed it and made it more little, like a walnut.

My aunt was always inquisitive about my school (still is), asking if I was lonely, or making friends, and how I was doing since my dad moved out. I liked her interest because no one would ever ask me those questions and she *really* wanted to know the answer to how I was feeling. If my mom and dad did ask me a question during the divorce and I told them the answer, their attention would float in another world, like when you're in a pool on your back and your ears are in the water and someone asks you if you're hungry or tells you to get out of the water because you look like a prune and everything sounds muffled and you say "What? I can't hear you." My Aunt Ru makes me feel seen and heard instead of seen and not heard, which children were supposed to be.

"So, tell me what you're up to?"

"Four foot three," I teased.

"How's your new school? Have you made any friends?"

"Yes. I have some friends on my street and in Bluebirds."

"Oh, how lovely. You're in Bluebirds. Isn't that fun," she said.

I was a proud Bluebird. I wanted to be a Camp Fire Girl. They said I had to wait until I was bigger. The weird thing about the Bluebirds was our jumpers were blue and *orange*. Why? We were bluebirds. Bluebirds don't have orange. We wore blue caps with white socks that had little bluebirds on them. My pin was a bluebird too. I loved the bluebirds.

"Do you see your old friends?" my uncle asked me. When we moved to Los Angeles on my seventh birthday, I still went to first grade at Fulbright in Canoga Park, until I finished. Then, after summer, I started second grade at Third Street Elementary on June Street.

"I still see my best friend, Parker, in my old neighborhood."

"We saw him last weekend, right?" my dad reminded.

"Yep." I went quiet for a minute. Thinking back, I didn't want to leave his house but stay there forever. The pictures of a happy life on Kittridge Street played in my mind like a silent movie. Moving from my old house, my neighborhood, and my friends made a hole inside of me. Being back on Kittridge Street, I saw all the kids still living with their families doing the same things. I wanted that back. I felt like one of those hippies that were drafted to Vietnam; they protested in a hippie parade because they thought it was wrong to be taken away from other hippies, and they held posters that said bad words or had boss peace signs scribbled on them. Some even stuck daisies in machine gun barrels that army men held outside of a hardware store. But I wasn't a hippie or old enough to protest. I didn't know how to stop the war.

My family had been bombed, like when Parker and I would take a pile of his army men, light a cherry bomb, and blow them all apart. Destruction of plastic arms and heads strewn all over the middle of the driveway, and we couldn't put them back together. It didn't matter. We had a whole bag of army men. Except, I only had one family. I couldn't talk about the hurt because it was too deep to understand, buried like a treasure chest never wanting to be found. Without even knowing where it could be buried, I had no 'Xplanation' to mark the spot. Opening a can of worms, when you weren't fishing, sounded like a messy business, and I wasn't prepared for what that would mean. I hadn't been in Bluebirds long enough to learn certain survival skills or how to deal with a can of worms.

"Have you made any new friends? It's important, you know," my uncle said as he took a puff on his cancer stick. He smoked too, like two chimneys at once that were the size of a smokestack at a coal mine.

"The Clampetts. They live across the street and down two houses. Their dad, Bob, makes the *Beany & Cecil* cartoon. You know that one?" I asked.

"Oh, sure," my uncle said.

"I met him. Bob told me I could come to the studio and see how they make the cartoon. You know what?"

"What?" My uncle smiled. I think he was really interested in my story.

"They have a drawing of Cecil on the bottom of their pool. Cecil likes the water, you know? So, it makes sense he's painted at the bottom of the pool. It's really neato," I told him.

Beany & Cecil was one of my favorite cartoons along with *The Flintstones*, which was my super-duper most favorite. Except, Fred and Barney didn't have a beanie and couldn't fly, so they used their bare feet to get their car around, which seemed like a lot of work. I liked Beany's beanie. It had a propellor on the top of it, and he could fly away anytime he wanted.

"That sounds exciting, Audrey. I'm glad you made some new friends on your street," my aunt said.

"Yep. I guess."

It wasn't the same, though. On Kittridge Street, I knew all the kids and could go to anybody's house for lunch or dinner. On Detroit Street, it was different. There weren't a lot of kids, and the only house I'd go to dinner at was Mrs. Porter's house; she babysat me after school because my mom worked near where my aunt and uncle lived.

Mrs. Porter was old like a mummy and lived in a brick duplex down the street, almost to the corner. She had a hunched back, shuffled as she walked, wore nude stockings that sagged at the ankles and knees, and always wore a sweater because her blood was cold. Her house smelled like burnt toast and still water that had been sitting for too long. I would go to her house after school, and she would make me sit in the living room in front of the TV without any lights on, watching *Dark Shadows*. It's a weird show about Vampires and people who argue; sometimes it's super scary, especially when a vampire is feeling hungry. They call it a soap opera, but there's no soap that I could see. It has a big staircase and a forest full of fog, which makes it hard to see anyone coming. There's this man named Barnabas, a vampire with sharp teeth like a lion who has ugly hair plastered to his head like Eddie Munster – and he would bite people! I didn't think a kid my age should have been watching that back then, but Mrs. Porter turned it on when she babysat me and left the room. I didn't move from my chair until it was time to go.

"Hey . . . can I ask you a question, Aunt Ru?"

"Sure, sugar. What's up?"

I wasn't sure I was supposed to ask, but I wasn't afraid of my Aunt Ru – like I was of my mom. She was small and thin, like a graham cracker, and she had a really big smile with big teeth that made her look happy. She never ever raised her voice at me or sent me to my room. My Aunt Ru gives me confidence, whatever that is. Maybe it's like common sense, which my mom told me about. I love it when my Aunt Ru strokes my face and calls me 'sugar', but her hand smells like cancer sticks. She smokes too much, always having a cigarette between her fingers, puffing away like a train.

Shelly would say it's boss to smoke. I smoked twice. The last time was on Kittridge Street when we found a cigar on Parker's front lawn and tried to smoke it. It was like trying to suck a marble through a garden hose. We gave up. The very first time I smoked, I was five with Parker and the Meets kids in their kitchen. We used to do all sorts of bad stuff when we would be at their house and their parents weren't home. Sometimes, it was confusing and didn't feel right, like little kids shouldn't be doing that. But Heidi would take me in her room and make me. She was eleven. She made me do stuff that I didn't think I should be doing and, to be honest, it made me scared. I got a feeling of a giant avocado pit in my stomach, if I swallowed one . . . which I wouldn't do. But that's what it felt like. I never told anyone. I never told anyone a lot of things that made me scared or that felt wrong.

Playing at the Meets' house always felt surprising, not knowing what exactly would happen that day. Kind of like a Cracker Jack's prize: you never knew what you were going to get. We'd smoke and do some other stuff we weren't supposed to – stuff that felt weird. One time, we tried to dig to China in their driveway. We only got up to my knees when realizing it might take longer than we thought and decided to go to Parker's house instead and swim.

As I was enjoying my ice cream (ready for thirds I'd never get), I somehow mustered up the courage to just spill it and ask my aunt why I had to take this pill that I didn't want to take; I said that I didn't know what it was and why I had to swallow it.

"It will help you, sugar," my aunt said.

"What is it? How will it help me?" I wondered. "Do other children have to swallow it?"

"She doesn't need to know, Ru," my dad said.

"Lee, don't keep it from her."

"Keep what?" I asked.

"Audrey, the reason you take that pill is because you have a hard time staying in your seat and it will help you," she sweetly said to me.

"No, it doesn't! I still get out of my seat! I hate that pill!"

"Ru," my dad interrupted, "now's not the time."

"Lee, I know how to handle this," she said to him. She was bigger than him, even though she was shorter. "This is what I do."

My aunt and uncle have a nursery school on Robertson Blvd, across from a school that has a playground. IT'S A CHILDREN'S LAND. That's what they call their school. I loved to go there and eat lunch and paint or make things out of Play-Doh. I loved the smell of Play-Doh. It smelled good enough to eat, but you weren't supposed to eat it (although I saw little kids do it).

Lula and Mildred work there. Lula is the cook and Mildred is the boss teacher. They're called black people, just like Edgar, who'd take me riding through the orange groves near Papino's Pizzeria out on the way to Santa Paula, when we lived in Ojai.

Mildred and Lula are my favorite people to visit at the school when I go. Lula wears thick glasses and always looks so happy to see me. Her eyes roll back in her head and flutter. All I can see are the whites of her eyes and her smile. "Ooo, child, it's so good to see your sweet face." That's what she says every time. Ever since we moved to Seattle, I don't see her as much, but she still tells me how happy she is to see me. I love her. I think she likes that I can be so helpful, too. Sometimes, when I ask, she lets me help her in the kitchen. She makes butter sandwiches on Wonder bread or hot dogs, and there is always Jell-O or some kind of pudding that she makes herself. It's all delicious. I'm the oldest kid there, but I don't mind. I find things to do. When it's nap time, I lay down on the floor with the little children and take a load off (I never actually napped, even when I was four). Mildred turns down the lights, and it's so quiet and peaceful; I feel safe.

Back when I was taking the orange pill, things were different.

"Don't keep things from her, Lee. You'd be surprised what children can understand," she told him.

"I'm not keeping things from her. You're wrong. She's too young to understand," he said.

"No, I'm not. I want to know, Daddy."

I did. I didn't like the secrets, because there were too many of them. If you want to know the truth, I'm keeping two big ones myself because I'm too scared to tell anyone.

My dad looked at my Aunt Ru. "Ok. If you think so, you can tell her," he said.

My Aunt Ru put out her cancer stick. The ashtray was full and stunk to high heaven. That's what my mom says when something really smells.

"Audrey, you know your mom and dad are getting a divorce, right?"

"Yes." I knew that. "My mom is going to get married again."

Out of the corner of my eye, I saw my dad lean back in his chair. I looked at him. He was pushing against the table like he was going to shove it against the wall. I saw his jaw tighten. I think it was a sore subject. I guess something happened when we lived on Kittridge Street. I heard Shelly and Lana whispering one day outside of the bathroom. It was after Lana got lost driving my mom's car home one Saturday. I asked them what they were whispering about. Lana told me I was too young to know about what they were saying. I said, "I already heard you say something about Mom's car, and a motel, and David's wife told on him. What does that mean? Is David's wife a rat fink?" They wouldn't tell me. But whatever it was, it changed everything. I know that. And we moved.

"How does that make you feel, your mom getting remarried?" she asked.

"Oh, Ru, what are you, a psychiatrist now?" my dad snapped at her.

"I did take child psychology at UCLA, Lee." She lit another cancer stick.

"What's that?" I asked.

"When they shrink your head," my dad said.

"Oh, Lee. Don't say things like that. Audrey . . . it's just someone who wants you to talk about your feelings."

"Aunt Ru, do you ever spank Bart or Stewart?" They were my big cousins who were in college up in Frisco, where the hippies liked to protest.

"Never. But we're not talking about your cousins. We're talking about you. How do you feel about your mom getting married to David?" she said to me again.

I didn't know how to answer. No one had ever asked me that question before.

20

"Beats me," I said. I didn't like talking about it because I didn't want to say something that would get me in trouble; I felt like running out the door right that minute, hoping no one could catch me.

"Well, we think you might be feeling bad about all of the changes and that little orange Ritalin pill will help you not feel so overwhelmed. Do you know what overwhelmed is?"

I thought a second.

"Sad?"

"Sometimes, when we're overwhelmed, we can feel sad too, girlfriend." She called me 'sugar' and 'girlfriend'. "But, mostly, we think it will help you focus in school and feel more calm and grounded."

"Grounded? I don't want to be grounded," I replied.

"No, kiddo. You're not grounded. This grounded means you have your feet on the ground," my dad said.

"Do you understand, Audrey?" my aunt asked.

"I guess so." But I didn't.

"So, will you take the pill?"

"Ok, Jose," I quietly said. I knew her name was Aunt Ru.

My mom would set the orange pill on the kitchen counter, but I would refuse to take it; I'd cry and protest, screaming "I'm not taking that orange pill!" I could go for hours. My mom looked so mad, but I wouldn't care what happened to me. I was scared. I was. That's why I'd throw a tantrum longer than a baseball game that went into thirteen innings. But I couldn't tell anyone that. I would hang onto her, wrapping my arms around her, pleading with her not to make me take the pill. But she would peel me off of her like when you pick up a snail and it's stuck to the ground; she would push me away from her. "Get away from me," she would tell me. I would try again to hug her because she was my mom, and I wanted her to love me. "Don't touch me." Again, she'd push me away and tell me not to touch her. Then, she'd tell me to stop throwing a tantrum and to go to my room; I was told to not come out until I stopped crying and could talk in my regular voice. She hated me.

My mom didn't want to understand what I was going through. My behavior escaped her as slimy as a slippery frog, or a scared cat scratching its way out of your arms. No one understood why I could act like that sometimes. Even me. All I know is I couldn't control myself. I swear. Cross my heart and hope to die, stick a needle in my eye.

Pretty soon, my mom stopped giving me the orange pill. I think I wore her out.

I wish I was Superman or Mighty Mouse. I would spin the world backward and change everything bad that happened to me and make my mom like me again.

3 RAT FINK

TWENTY-SEVEN TIMES NINE IS ONE HUNDRED AND EIGHTY-THREE. No. That's not right. I forgot to carry the six and add it to the one hundred and eighty-three. Twenty-seven times nine is two hundred and forty-three.

That's right. I get that number because I take my birthday, February twenty-seventh, and I times it by my age (nine years old). That's what I do when I'm bored. I do math in my head and count numbers. When I can't sleep, I count backward from fifty over and over until I am sleeping. Then I can't count – because I'm asleep and I'm dreaming. No one counts when they dream. You see discombobulated movies that play in a scribbly, imagined way; meaning, half the time they don't make any sense, AND you forget once you wake up – like they never existed or mattered, kind of like etch-a-sketch after you've shaken it and what you drew disappears. Sometimes, dreams are even scary. Discombobulated stuff happens all the time because discombobulated has six syllables and is a big word I like to say when I'm trying to make a point about stuff being weird and confusing.

I had a scary dream once when we were living back on Kittridge street; I bolted out of my bed, ran out of my room, down the hall, through the living room, past the table that looked like a bale of wheat and scratched you with the pointy wheat things if you rubbed up against it, and I opened the front door that wasn't locked because no one locks their front doors. I ran out of my house, down the driveway, across my dad's perfect dichondra lawn that he always picked out all the weeds from and was so proud of, dashed across the street to Georgia's house, and I knocked on the door.

I wasn't wearing any shoes.

Georgia opened the door a crack, and I could see through the sliver (less wide than a Twinkie) that she wore an orange and blue moo moo with hair rollers cocooned under a plastic cap. She looked surprised to see me. I wasn't sure why. Maybe no one saw her in rollers outside of Mr. Gunn, or she was expecting someone else, like the milkman. But it was too dark to be delivering milk.

My heart was pounding so fast from running and being scared that it took a moment to get my words out. I told her no one was home at my house.

She made a confused face and said, "Again, Audrey?"

I was still half asleep. She looked me over.

"And where are your shoes?"

"I don't wear shoes to bed, Georgia," I told her.

"Come in here," she said with an impatient growl.

She opened the door wider so I could get in. It was late, and the Santa Ana winds were beginning to kick up the oleander hedges my dad planted along our driveway; the bottlebrush trees were shaking in her yard.

"Stay here," she commanded, pointing to a spot near the door. I knew not to step any further, sensing my interruption would be fleeting. My time in Georgia's house never seemed very long, as long as I knew her. In all the time we lived across the street, I never saw past her foyer.

I could hear the rotary phone making its rotations, sounding like chalk writing on a blackboard. I heard some mumbling then the hanging up of the receiver. I stood patiently listening for my heart to settle down. Minutes later, my dad came over in his plaid pajama bottoms and a white undershirt to get me. You could see the stains in the armpits from sweating, probably from all of that weed picking in the dichondra lawn.

My dad isn't a tall guy, but he's fit enough. His body isn't like Jack LaLanne, and he'd never be caught dead in a leotard like Jack LaLanne wears, but my dad is strong. His hair is barely hanging on, like it's afraid of the unknown and fears letting go; he has a few strands still holding out, swept to the side with purpose – his shiny head peeking through. He has more hair on his arms than he does on his head. He has piercing blue eyes that look like pretty marbles and a kind, crooked smile. But my dad can have a temper. Especially back on Kittridge Street when he caught the Watkins boys stealing some money out of his car and kicked Robby really hard in the butt as he scrammed down the driveway yelling, "Don't ever set foot on my driveway again, you little bastard!" I'm not sure what a bastard is exactly, but if it's anything like my neighbor's dog pooping on my dad's perfect lawn, it's really bad.

Other than kicking Robby in the butt, I never saw him get mad enough to strike someone – except when I got spanked. He only spanked me one time ever. Can you believe that? I deserved it; I tell you. I lied to him. When you lie and you don't get away with it and get caught, well, that deserves a spanking – I'm told. See, I took my bike to Pierce College with Parker and a couple of the other neighborhood kids when I wasn't supposed to. We were never allowed to go to the college without our parents, but we snuck over all the time to see the farm animals or to use the bathrooms for fun. One time, I tried to pee in the urinal like the boys. I pulled myself up because I was only five and not tall enough to reach standing up. I wrapped my arms around the cold porcelain like I was climbing a tree and strapped my knees around each side, squeezing to stay in place and I peed. Except, I peed all over my capris because that's not how urinals work and I'm a girl. But I gave it the ol' college try, seeing I was at Pierce.

We dug riding our bikes around the campus. The sidewalks were wide and smooth and perfect for bike riding, with no rocks to put you off balance or curbs to run in to (at least not on the walkways where the big kids walked with their books). I remember it was on a Friday because school was over for the day, with no college kids in our way to accidentally run over. We made our way to the far side of the campus, near where the sheep were, and there was this hill down to a driveway. It was steep. I hadn't been riding my bike for very long, and I was not so sure of myself.

Parker went first and got to the bottom. He looked up at me and told me to get off my bike and walk it down – that it was too steep for a little kid like me. But I didn't listen. I liked to show off, sometimes. I took a deep breath and started down the hill when, unexpectedly and unplanned, I slipped off my seat into the well of the bike and got a rupture. Do you know what that is? It's when you slip off the seat and your privates hit the metal bar; it hurts like getting your finger caught in the car door or the T-Bird's electric window.

Now I'm in pain as I'm careening out of control down the hill, my bike wobbling, me barely steering straight. My feet were trying to control the speed of the bike like Fred and Barney do when they're driving their cars. I'm stuck in the well of the lower bars, and all I can see is all the kids with their bikes, blocking a hedge, as if they were trying to stop me. At the last minute, they darted out of my way, and I went off the curb, across the asphalt, bounced in to and over a curb, then crashed into the oleander hedge that looked freshly pruned.

Buried deep in the hedge, they pulled me out; I had a bloody nose and my heart was still leaping out of my chest. Then, like a little girl, I began to cry, blubbering through my tears, "Can we go home, now?"

We pulled up in front of Parker's house in a pale-yellow VW Bug that some nice man from Pierce gave us a ride home in. He took us up to Parker's front door and knocked. Parker and I looked at each other, shaking like wet dogs, knowing we were in so much trouble. We would be grounded for life. Pam answered the door and looked at us. She looked me over one more time.

"What happened to you, Audrey?" She asked.

The man told her what happened, and she pulled Parker into the house by his collar, pointed at me, all covered in dried blood, and said, "That one is not mine."

The man shrugged and said good night. Pam thanked him, then yelled, "Paul! Take Audrey home!"

Paul was Parker's second oldest brother and one year older than my sister, Shelly. He was signed up to go to Vietnam and was spending the summer stocking up on fun before they shipped him off. That's what Parker's dad called it – shipping off – one night while sitting at their dinner table after a day of swimming.

"Paul is being shipped off to Vietnam," like he was a care package of cookies being sent to summer camp.

He didn't sign up on his own. His dad took him. Ned, also Parker's dad's name (like my brother's), made him put on a nice shirt with long sleeves and a pair of slacks – and even comb his hair. I was there. I spent the night; I often did. Parker was my best friend, and we were like two brothers even though I was a girl. When Paul came out of the bathroom, his hair looked funny and was slicked down like when we'd put one of Pam's nylon stockings over our head. Most of the time, Paul's brown hair looked like a bird's nest or when our cat, Suzuki, would scratch up the couch and threads would be sticking out like thorns.

I heard a few years later that Paul went AWOL before he ever made it to basic training, where they teach boys how to shoot guns and kill people. Can you believe that? I can't even hurt an ant, or a bee, or a caterpillar. I can hurt a mosquito though. I hate itching, and mosquitos like to bite me.

Paul walked me home, and even though it was only four houses away from my house, it was the longest walk of my life. Actually, it was the second-longest walk of my life. The first one came months later. It was the same four houses, but it was the most awful night of my life. I think you should know. I will tell you about that when I'm ready. I'm not ready yet.

This walk with Paul felt like it was as long as the walk from the Magic Castle down Main Street to the front gates of Disneyland. I felt the same way – like I feel when we have to go home after a long day at the happiest place on earth; I didn't want to go. I trailed behind on his boot heels because Paul was tall and had big walks like Mean Ned; I had to practically run to keep up with him because my walks were little. I ran alongside him, struggling to match his pace, begging him not to tell my mom or dad. I knew what I did was wrong. I didn't want a spanking. I didn't want to be grounded. I promised I would be a good girl and never take my bike to Pierce College ever again, even if Parker twisted my arm behind my back or gave me a rope burn (which really hurt); he'd wring my forearm as if he was trying to get water out of it.

Paul was really nice. He was too nice to go to Vietnam. I saw pictures on the television of fire and explosions and the sound of guns – and not the pretend machine gun sounds that Parker could do with his mouth. Ratttaaattatatatatatatata! Parker was really good at making those sounds and not spitting on me. But in Vietnam, there were real guns that killed people, and their parents would cry and scream, "NOOOOOO!" like I heard Mrs. Slauson do on her front lawn when she heard her son, Donny, died in Vietnam. Mrs. Saluson's dog would look so sad and would lay down on the lawn and never move, like he was just waiting for Donny to come home and play with him. But he never did. Never ever again. Donny was dead. Later, Sylvia, Mrs. Slauson's daughter, died. Not in Vietnam. In the bathtub. Ned said, "She did herself in." I wondered why she didn't do herself out. When I got in the bathtub, I got out.

Paul knocked on our front door. I felt like a contestant waiting to see what would be behind door number "Oh, boy, am I in BIG trouble" and the anticipation feeling longer than the entire game show *Let's Make A Deal.* Then Shelly answered. I was relieved it wasn't my mom or dad. I have no idea if I'd still be here telling you my story if my mom answered the door. Seeing Shelly and her bright smile, I knew I won the big prize; my heart started to settle, feeling the worse part was over. Shelly looked at Paul and smiled in a girly way, playing with her blond hair, tugging at it like gum got stuck in it or something. It was weird. Then she looked at me and said, "What happened, Audrey? Did you get in a fight?"

Paul told her the story of how I took my bike to Pierce College when I wasn't supposed to and crashed in a hedge and got a bloody nose; he said not to tell on me and that I promised not to do it again. I nodded my head and I smiled, flashing my missing front tooth that I had lost three days before.

"Let's get you cleaned up," my sister said.

Yes! I did it. I escaped being grounded.

Now, this is where I made my big mistake. I couldn't just be happy that I got away with not being grounded for taking my bike to Pierce College (even though I wasn't supposed to).

After my sister cleaned all the blood off my face and hid my shirt in her closet, for some stupid reason I walked back to Parker's house; I found him crying on his front lawn because – guess what? He got grounded. There I was, free as a bird, walking on the sidewalk along Kittridge Street and not banished to my back yard behind a fence and gate like I was in prison. I was out in the open air, kicking my heels up, feeling like Bonnie & Clyde. Well, at least like Bonnie, because Clyde got caught.

You would have thought I learned by then that sarcasm gets you nowhere and not to push my luck. But I was only six and still had a lot to learn about seven-year-old boys, about how mean they could be and how mad they got when you made fun of them. Gosh, my mean brother, Ned, should have taught me that. He would get so mad at me when I'd go in his room when he was sleeping. I couldn't help myself. It was like if there was a giant magnet in his room and I was made of metal, like the Tin Man; when I walked past his door on the way to the kitchen, this powerful force would start drawing its magnetic power on me, and I would get pulled into his room. Feeling lured by the invisible magnetic pull, it wasn't even me opening his door and creeping inside. My mom said I needed to not go in his room, like he asked me. But I don't think she ever understood the magnet thing.

See, I'd get up early and get bored being the only one awake, especially when no good cartoons were on. I'd ask my mom if I could wake up Ned. She would say, "No." But did I listen? I'd tiptoe down the hall and sneak up to Ned's door like Kelly Robinson from my favorite nighttime show, *I Spy*. Softly turning the handle, I'd quietly open it, not making one rattle to wake him.

Just so you know, next to *I Spy*, I liked *The Ed Sullivan Show* too. That was on at night. I loved all the performers, and I dream of being on television one day too. My grandma worked for a man named Robert Stack, who played a part on a tv show. When I was born, Mr. Stack and Mrs. Stack gave me a little stuffed lamb that I have on my bed. My grandma said they were nice. But after a few years, she went to work for another lady who was a big actress and a singer. I went to her house a few times when I was little. What was her name? Judy. She was Dorothy in the *Wizard of Oz* when she was a little girl. She had a dog named Toto and red shoes. I love that movie.

When I opened Mean Ned's door, I could see him lying in bed on his back with his hands up over his head behind his pillow. He always seemed to sleep like that when the magnet pulled me into his room. His twin bed faced the open door, so I could see him really good. I'd sweetly whisper, "Ned . . . Ned . . . Ned . . . wake up." One time, I climbed in bed with him when I was scared over something I dreamt, and he let me, moving over so I wouldn't fall off the edge. I don't know why he let me. Maybe he had an earache and wasn't feeling like being mean. I know when I get earaches, I can't do anything mean.

I was determined to wake him because I just couldn't help myself. Magnet, magnet, magnet. I liked to bug him. I think it's because I wanted him to pay attention to me and like me. He said he was mad that I was born. He wanted a little brother, and I came out a little girl; he hated that. My dad said Ned cried when I was born, like when your toys are taken away or your ice cream flops on the floor just after the first lick. That's a bummer.

"Ned . . . Ned . . ."

It would happen so fast. Every time.

Out of nowhere – and this happened every single time I'd go into his room when he was sleeping – he'd launched his pillow at me like a rocket. It weighed two pounds at least, and it would hit me like a bullseye, knocking me into the door; my head would bang against the door, and I buckled like a house of cards collapsing to the floor. Wipeout. Every time.

I would go crying to my mom, "Ned hit me with his pillow, and I banged my head against his door; he's mean and hurt me."

"What did I tell you, Audrey?"

"Not to go into his room," I whimper.

"And what did you do?" she'd ask.

"Went in his room."

It made sense when you said it out loud. But did I listen inside? See, being clever isn't always clever.

So there I was, standing on the sidewalk of freedom, and there sat grounded Parker, sitting Indian style on his front lawn, sniveling like a cry baby. I pointed at him and said — oh, I get so frosted at myself because I should have just kept my big trap shut — I said really sarcastically, "I didn't get grounded, I didn't get grounded."

Actually, I sing sang it over and over again.

"I didn't get grounded, I didn't get grounded . . ." and even put a little dance to it, swaying my hips. I think I even twirled once or twice.

"I didn't get grounded . . . you got grounded . . . I didn't, I didn't . . ." I sang over and over again, like I was on American Bandstand.

Do you know what baiting someone is? That's what my mom would call it when I'd go into my brother's room. She said I was baiting him like when you put a worm on a fishhook; it wiggles in the water and the fish wants to grab it and eat it.

My mom loved to fish. We would go up to Ojai or Wheeler Hot Springs, and she'd take me down the washed rocks to the river into these quiet pools where she'd fish. My mom's thin and lanky with shoulder-length brown hair that she sprayed with AquaNet and brown eyes that looked like the color of a Hershey bar. She looked so happy when she fished. She looked at peace – as quiet as the pools she fished in. And she was good at it. She bought me a little red fishing pole, and I'd sit on a big rock by the river waiting for a nibble. I'd watch my fishing pole so closely I'd sometimes turn cross-eyed, seeing if it would move. Bowing, bending down, the pole was like a kid trying to dive off the diving board for the first time, leaning so far over it's not even diving anymore. That's what happens when the fish takes the worm. The pole bends, being pulled down. Then you have to slowly reel in the fish, letting out the line a little bit, giving it some slack so the line doesn't break or the fish doesn't escape the hook.

One time, when we were fishing near Camarillo, my mom caught a big trout – as long as my arm. It was shiny and beautiful with rainbow scales that look like a kaleidoscope. At first, I felt bad because it couldn't breathe, with its gills opening and closing, pleading to live. It scared me. It made me sad. Truth be told, I don't fish much because it breaks my heart. Why separate the fish from their family and make them suffer when all you have to do is go to the store and buy fish sticks, already made? But my mom said she'd make sure it didn't suffer and made me turn my back. I'm not sure what she did, but the next time I saw that trout was the morning she shared it with me for breakfast. Yep . . .we ate trout for breakfast before anyone woke up. It was really fun; I don't have many memories like that of my mom, back on Kittridge Street. Mainly, it's just of her being mad and yelling at my dad or my sister, Shelly, or grounding me.

I remember her showing me how to clean the fish. She was at the kitchen sink, and I was sitting at the counter on a counter stool watching her intently. She scraped the scales with a sharp knife and then rinsed them off under the water faucet. Then, putting a big iron skillet on the stove with some Crisco oil, I watched her fry it whole. Head and eyeballs and tail and all. That's how you cook a fish. My mom loves to cook. She's called a gourmet cook. She told me it's a name for housewives that don't work cooking in a restaurant. Sometimes, we'd watch a lady named Julia on the television. Julia sounded like a man. But boy did she make delicious things. My mom used to tell me to pay attention because one day I would cook like a grown-up and not just make cakes with my easy bake oven, and I needed to know how. I watched Julia with excitement and liked that she used so much butter. I love butter.

I remember the sizzling of the fish in the pan, how it became a brownish color, and you couldn't see the eyeballs any longer, becoming white. The fish made the kitchen smell stinky, but I didn't care. I was alone with my mom while everyone was sleeping, and she was sharing her trout that she caught in the river of Ojai with me; I felt very special. After, when we were all done eating every bit of that fish, my mom gave the head to Suzuki, our Siamese cat, to eat. Suzuki took it outside on the patio. She wasn't good at sharing. After she was done, she licked her little fishy cat lips. I knew how she felt.

As I continued baiting Parker, soon he stopped crying and got a funny face like he was about to sneeze. His eyes got squinty, as if he was using X-ray vision on me, and he stiffened his lips. I did one more twirl and a double finger point at him, just like a gunslinger; but, bringing my point home, before I could finish my sentence, "I didn't get grou –" Parker bolted up and started running off the lawn, onto the sidewalk, out of grounded boundaries, and down the street.

I was startled. I couldn't move for a sec. Then, I could see he was running past the Minors' house next door, and I got the lead out. I went running after him, screaming, "Hey, wait! You're grounded! You're not allowed to leave your front lawn!"

But he didn't listen. Clyde was back, like an outlaw.

He ran down the sidewalk, past the Turners' house, the Phelps' house, and the Shaws' house, then turned left around the oleander hedge, into our driveway, past my dad's T-bird and our trailer that we'd take camping, scrambled up to my front door, and banged on it. Shelly answered, again, and he spilled the beans about what had happened; he told her that, even though we weren't supposed to, we took our bikes to Pierce College, I fell off my seat, ran into a hedge and got a bloody nose.

"What a rat fink!" I shouted at him.

"I am not a fink!"

"You are too a fink!" I let him know.

"Am not!"

"Are too!"

But my sister already knew the story. I wasn't worried. I just wanted to make Parker feel bad for being a fink.

Then, I felt something burning on my back; it was like we'd do with a magnifying glass in the sun when we would torch leaves on the sidewalk or when my mom would stare at me with those angry eyes when she didn't like something I did. All I know is I just felt this burning sensation – an X-ray vision feeling.

I slowly turned to my left, over my shoulder, and there he was: my dad, standing at the den window. He heard everything the fink said, and he came unglued. I remember the look on his face. I remember seeing steam coming out of his ears and fire coming out of his mouth; his nails turned into claws and his muscles bust out of his shirt, ripping it to shreds, and he screeched like a dragon.

I blinked in fright. I can still feel my heart beating so fast.

My dad was dressed in a white undershirt, with stains in the underarms like there always were, and slacks, having just gotten home from work. He stared at me through the glass window, his blue eyes turning black with disappointment. Parker was told to go home, and the fink split like a banana, skipping away, acting proud to be a big tattletale.

That was it, my one and only spanking that my dad gave me – because I didn't tell the truth. And guess what happened next? Yep. I spent the next week behind the back gate, crying and sniveling like a pointing and twirling bozo, grounded – all because I couldn't keep my trap shut.

That night wasn't the first time I had a nightmare, and it wasn't the last time I ran over to Georgia's, still half asleep. I stood still in Georgia's entryway, hearing her foot tap on the linoleum. I was looking her over, wondering how she learned to put her hair in little rollers, seeing she was a housewife and not a beautician. My thoughts were getting tired listening to her and my dad blab on about how, maybe, he should put a lock on the top of the front door, so I can't get out – that what if something happened to me and I ended up at a stranger's house.

My dad apologized to Georgia, then he turned to me with a concerned looked. "What's going on, kiddo?"

I didn't know what to say. Nothing came out of my mouth. He shrugged to Georgia, then he swept me up in his arms and carried me home.

"Sorry, Georgia," he called back.

"Get some sleep. See you at the Stevens' cocktail party tomorrow," she called back. Maybe that's why her hair was in rollers.

I was exhausted and started to fall asleep on his shoulder, the odor from his armpits lulling me to sleep. I loved it. It smelled like my dad when he was working on the lawn or when he was waxing the car; that's when he was happy. He was proud of his work. He'd tell me in an earnest voice, "If you take care of things, they will last a long time."

I wondered whether if you took care of them, would it work with people, or my cat, Suzuki. Regardless, that armpit smell was stinky happiness, and I felt like I was safe in my daddy's arms.

He carried me into my darkened bedroom, past Shelly's pet rat cage, her pet snake cage, my turtle bowl, and carefully put me in bed. He sat on the edge, stroked my forehead, and quietly whispered, "Who loves you?" We'd play this game all the time, but I was sleepy and could barely get the words out.

"Who loves you?" he asked again.

"You do."

"How much?" he playfully questioned me.

"The world, Daddy."

"That's right."

He kissed me good night. "Sleep tight. Don't let the bed bugs bite." That woke me wide awake. Now I was worried about bed bugs biting me. He left, quietly shutting the door.

You know what the silly thing was about me running over to Georgia's and saying to her that no one was home? My big sister, Shelly, was sleeping right beside me, and everybody was home, including Ned, when I ran out the front door thinking my house was empty. Everybody was home. That's what dreams do. They fool you.

But if you want to know the truth, I felt very alone. Like I said, my mom and dad were always mad at each other, and there was a lot of yelling. "You get out of this house right now!" My mom would say that to my dad, and he would leave. Before he would go, he'd come into my room, sit on my bed, lean close to my ear, and whisper, "I have to leave now," not wanting to wake me up. I could feel his breath on my cheek. Sometimes, he would cry. But I was awake. I was pretending to be asleep. Actually, I was counting backward, but it wasn't working. I didn't know what to do. I just kept my eyes closed.

Then he would leave. A few days later, he would be home again. Then a week or more would pass and more yelling. A plate would break. A door would slam. "I'm going to kill you!" would be shouted. Later in the night, I'd hear my door creak open and footsteps coming to the side of my bed. A whisper. A tear. Gone. The house empty of my father and most of his things. It was confusing – and scary. I didn't understand any of it and wondered why, if my mom and dad really loved each other, they were so mean to each other and broke so much stuff?

I knew it couldn't last much longer.

Especially after that night that changed everything . . . and me, forever. It's why I don't play with dolls anymore.

4 FLAT TIRE

ALL IT TOOK WAS FOUR WORDS TO PUT A SMILE ON MY FACE AND GET me out the door lickety-split.

"The ice cream truck! The ice cream tru – ?!"

I could hear it as far as Dr. Kudrow's house, all the way up the block and around the corner. Ice cream truck grinding music to kids is like a dog whistle to dogs, or throwing a ball, or shaking a bowl full of kibble. It's like a superpower. I could hear it even when my mean brother was playing the drums: that grinding tune carved in my brain like an etch-a-sketch.

You'd stand on the curb, hold out your hand and the Good Humor ice cream man would stop his truck; the neighborhood kids would gather around the side looking at the board with all the choices, salivating and drooling like Parker's Great Dane, Ripple, knowing ice cream delight was safely inside the truck – every bar ready to be inhaled like oxygen. The ice cream man was dressed in white, wearing a white cap, with his changemaker on his belt. He waited patiently for us kids to decide, then reached inside the icebox door, pulling out whatever was screamed for. He was good at knowing what kids were screaming. I loved the push-up, which is ice cream in a toilet paper roll that you pushed up with a little stick. And let me tell you, the ice cream does not fill up the whole cardboard tube; it's a gip.

All of us neighbor kids, we'd gathered 'round. There was Parker, me, all the Meets kids, Sheldon Shaw, mean Rebecca Watkins, who was the neighborhood bully and liked to beat me up whenever she got the chance, and Sonya, who hurt my feelings so badly; I'll probably remember *her* until I'm as old as Mrs. Andrews, who was my second-grade school secretary and wore cat glasses.

Even though we lived on the same block, I didn't even know Sonya, and I still do not understand why she picked me that day to be so mean to. Parker and I were riding on my bike. He was standing up steering, and I was sitting on the seat. We'd do that a lot. I'd steady myself, balancing with my feet out so my bell-bottoms wouldn't get caught in the chain and tightly holding on to his Levi's belt loops. I was wearing no shirt – just my jeans. I saw Sonya and a few girls up ahead with their bikes in front of her house on the sidewalk, and I said to Parker, "Stop!" He stopped my bike in front of Dr. Kudrow's house, and I got off.

"What's up?" he asked.

"Give me your shirt."

"No."

"Yes," I demanded.

"Why?"

"Because."

"Because why?" he pried.

"Because I said so."

I don't know what happened on that day. I often played without a shirt on, especially on a hot summer day, and I never thought about it. Parker didn't wear a shirt, so I didn't either. A lot of kids ran around shirtless. Sometimes, I would turn my jeans backward with the zipper in the front so I could be like Parker. One time, after I fell in the pool with my clothes on, his mom told me to get out of my clothes, and she gave me a pair of Parker's underwear to put on. They were comfortable and padded. Not like girls' underwear. They felt more like a diaper and dependable.

But all of a sudden, there I was out on Kittridge Street, on a hot summer day, and I became aware that I wasn't wearing a shirt; I was a girl, and I wasn't supposed to not wear a shirt – even though it was hot, and I was six.

"Please, Parker. I'll buy you an ice cream."

"You promise? Stick a needle in your eye?"

I certainly didn't want to stick a needle in my eye because that would hurt. My mom would say, "It's better than a poke in the eye with a sharp stick." I agree. I once poked my eye on a big stick.

"Yes. I promise, Parker. Swear to God."

"Let me see your fingers." He was suspicious.

"I'm not crossing my fingers or my toes. Just give me your shirt, would you?"

He took off his T-shirt, handed it to me, and I put it on. I felt different. I felt normal. I was a girl and not a boy, and I should wear a shirt. After I put it on, he got off my bike and said he was going home. I told him I'd see him later and to listen for the ice cream truck.

I rode my bike over to Sonya's, and she was there with two other friends of hers; they were little girls from another street I didn't know. Sonya was wearing a pretty dress and riding a pink bike with streamers and a white basket on the handlebars. The other girls had nice bikes too. Sonya looked at my bicycle and made a face.

"Where did you get that bike?"

"My dad got it for me," I said.

"It's ugly – and old," Sonya told me.

I didn't know what to say. It was old. There was some rust, even. It was blue with a blue and white seat and white wall tires. It wasn't groovy like Sonya's or her friends' bicycles. The handlebars weren't like a stingray. It didn't have a banana seat either or pretty streamers coming out of its handles. But it was my bike, and I was too little to ride Lana's blue and Shelly's red matching Schwinn three speeds.

"What are those things in the wheels?" another girl asked.

"They're cards," I said. Parker and I had used close pins to attach the playing cards to the spokes. "They make a neato sound when you go," I told them.

"Let me see," said the other girl.

I slowly wheeled over to her; as the wheel turned, the cards made a shuffling, ticking sound. I stopped in front of the little girl. Sonya was behind me with the other girl.

"See?" I said.

"Neato," said Sonya.

I smiled. I felt proud. I always wanted to play with Sonya, and now here I was, finally.

"So, listen girls . . . be careful with your bikes."

"Why, Sonya?" the girl next to her asked.

"I accidentally dropped a thumbtack on the sidewalk."

My eyes scanned the ground carefully; then, before I lifted my head up or anyone could say anything back, I heard the supersonic whisper of air hissing and saw that my back tire had started to go flat. I'll never forget that. I knew I didn't wheel over the tack. I hardly moved my bike. I had this sick feeling in my stomach. I knew, when I wasn't looking, Sonya or someone put the tack in my tire. I'll never understand. I didn't even know Sonya. We didn't even go to the same school. I never did anything to her. Why did she do that to me?

I wheeled my bike home, crying. I was sad. My feelings were hurt if you want to know the truth. I can tell you that. I can't tell anyone else though, especially Mean Ned. He'd just make fun of me and probably rub it in.

I wheeled my bike into the garage; the flat tire was making a squishy sound on the cement floor, reminding me of my deflated spirit. I leaned it up against the wall because the kickstand was broken. I walked into the house, and my dad was in the living room reading the green sheet paper. I was afraid to tell him that my tire was flat. Without looking up, he felt me come in.

"Hey, kiddo. What are you up to?"

"Dad . . ."

"Yes, Audrey?"

I wasn't sure I should say it. He lowered the paper.

"What's up?"

"Nothing." I was stalling.

40

"Okay," he said and went back to reading the paper.

"Daddy?"

He lowered the paper again and looked at me.

"You're not getting ice cream," he told me.

"That's not it. My back tire's flat."

"How'd that happen?" he scoffed.

"Beats me. I must have rode over a tack when I was with Parker," I quietly confessed. I started to cry. I didn't want to be grounded.

"Hey, there . . .no reason to cry." He set the paper down. "I'll take the inner tube to the gas station and have them patch it."

"Really?" I said. I was shocked. That was easy.

"Of course, sweetheart. It's not your fault."

"Can I come watch them do it?" I asked.

"Sure you can," he told me.

I went over to him and wrapped my arms around his neck.

"Thank you, Daddy."

"Who loves you?"

"You do," I told him.

Before he could get the next words out (asking me how much I loved him and me saying the world), right then I heard it, while I was giving my dad a big hug because he wasn't disappointed with me. The faint sound of the music box grinding song – the ice cream truck.

"DAD! The ice cream truck! The ice cream truck!" I screamed. I jumped in place, like the living room carpet was a trampoline, elated, hearing the sound of such a sweet, delicious song.

He reached in his pocket and gave me fifty cents (enough for two, I thought). I owed Parker an ice cream, like I promised him.

You're a *popsaholic*, Audrey," my dad said with a smile. That's a kid that loves ice cream. And boy oh boy, do I ever. Popsicles are my favorite because I can eat the whole box. After popsicles, fudgesicles, pushups, strawberry shortcake, big sticks, orange creamsicles, sundaes, and snow cones – in that order.

On that day, I remember exactly what ice cream I had because that day started out so good and ended so badly, with the tack in my bike tire and what happened that night. That's the day I'm still not ready to talk about. But I will tell you that we moved on my seventh birthday, and my dad left our house for good.

That was about two years and seven months ago. I asked my dad yesterday when I talked to him on the phone because I wanted to know how long he has been living in his apartment. He got a studio apartment by Century City when he left. It's a very tiny city that has an outdoor mall and a movie theatre. There are tall buildings and a big hotel that curves like the apartment building he lives in, like a half-circle, and his studio apartment smells like my grandma's mothball sweater – I guess because my dad puts mothballs in his closet. The building has a really big swimming pool and a diving board that I dive off when I stay there. My dad says I'm a good diver. I think I am. I point my hands into the water and try to keep my ankles together. I don't bend over so I'm only three inches from the water. I dive like a swan. Sometimes, I belly flop. But that's just part of being a show-off.

Before we moved to Grand Avenue, I'd sleep at my dad's every other weekend, and we'd go to Kiddieland every Saturday. It's an amusement park for kids that has all sorts of rides and roller coasters. Next door, there is the pony ride. I'd like to ride the pony too. There are so many kids with their dads. I asked my dad once why there were so many dads and not many moms. He said it was because their moms have a new husband. It seemed like there are a lot of moms with new husbands. Moms like new husbands, I guess. Then again, new cars smell better and drive better than old ones, so maybe that's it.

At Kiddieland, my favorite ride is the bumper cars. I ride in one car because I'm big enough to ride alone, and my dad rides in another. I like to ram into him. He says I better not drive like that when I'm older. I won't. I don't want to go to jail.

After a day with all the divorced people and kids, we'd go to Pink's for a chili dog. Pink's Hot Dogs takes up a tiny bit of the block on La Brea and makes the best hot dogs. But if you want chocolate malts, you go to Bob's Big Boy. Bob's has this chubby kid dressed in a red race car outfit out front, holding up a giant hamburger. The malts come in a big steel vase thing that keeps it cold for a long time, and they're thick and creamy like ice cream, which is a plus. When we lived on Kittridge Street, Lana work as a carhop at *Bob's Big Boy*. On roller skates – carrying a tray – she delivered hamburgers, and malt milkshakes, and French fries. Bob's was all about speed. I think they wanted their food out faster than McDonald's, so they thought the roller skates would be just the ticket. We went a few times and ordered from Lana, parking the car in one of the stalls. She arrived with our food and never fell, or wiped out, or got lost coming from the kitchen to the car. I was shocked.

For a delicious hot dog, Pink's is the place. When my dad takes me there, I squeeze up to the counter, and I order mine smothered in chili and onions. My dad thinks it's strange I like onions because I'm just a kid. Sometimes, I eat two chili dogs. After I eat both chili dogs smothered in onions, on purpose, I breathe on my dad; with my huffy words, using my breath like the Big Bad Wolf, I say, "*Hi*, Dad. *How* are you? *How* old are you? *How's* everything? *How's* it going?" just to bug him, because my breath reeks of chili and onions and could kill a hippopotamus. The secret is the bun, which feels so soft like my old doll's tummy, and the wiener dog thumps when you bite it. It's like if heaven could be a hot dog and the clouds were onions and the skies were chili. My mouth is watering just thinking about it.

The hardest part of weekends with my dad was when he would take me home to Detroit Street, idle the car in front of our duplex and just stare at the front window. Sometimes, we'd sit there for five minutes or more. He'd just stare.

Then, without looking at me, his eyes still fixed on the window, he'd ask me, "Is he there now? Do you like him?"

I'd never know what to say because I would get scared that I might say the wrong thing. So, I shrugged. It seemed safer.

My mom had met someone else – David. He was really nice. I couldn't tell my dad that. I was too afraid he might get angry and slam his fist on the dashboard. I clammed up like a clam. It's like the cat's got my tongue. But don't worry – I still have my tongue. It's just I'm not sure what I should say when something like that happens.

They had gotten married in August right after my dad's birthday and eight months after we moved to Detroit Street. They'd gone to Acapulco and came back with tans and these pointy red and black suckers that taste good, and my mom had a ring on her finger. I guess they stopped at the Rabbi's office before they got on the plane, saying they'd love each other until they died and they meant it. I got five of those pointy suckers, maracas, and a poncho with rainbow colors. My mom and David liked to kiss a lot. It wasn't that weird, even though I never saw my mom and dad kiss like that. I got used to it. They laughed too – a lot. There was no yelling. She liked to squish up next to him in the front seat of the car. He'd put his hand on her leg and drive the car with one hand.

David was a good driver. I'd stand in the back wheel well resting my hands on the front seat, and I'd watch him turn the wheel. Sometimes he'd just use one finger; it was really groovy. One time, he parked the car in front of our neighbor's house, and it was too small for his car to fit. He backed in and squeezed into the space, pushing the car behind him with his big chrome bumper – the wheels squealing like a drag racer until the neighbor's car moved just enough to make his car fit. The burning rubber smelled like that machine they use when the men come and put tar on top of the roof. It stunk.

Mr. Mathers came screaming out of his house, "What the God damn hell are you doing, Saltzman?!" I remember those words because Parker's brother Sean said them to me when I was in his room playing hide and seek. "What the God damn hell are you doing in my room, Audrey?!" Sean was lucky Pam wasn't home to hear him say those words. I heard her say 'hell' once when I accidentally knocked over the Christmas tree when we were playing – you guessed it – hide and seek. I thought hiding between the tree and window behind the curtain was a good spot. It was . . . until I knocked over the tree, and the noise of all the breaking ornaments gave me away. Pam came running in and said, "Holy hell" and another bad word which rhymes with Chuck. I know the word. We knew people with the name Chuck. We'd sing the

'Name Game' song: "Chuck, chuck bo buck banana fanna fo . . ." you know what comes next, right? That bad word. Oh, we'd start laughing because we knew it was a bad word. And Pam said it that day I knocked over the Christmas tree. I think that's when I knew I was in big trouble.

I climbed out from under the tree, stepping over the broken ornaments, the tinsel and crushed candy canes, and ran into Parker's room, where I ended up crying on his bed. I was so scared and sorry. Mostly, I felt stupid and embarrassed. Pam came into the room, walked over to the bed and rubbed my back, telling me that "everything would be alright" and that she wasn't mad at me. Pam was really nice. She always had a smile and never got mad. She was smaller than my mom and was half the size of big Ned, it seemed like. I wiped my tears, and I crossed my heart and hoped to die, swearing I'd never do that again. And I didn't.

I heard Mr. Mathers mumbling to himself as he walked back inside. David chuckled and smiled at my mom. I wonder if Mrs. Mathers washed Mr. Mathers' mouth out with soap. 'Hell' is a bad word. I had my mouth washed out many times for just talking back, and I never said any bad words.

We got out of the car and walked to the house. Before we got to the front door, David kissed my mom, mushy like. She looked at me, and I rolled my eyes. We laughed. Then we walked inside. David set his car keys on the side table next to the door, took a step and suddenly went down on one knee.

"David, honey! Are you okay?" my mom loudly said. I felt this panic sound in her voice, like when she was in the car that time and saw the plane she thought was going to crash . . .or when Shelly fainted before she went away to that place I don't want to say the name of.

"Mom, is David okay?" I asked.

"He's fine, Audrey. Go to your room."

I left the living room and stood on the step to the hall that led to all of our bedrooms, watching my mom grab David by the arm and help him back up. I heard him say he was fine, that he just got dizzy

for a moment, but he looked like me when I ran my bike in the bushes
– hurt and like he wanted to cry.

"David, do you want some ice cream? That will make you feel
better." Actually, I wanted some ice cream, but I wanted to share.

"Sure, Audrey. That would be peachy," he said, trying to stand
upright and not hunched like a caveman. But David wasn't hairy. He
had grey, short-buzzed hair and no mustache.

"Can I, Mom?"

"Yes, Audrey."

I saw my mom put her hand on his face and stroke it. She loved
David. I could tell. He took her hand and kissed it.

"Go get the gallon of Neapolitan in the freezer and bring three
spoons," she said. "We never celebrated your birthday."

5 PRINCIPAL'S OFFICE

I'VE ALWAYS HAD A PROBLEM SITTING STILL AND THAT DAY WAS NO different. I didn't do anything wrong, so why was I waiting for the principal to see me? During second grade at Third Street Elementary, I spent more time in the principal's office than I did in the classroom. I was perplexed – spelled p-e-r-p-l-e-x-e-d. I'd win the spelling bee in my third grade a lot. It was either me or Grant Winters. Math bee, too. I loved third grade.

I was perplexed, as any child could be, mulling over in my ever-inquisitive brain what I could have done to be sent to the principal's office . . . again. Gee whiz, it wasn't my first time. I got to know the principal pretty well. Our chats were always about how I was a Mexican jumping bean, and I couldn't sit still.

He'd ask, "Do you have ants in your pants?" I told him that I did have an ant farm, but I didn't think any had gotten out and into my pants. No, I was just wound up like a top, like the Looney Tunes Tasmanian Devil, not meaning to be bad or ruin things. How can I say it? It's like I'm going to visit George Jetson for dinner, and I'm flying with a jet pack from my house to his house. Then, when I make a sharp right turn, the jet pack falls off and now I'm in space, floating, with no jet pack; I can't control anything or ever get back home to my house or my mom, hoping she wouldn't be mad at me for losing my jet pack.

47

I sat on the hard bench and kicked my feet in a running motion, wishing I could run. My untied shoes dangled. As one of the smallest in my second-grade class, my blue Keds could barely touch the floor. I was restless. The bench rocked every time I kicked, and the wooden legs made a thumping sound.

Mrs. Andrews busily typed on her typewriter, taking a quick maneuver to push her black cat-eyed glasses up on her nose, staring up at me as if my thumping was more annoying than her typing (which sounded like gum snapping). My dad hated gum snapping. Boy, did that get him streamed up. Anytime Shelly would snap her gum, he'd stick out his hand and tell her to spit it out. She liked to braid bracelets out of string and chew gum – and pop it. She was really good at snapping her gum like a machine gun. Pop, pop, pop! Yet she never learned that if she wanted to keep her gum, not to pop it when my dad was around. Once my dad said, "Spit it out," you could not protest. Out with the gum. It was over. Obliging, she'd dribble the wad into his palm, and he'd toss it out of the window of our T- Bird; minutes later, she would unwrap another piece of Juicy Fruit, stick another stick in her mouth, and, after about five minutes, she'd forget and pop her gum. Guess what? Yep. My dad would make her spit it out. I think she kept Wrigley in business.

Bored, bored, bored. I sat on that bench waiting for my crime to be declared and thinking about what my sentence would be. How much longer would I have to wait? The suspense was killing me.

"How much longer?" I finally asked.

"Patience is a virtue, Audrey," Mrs. Andrews mumbled and continued typing, pushing her glasses up as they slipped down her nose.

I thought back then: What does that mean? Virtue? In second grade, I didn't even know how to spell it to even look it up in the dictionary. V-e-r-c-h-e-w. That's what it sounded like. Still, my mom always makes me look up words in the dictionary when I don't know what they mean. How do you look up a word you can't spell? Why can't she just tell me? It makes more sense. And, it's faster. No, I have to sound out the word. That makes it hard. Sometimes I don't sound it out right, and it takes me a year to look it up; my mom gets tired of me asking how to spell it and finally tells me.

I listened to the snapping of the typewriter and watched Mrs. Andrews push her glasses up *again*. Boy, was it annoying.

"Why don't you get new glasses, Mrs. Andrews? Those are too big. And, one of the fake diamonds is missing."

It was a super-duper observation on my part. There were seven fake diamonds on the right side and only six fake diamonds on the left side. I knew they were fake because Lesly Pullman, my third best friend in the second grade, told me that nobody has real diamonds on their glasses unless they are a movie star. Lesly told me that millionaires have real diamonds on their glasses too. Not the Beverly Hillbillies because they were bad dressers – but everybody else who has a million dollars. She would know this. They lived on June Street in a big house, and they were millionaires. We had our Bluebirds meeting there one time, and I brought chocolate cupcakes that I baked in my easy bake oven and a box of Milk Duds that were half eaten because I couldn't wait. Their backyard was as big as a baseball field, and it had a pool that had a fountain in it. Can you believe that? A fountain in your pool – like that makes sense.

Frances Hardy, who was in the third grade, threw a penny in the pool and made a wish. She said she wished for a little brother. Lesly's mom got really mad and said that Frances needed to learn some manners; she said the stork didn't take wishes like Santa Claus and that the fountain wasn't for wishing but for looking. So, I looked. Even though I had $18.31 in pennies in my piggy bank and could make a lot of wishes, I wasn't about to make Mrs. Pullman mad.

Mrs. Andrews wasn't a movie star or a millionaire; she was the school secretary. So, I felt pretty safe with my observation about her fake diamonds on her glasses, as well as my advice that they were too big, so she should get a new pair that fit better – and that weren't missing a fake diamond.

"Did you hear me, Mrs. Andrews?"

Mrs. Andrews stopped typing and stared at me. Then pushed her glasses up once more, like she was doing it on purpose to bug me. Her eyes narrowed a bit. She got this really mean look on her face, like my mom does when I talk back. Mrs. Andrews was really old and mean, and now she was mad.

"Why don't you mind your own business, huh?" She went back to typing.

I tried to mind my own business for the next thirteen seconds. Then, I dug myself in a little deeper.

"Mrs. Andrews?"

Oh, she was getting huffy and irritated with me. I felt like I was home and my mean brother would tell me "You're cruisin' for a bruisin'."

Through gritted teeth, "What, Audrey?"

"How old are you? Because I know you're not a spring chicken," I told her.

Her mouth made a crooked smirk. She looked lopsided by my question. "How old do you think I am?" She pushed up her glasses again.

"*Old*. Not like my grandma, because she's a hundred and twenty. Or old like Cruella De Vil, who's a mummy. But not old like my sister, Lana, who looks like Snow White and is old enough to kiss a boy."

"Uh-huh. I can you tell what, Audrey, I'm not a mummy," she said with a calm voice. Looking closely, I could see the tornado building under her skin; her face started to grow angry, contort, and freak out like it was a cartoon on television with its eyes popping out. I thought about how old I thought she was, not wanting to rile her up some more. Whatever I said didn't look like it sat well.

"Well, if I'm eight years old . . . I think you have to be sixty. Eight times sixty is four hundred and eighty," I blurted out.

I told you I was good at math – adding, subtracting, times table and division. I always liked math. On Detroit Street, I had a piggy bank with eighteen dollars and thirty-one cents in it that I saved from doing chores around the house and our other neighbor, Mr. Bennet's driveway. Mostly, they were pennies. I counted them all the time to make sure my brother didn't steal any. He could be a butt that way. You have to know your math and be able to add up pennies because they are only one cent and it takes one hundred pennies to make one dollar. Not a penny more.

"SIXTY? You think I'm SIXTY YEARS OLD?" Mrs. Andrews' jaw dropped. She looked bent out of shape. She shook her head a second. Furrowed her eyebrows. Cleared her throat. Cocked her head. Fluffed her hair. Made an ugly face. AND . . . pushed up her glasses.

"For your information, I am twenty-one years old. Not sixty. My grandma isn't even sixty. Do you even know what sixty is, Audrey? Criminy. Twerps." She went back to typing in a huffy way, like I'd insulted her or something. She stopped again.

"And, for your information, Audrey, that's STILL a spring chicken."

I didn't even know what a spring chicken was. I just heard my aunt say it to my mom once when they were trying on bathing suits: "Sophia, you're not a spring chicken." We had three chickens we called The Girls; I got them for Easter when they were just little baby chicks. That's in the spring. Maybe that's what it means.

Just then, Mr. Block came out of his office. I felt a certain relief seeing him because Mrs. Andrews seemed really furious, and getting a long sentence seemed safer at that point.

"Audrey?" he said.

I reluctantly got off the bench and walked toward his office.

"No, no . . . sit. I just wanted to tell you that your sister should be here in a few minutes to pick you up. She's late."

"Why?" I asked.

"She'll tell you when she gets here. I just didn't want you to worry," he said.

"You mean, I'm not in trouble?" I asked, surprised.

"Not today, Audrey. Not today," he smiled.

I was stunned. I squeaked by. I survived another day of second grade, at Third Street Elementary School, without having to clean chalkboards.

Right then, my big sister, Lana, walked in all frazzled and out of breath. She was nineteen then and still liked to wear her hair high and put that weird flesh-colored concealer on her lips that made her look dead.

"Sorry I'm late. We got to go, Audrey," she said through her breath.

My sister is ALWAYS late. My mom said she was born late (that's why) and with no sense of direction because she came out feet first like she was going down a slide. I knew I was in for a long haul. She got lost in the car all the time. When I was five and she got her license, my parents would ask her to go to the store to pick up milk or go get my mean brother at baseball practice; they would make me go with her just so to get her back home in one piece, and by sundown. I was only five and knew the valley better than she did, even though I barely left my neighborhood. I have a really good sense of direction. I don't know why. Maybe I was a bus driver in a past life. I'd stand in the back seat wheel well, my arms resting on the front seat, and direct her like a conductor. The roads were my symphony, and I loved to go places. "Turn right here. Turn here. Turn here." I knew how to get home from almost anywhere. I don't know how I knew. I was born like that. I probably told the stork how to get to my house when I was delivered.

Lana handed Mr. Block a piece of paper, and he put it on the counter for Mrs. Andrews, who turned and pushed up her glasses. Then he walked into his office mumbling, "My best to your family in these difficult times."

"Why are you here? Where are we going?" I asked. I was frothed, missing math class. She put her arm around my shoulders to escort me out of the office, looking at me with a look of guilt.

"I'll tell you in the car, Porky." She called me Porky after Porky Pig, even though I was a scrawny kid and didn't even eat bacon. I didn't want her to tell me in the car. If she didn't pay attention, we'd get lost and I didn't even know where we were going.

Outside, walking to the car, I pried. "I want to know now, Lana.

Please tell me."

Lana stopped, bent down, and looked in my eyes, "The hospital . . . so you can say goodbye to David."

"Why? Where's he going? To the beach?"

Before David and my mom got married, we'd go down to his house in Palos Verdes and climb down to the tidal pools below the cliffs and see all the sea life. There were crabs and sea urchins and starfish and cucumbers. Not like the ones you grow in your backyard, or buy at the Market Basket, or IGA, and eat. These were alive, and cute, and were not green. I loved going to the tide pools.

"He's not going anywhere like that," she told me.

"Then why do I have to say goodbye if he's not going anywhere?" I said.

"Audrey . . . he's dying," she said.

I didn't understand.

"How? I just saw him. Mom just got married. Why would he die?" I felt my heart pounding fast, big enough to explode out of my chest.

"Doesn't he like her?" I asked.

"Of course he does. He loves her. It's not about that. He's very sick. He has an aggressive cancer, Porky."

"I don't know what that means. I'm just a kid."

"It's when you're really, really, really sick and you won't get better," she explained.

"Why didn't he stay in bed and eat ice cream? That would have worked. I get better when I do that," I told her. Everybody knows ice cream is the best kind of medicine and makes your tummy feel better.

"Because he didn't know he was sick" she quietly said.

"Don't tell me that! He must have known! How could he not know? What's going to happen to Mom?!" And just like that, I took off running. I've always run. Mostly because I didn't want to take a bath. Sometimes, I'd make it out the front door and halfway down the driveway before I was intercepted and dragged back to the tub. Now, instead of running because I didn't want to take a bath, I started running when I was sad or scared and didn't know what to do. My sister was used to chasing me from when I was little, and she soon caught me in no time because she was bigger than me and her legs are as long as a giraffe's.

She grabbed me tightly in her arms and held me. I didn't want to be held. I felt trapped.

"Stop running, Audrey. Everything's going to be okay."

I remember my mind being so confused. And angry. Before that, I'd never known anyone who died that was still alive.

"It's all my fault!" I cried.

"No . . . no, it's *not* your fault."

She held me tight as I cried. I knew at that moment my life would change again.

"It's not fair," I sobbed.

"Shhh . . . it's okay, Porky. Everything's going to be okay." She rocked me.

"Everything's going to change again," I said.

The truth is, and I never told anybody this, the truth is I didn't want David to die because I didn't want to move again; when we moved, people left me. When we moved from Kittridge Street to Detroit Street, my dad had already left. Lana went to live with some family for six months in Acapulco, taking care of their kids. Even my sister, Shelly, left for a while. And my mom would get a job and have to be away at work. See, everybody was leaving – every time we moved or if I loved someone, they left.

My mind was remembering all the times someone left. After that night on Kittridge Street, after the first longest walk of my life, something terrible happened and Shelly fainted. After, she left too. I can't talk about it right now. I'm still not ready. But they sent her away to . . . juvenile hall; that's the place I didn't want to say . . . and then to a girl's school she had to live at, not far from Pink's and the Kentucky Fried Chicken my brother worked at. Ned knew the Colonel's secret recipe and would never tell us because he made a promise to the manager. We'd try to get him to spill the beans, but he would tell my mom, "I can't tell you or I'll lose my job, Mom."

I didn't want David to die, because I really liked him. He was nice. He made my mom laugh and smile; he'd take me to the tidal pools to look at the sea urchins and could drive with one finger. I was afraid that when he died, someone else would leave or die too.

My sister held me tight; I tried to wriggle out, but her strength bound me, and she wouldn't let go.

"Let me go." I fought back the tears. I was so scared. I just wanted to run again.

I squirmed to get out of her grip on me, trying to peel her off like a wet pair of jeans after we'd play at the ocean on the sand; we'd walk on the beach and get too close to the surf when a big wave broke and swept onto the sand. When peeling out of her grasp didn't work, I went to my next move of defense, and I pinched her hard. That always worked. But Lana just made an agonized face and let me do it.

"Lana . . . let me GO!"

"No. I'm going to hang onto you, Porky. I'm never letting you go. Everything is going to be alright."

I wanted to believe her. I did. I couldn't though because I knew she wouldn't always be there to protect me when I needed it most – or stop me from causing everybody to leave.

6 JEWISH FUNERALS

HOSPITALS ARE SCARY. THEY SAY PEOPLE GO THERE TO GET BETTER. Yet, people die in hospitals. So why would anyone want to go to a hospital if you can die there?

No one talks. It's like the cat's got everybody's tongue. There are hardly any people in the halls, just nurses who walk around in white dresses and with little white envelopes pinned in their hair. They are too quiet. Not quiet like a library, where anytime you say a word someone says, "SHHHH", but quiet like a funeral parlor, where the people keep their mouths shut and stare like they were told to go sit in the corner. I know; I had to go to a funeral parlor when David died.

Lana led me by the hand down the clean hospital hall. It was super shiny, like Mr. Clean, and it did not have one gum wrapper on the floor. As we passed by the ladies in white dresses with mail on their heads, they looked sternly at me like Mrs. Green would. She lived on the other side of the pink cinder brick wall behind Parker's house. We'd cross her backyard walking on top of the wall and pick plums from her plum tree; she would tell us to get out of her yard, but we'd say, "We're not in your yard, Mrs. Green. We're on the cinder block wall." She'd go ape, saying we were smart Alecs, and she was going to go tell our parents. But she never would. She never left her house. I think she actually looked forward to yelling at us. It gave her something to do.

I looked up at this one nurse. She reminded me of my kindergarten nurse, who once told me I needed to clean my ears better when I went to her office because my throat was sore. This nurse did not smile or say anything to me. She just stared with her big beady eyes following me like the moon.

I turned to Lana and asked, "Why is she looking at me like I'm not supposed to be here?"

"Because you're not," Lana said. "Squirts aren't allowed in hospitals."

"Are pets allowed in hospitals?" I asked.

"No. Just adults."

Lana stopped in front of a door and knelt down so she was at my eye level. She did that when she had something important to say and wanted me to pay attention.

"Okay. Now, don't be afraid. David looks a little different, but everything's going to be alright, Audrey."

"Where is Mom?"

"She's in the room with David. I need you to hang tough for Mom, okay?"

"I will. Cross my heart." But I was a little afraid, as if we're about to go on Pirates of the Caribbean ride; I know at some point after that big pirate ship battle, when you're floating through that town on fire and that one pirate teetering on the wall above you, holding his whiskey bottle, sings, "Yo ho, yo ho!" He looks like he's about to fall off the bridge on to you because he's drunk, I guess. That's what my dad told me, anyhow. I know it's going to happen, but it scares me, still, every time.

She led me into the dim room, the curtains drawn, shutting out the real world.

There he was. David was lying in a hospital bed with all of these wires coming out of him. He looked like he hadn't eaten in a year. My mom was sitting in a chair in the corner of the room, looking sadder than I had ever seen her. She looked up at us when we walked in and tried to smile and put on a happy face. But little monsters were pulling the corners of her mouth down, and she could not fight them. She looked away. The monsters had won.

My sister walked over to her and hugged her. I never saw my mom like that before. She seemed so limp, like wet spaghetti or when I'd play dead and Parker would try to pick me up.

I tiptoed over to David. His eyes were closed. I looked at all the wires and tubes coming out of him like Frankenstein and wondered if it hurt.

I asked, "Does it hurt?"

He didn't say anything. There was just a beeping sound coming from one of the machines.

I got close to his ear and whispered, "David . . . wake up."

David opened his eyes and turned to look at me. His eyes weren't as blue as I remembered them – when he was home the month before, after he came to live with us forever. His hair was longer and more white grey, like a melting snowball with some tinsel in it.

"Does it hurt, David?" I asked again, concerned.

"Hi, pickle." He called me pickle because he loved them, he once said. "No, Audrey. They've given me some medicine to make me not feel any pain."

"Ice cream?" I asked. I hoped so.

"Something like that." He was so tired he could barely speak.

"Can I have some?"

"No, pickle. It's grown-up ice cream," he replied.

"Can you still drive with one finger?"

I wanted to know. I wanted to know if he was still strong enough to drive with one finger because if he was, I knew he would be alright.

My mom walked over to the end of his bed and stood there.

David looked at my mom and a smile came to his face. It's almost as if she was the sun shining on him, and he felt all warm.

"Look at her. Isn't she beautiful?" he said. I'll remember that forever. David looked like he was in so much pain and all he could think to say was that he thought my mom was beautiful. My mom smiled at him like I've never seen her smile at my dad. She put her head down. Then I saw a drop of water fall on the white blanket covering his feet. I think my mom was crying.

"Audrey . . . say goodbye to David," I heard my mom quietly say.

I looked at David and I grabbed his arm, trying not to touch any of the wires and tubes.

"Bye, David. I'll see you later, alligator." We'd say that to one another.

"See you later, alligator," he replied. I smiled. I really liked David. He was nice. And, he made my mom smile and laugh.

"Write me, okay? And I'll write you," I told him.

He blinked his eyes; it was like he was telling me he would.

Lana walked over and kissed David on his forehead. She took me by the hand and led me out. As we left, I looked back and saw my mom climbing onto the bed, carefully lying next to him. She wrapped her arms around him like she did when I fell down and skinned my knee. He put his hand on her leg like he always did when they'd ride side by side in the car. She pulled herself close to him, burying her face into his neck and held onto him like a life raft that she didn't ever want to let go – like he was the only thing that could save her.

Jewish funerals are weird. At least, David's funeral was. The family sat behind a black curtain so the other people in the funeral parlor couldn't see them. And they cried. My mom cried. I couldn't see her crying, with that black veil covering her face. But I could hear her crying. I never heard my mom cry like that before. She sounded like me when I was grounded or put in my room and couldn't come out until I was ready. I was always ready to come out of my room, but my mom said I wasn't. How did she know? I was the one stuck in my room and wanted to come out.

Frankly, hearing my mom cry made me feel worried and antsy because I didn't know how to make her stop. My grandma tried to make her stop. If my grandma couldn't do it, no one could because all she had to do was look at you and say, "I'll give you something to cry about," and suddenly you stop crying in between sniffles; it's confusing because you're thinking, 'But I'm already crying about something, so what else is she going to give me to cry about?' And you get scared. And instead of crying, you stop and go super-duper 'You Sunk My Battleship' alert and get real suspicious that there's going to be a secret missile that will sink your battleship – and you stop crying. My grandma was good at Battleship, and I was always on high alert. I'm not sure that's a good thing.

I did go up to my mom and wrap my arms around her like she would do to me to make my crying stop when I hurt myself. But she cried harder. I didn't know what to do. So, I decided to go and drop my letter in David's coffin. That's where they put dead people – in a coffin and not in a shoebox like we did when my cat, Suzuki, died; we dug a hole in the backyard and buried it. Suzuki was a Siamese cat that looked like those two cats in *101 Dalmatians*. I love that movie.

"We are Siamese if you please. We are Siamese if you don't please."

They were bad cats in the movie. Suzuki was a good cat. She didn't destroy our house or knock over stuff, otherwise my mom would have gotten rid of her like she did our poodle, Jacques, when he peed on the carpet. We had off-white carpet in the living room on Kittridge street and Jacques liked to pee and poop on it. It was like he did it on purpose. He would wait for my mom to get home and go in the corner, right in front of her.

"His poodle paws are on thin ice," Shelly would say. She liked to ice skate. So do I.

Every day, it seemed like my mom would get down on her hands and knees, scrub the carpet trying to clean up the pee, and say to him, "Are you listening, Jacques, because you better listen." She was mad but had that nice mad voice when you clench your teeth and you're trying to pretend you're not mad. "You better not pee again or else." Or else. That gave you something to think about.

He'd look at her in a dumb way, but he could understand her because his ears lifted up like a pop tart coming out of the toaster. So, he wasn't fooling anyone. Poodles are smart. Shelly's poodle, Scooter, knew how to do tricks. She'd roll over and dance in a circle on her back legs like a circus bear.

One day, when my mom was cleaning up Jacques' poop, she told him, "Next time you pee on the carpet, I'm going to get rid of you."

Jacques blinked, pretending he didn't know English because he had a French name. You know what? He didn't listen. But he should have. Otherwise, he wouldn't have gone to live with some people in Reseda. These people didn't have carpet. I drove with my mom to his new house. She drove really slowly and carefully, reading each address, making sure we stopped at the right one. We took him up to the door. I was really sad. He may have been a pooper, but he was cute. I got down and hugged him. "Adios, Jacques. Be a good boy and stop pooping." After the new owner took him in her house, I asked if the lady knew why my mom was giving Jacques to her.

My mom didn't say anything, grabbed my hand, and led me back to the car. As we drove away, I looked out the window and waved goodbye to Jacques' new house.

"I'm getting new carpet," my mom said.

And that was that. No more Jacques.

There were only three things we were supposed to do as kids.

1. *Don't take candy from a stranger.* One time, when we were playing on Mason Avenue near the wash at De Soto Avenue, a stranger stopped his car and offered me candy. I didn't take it because I was told not to.

2. *Don't talk back.* I'm still working on that one.

3. *Look both ways before you cross the street.* I forgot, once, after we moved to Detroit Street and almost got hit by a car. I went between two parked cars, which I wasn't supposed to do either, and ran into the street. The car didn't see me and slammed on its brakes, screeching. My mom saw from the front window and grounded me. But as kids on Kittridge Street, we'd play that game when we'd all lay in the middle of the street, in a row, waiting for a car to come. Nothing happened. We'd get up and run once the car got too close. Our parents never saw.

I guess that's why I never got grounded.

A few months later, after Jacques went to live in Reseda, Suzuki got hit by a car. It was just a week after she had kittens. She was a cat and not a kid, so she didn't look both ways.

I was walking home from school and saw Lana and Shelly were out front of our house, and Lana saw me coming down the street and screamed, "Audrey, don't come here! Go to Parker's!"

"Why?" I asked. I always had a hard time doing what I was told.

"Pretty please, Audrey. Go to Parker's," she said. Pretty please was a super-duper please, and I knew she was serious. I turned around, went to Parker's and swam in their pool until the coast was clear and I could go home.

She didn't want me to see Suzuki because she was bloody – and dead. I loved that cat, and she was a good mommy to her little kittens. Two were black and two were black with brown spots that looked like syrup you put on pancakes.

Lana found the shoebox in my mom's closet. I cried when they put her in it. I told them to be really soft with Suzuki because I loved her. I didn't let the kittens see because I didn't want them to cry, even though their eyes were shut. When we buried her along the backyard fence, my mom said she'd grow into a flower. Every time I see flowers, I know they were once dead cats, and I think they look so pretty; it makes me smile.

We had to feed Suzuki's kittens with one of my baby doll bottles. They were so tiny and cute with their eyes still trying to open. But you know what happened? Scooter, Shelly's miniature black poodle that I told you about – I don't know if you know this, but poodles come in different sizes, like sweatshirts. Scooter was size medium. Well, a few days later, Scooter started nursing the kittens! My mom said it was a miracle because Scooter couldn't be a mommy – that the vet took away her mommy parts. The kittens would climb all over her and find a spot on her belly and get milk. Scooter loved those kittens. They would purr and knead her with their little paws. Their tiny nails would dig into her, and she wouldn't bite them, even though it looked like it hurt. When their eyes opened and they started getting bigger and walking away, she would go get them, carrying them by the back of the neck, hanging from her mouth like a Christmas ornament. She'd bring them back to her bed and lick them until they were all wet. One time, she found a kitten in my brother's closet. Did you know kittens' eyes are blue when they are born, and then they turn color as they grow up? My mom told me that so I could learn something.

Coffins are like drawers you put your pajamas in, except they put people in them instead for safekeeping. David's coffin was made of wood, like the counter in our old trailer that my dad would pull behind the family station wagon. There was no top. Just a piece of plastic over it and David was laying inside. I took a moment to muster up the courage to look inside. I was afraid he was going to jump up and try to scare me like my brother does when I don't expect it. I inhaled and looked. I was really quiet and careful. I hung on to the top edge, got on my tippy-toes, and peaked over the rim through the plastic. I could see his eyes were closed, and he was sleeping. He looked different. Like he had been sleeping for too long. Shelly said that he died and went to sleep forever, and when he finally woke up again, he would be in heaven playing a harp. My sister says it's like a guitar, only smaller, and it sounds angelic, like a dream.

I lifted up the plastic very quietly because I didn't want to wake him up and slipped my letter into the coffin. I wrote him a letter telling him how much I liked him and that he was a good driver; I told him that I wanted to grow up to drive like him, and I liked that he could make my mom laugh. I also told him that I would miss him, and asked that when he wakes up, could he give me a call and play me a song on the harp because I wanted to know if a harp sounded like a small guitar.

Then, some men came and asked me to step back from the coffin. This skinny man wearing glasses gently pulled me back. I looked up at him and noticed he was also wearing a little beanie on his head. I forget what those little beanies are called. I know they wear them to keep their bald spot warm. That's what my dad told me when he was wearing one at Aunt Chick's house for Passover. I think they should put a propeller on the top – then I'd wear one.

"I need you to go sit down."

"Why?" I asked.

"Because we have to take him," he said.

"Where are you taking him?"

"Please go sit down," he said.

"No. I want to know where you are taking him because he's sleeping, and I don't want you to wake him up," I said.

The skinny man looked frustrated like Mrs. Andrews would get when I asked her too many questions. Guess what? He pushed up his glasses.

"Audrey?"

I turned and saw my mom standing, with a black veil covering her face.

"Come sit with me," she said.

"But, Mom, they're trying to take David somewhere."

"These men are going to take David to the car," she quietly told me.

"And then what? Are you gonna bury him in the cement terry?"

"Yes."

"But I don't want you to bury him; then I won't see him again," I told her.

"Audrey . . . you can visit him in Ojai."

"But he'll be in the ground, and the worms and bugs will eat him! How will I see him?!" I shouted.

"Audrey . . . come here." I reluctantly walked over to her. "I know you are sad and don't understand. But you need to say goodbye to David so the men can take him."

I looked at my mom and she looked so weak – like she needed some ice cream to cheer her up. But there was no ice cream in the funeral home, which wasn't a home at all, but a strange, quiet place with people who whispered and cried and dressed in black suits. And just like that, I ran out of the funeral home, down the road to a pond

that was near some tall trees surrounded by all o
engraved with people's names because I didn't wai
David.

After David's funeral, they drove up to Ojai to
my brother if they could bury him in Grandma's ba
Ned said, "No, stupid, they have to bury him in the

I don't know what that is, but I told Grandma that I hope David would enjoy being buried in the cement terry; my grandma said he would because there are lots of old oak trees for shade, and he wouldn't get hot.

It made me happy that he would be shaded by the branches of old trees like the one in our old backyard, as if they were protecting him like Batman's cape so as not to get sunburn. David was too nice to get hot, especially if there was no lemonade in heaven. That's the only thing that tastes good. Not Fresca. Fresca makes you sick on a hot day. And, what bozo drinks grapefruit soda on a hot day, or at all? Barf.

I wasn't allowed to go to Ojai this time, even though we'd always gone (since I was little). My grandma still had a house there on Oak Street where my mom grew up and where me, my mom, dad, sisters, and brother would go to visit. One time, when we were driving up route 33 through Meiners Oaks, there was a small plane in the sky, and my mom thought it was going to crash into us.

She screamed, "Lee! Lee! Pull over! Pull over!" She was acting like a character from Looney Tunes.

My dad pulled over and we waited for the plane to crash. It didn't, so we drove to my grandma's house. But I'll never forget how scared she was. It was weird because a few years later, after we just moved to Ojai, my mom took me up in a small plane to Santa Barbara with her friend Nate, who was a pilot. He even let me steer. My mom didn't scream at all or think we were going to crash. She looked like she was having fun.

I loved going to Ojai with my family, before my dad left and moved to his own place. I liked hiking in Libbey Park or up in the hills. You had to be careful of the poison ivy. If it bit you, you'd itch for weeks.

...mes when we hiked, it was steep, and they'd pass me from one ...son to the other; my feet wouldn't touch the ground. I felt special. Even with Mean Ned. He didn't say, "Barf . . . she has cooties. I'm not touching her." He'd just gently pass me to my sister like I was a bowl of mashed potatoes, and he took his share. Hiking in Ojai was always fun. My parents didn't yell at each other, and we were all together as a family.

Mountains, horseback riding, streams, orange groves, Ojai's a paradise of adventure. I remember when my sisters swam in the river, and they were wearing these long dresses that women could wear if they worked on a cowboy ranch; the air got caught under their skirts and they rode down the river like it was an inner tube. It was a gas to watch. I can still picture them in my brain, seeing them laughing and having a ball. My mom couldn't watch. She looked like she'd was going to have a cow, making the same expression when she thought that little plane was going to fall out of the sky.

I wished I was big enough to wear a cowboy ranch dress and ride the river as if I was a part of it. I wouldn't get out of the water when my mom told me to. I'd keep going down the river until I glided into the ocean, then floated past the waves and the surfers and seals, into the big sea – ending up on *Gilligan's Island*. If I was big enough to wear a cowboy ranch dress, that's what I would have done. I'd have floated away to an island and never been found.

7 AUDREY FRIEDMAN

I WAS JUST A LITTLE GIRL, FROM A BROKEN MARRIAGE, WITH NO EXPECTATIONS.

The motor engine sounded like a movie projector ticking loudly, while dusty, exhausted, snail moving men smoking cancer sticks loaded the last of the boxes into the May Flower moving van. The idling of the clunky truck engine echoed through my empty house on Kittridge Street, losing speed, sputtering and dying out, the sound haunting and spooking me like a ghost from Christmas past. I stood in the doorway of my soon-to-be old bedroom, where I had slept for the last, nearly, almost, seven years of my life. Well, before my sister stole it from me for her stupid dance parties.

We moved on my birthday. Instead of throwing me a party with all of my neighborhood friends, playing pin the tail on the donkey, or doing the balloon relay, or clothespin in the bottle, and stuffing our faces with chocolate cake smothered in chocolate frosting and caked with vanilla ice cream, we were moving across the Santa Monica mountains and closer to my grandma, who was working for some new lady in Beverly Hills. We moved into a duplex not far from the Farmers' Market, where my mom would buy me hard black licorice buttons that took forever to chew and got stuck in my teeth. I spent more time picking licorice buttons out of my teeth than chewing them.

I stood in the doorway of my never-again bedroom, the orange walls still vibrant with holes from posters and pictures from when my big sister roomed there and had sleepovers with half of her twelfth-grade class. My mom put me back in that bedroom after Lana left for Mexico on a long trip with some other family, as if she wasn't part of our family anymore. On the floor where my twin bed had been, some dustballs had gathered for safety, I guess. In the lint, I noticed two M&M's, one yellow and one brown, and an old wrapper of Fizzies. I remember once when Parker and I were drinking lemon-lime, we laughed, and it came out our noses. We thought it was so funny that it made us crack up even more. In the corner, where my drawers were, I saw a pink slipper from my Chatty Cathy that I had lost two months before. I hated that doll now, and I never wanted to see her again after what happened on that night I'm not ready to talk about yet.

"Audrey . . . we have to go!" came echoing from my ever-growing impatient mom. I knew she was stressed out because she reminded me and Mean Ned every night at dinner that "Moving is one of the most stressful things."

Ned would snidely reply, "I thought divorce was." I remember my mom giving him that look like he was cruisin' for a bruisin'.

See, my mom decided to move us out of the Valley and to Los Angeles, where the dreams were bigger, the neighborhoods more pretty and more crowded – with new memories to make. Besides, she had met David, and she wanted to be closer to where he lived, near the tidal pools, way down below the cliffs of Palos Verdes.

My dad was already settled in his curved apartment building in Century City and only a ten-minute car ride downtown to the LOS ANGELES TIMES where he works in display advertising. He's really good at selling ads to stores. He's the Times best salesman. He told me the new mall at Century City wanted him to be the manager – that's the boss – because he knows Joseph and Ira Magnin and all the big, fancy stores in Beverly Hills, 'cuz he places their ads in The Times newspaper. But my Pop wasn't interested. He had another plan, he said. He had started law school at night and was going to become a lawyer.

"Are lawyers as old as you, Dad?"

"I'm only forty-seven, Audrey."

"What? Daddy, that's as old as a mummy. How can you be a lawyer if you are wrapped in cloth and your mouth can't talk? Perry Mason wears a suit and you can hear him talk," I said. I watched the show. I knew what he wore.

He laughed.

"Why are you laughing, Dad? I'm serious."

"I know, sweetheart. You wait until you're forty-seven. You'll see. It's not that old," he told me.

"If you say so, Pop." I honestly thought he was too big to be a lawyer and should just stick with selling advertising to fancy stores because he was really good at it – and at yard work. He always told me, "You have to take care of things. If you do, they will last forever." At first, I wondered if that included family, but he was talking about stuff that is yours, like a tennis racket or shoes – not people.

We were standing on the driveway one time and my dad saw a for sale sign on the house across the street, next to the Shaws' house. Those people were moving somewhere else. My dad said they were getting top dollar for their house. I looked at it and thought, 'But their grass isn't as nice as ours.'

"Do you know how much I paid for this house?" my dad asked me.

I shook my head.

"I bought it in '58 for fifteen thousand dollars. Do you know how much that is?"

I shook my head. I could only count to one thousand when I was six because counting to one thousand is only counting to one hundred ten times and changing the one hundred to the next number and counting regular and adding an 'and'.

"Nope."

"Guess."

I thought. "Can I buy ten candy bars for fifteen thousand dollars?" I wondered.

"You could buy all the candy in the store," he told me.

My eyes got huge, like the size of a frisbee. I couldn't believe it. ALL the candy in the store?

"What about licorice?" I almost loved red or black licorice as much as I loved ice cream.

"All the licorice you could ever eat," he said.

"Wowee!" I was elated. That's a lot of licorice. I love licorice. I could buy twenty-five whips for a quarter. Fifty licorice whips for fifty cents.

"See, Audrey? When you take care of things, they become more valuable and last," he told me.

I remember that morning when my dad was done packing the Thunderbird with his suitcases and toolbox and drove off. Rebecca Watkins, who was nine years old, and the neighborhood bully, and the little sister to the bad brother my dad kicked in the butt, said to me that my dad didn't love me anymore. She said he was going to live in paradise, closer to the beach because the life he had with us was not magical at all. I knew Century City had a new outdoor mall, but I didn't think it was magical or better than our life. But Rebecca Watkins said so, and I was too afraid of her to tell her she was a meanie and lying; I was a small fry compared to her, and she could pound me like she did to Sheldon, my neighbor who lived across the street next door to Georgia.

I told my mom what Rebecca Watkins said, but mom never showed any emotion about it. She seemed really happy, although she hated packing boxes and the moving men being rough with her furniture.

My dad leaving to go live in paradise without me – I'll tell you that it affected me in ways that would make me really sad. I didn't talk about it. See, I loved my dad. He only spanked me one time, way less than my mom did. I don't think I was ever the same kid, even though I was happy there was no more yelling to wake me up at night – and I didn't have to see him cry anymore. If someone asked me how I felt about my mom and dad getting a divorce, I'd just shrug my shoulders and say nothing. How do you talk about something you don't understand?

One day, about two weeks after my dad "walked out on us" (that's what Rebecca Watkins said he did), my brother threw away the surfboard my dad had bought him; he threw it into the garbage truck dumpster himself, on Friday trash day. I remember watching him from the den front window carry the surfboard under his arm, down the driveway, in the middle of winter, in the middle of a freezing day (around my birthday); it was before we moved from Kittridge Street, when the temperature could get to really cold in the Valley, and you'd shake like a dog who was yelled at for peeing on the carpet. Ned just threw the board in on top of the garbage, turned around, and walked back up the driveway without any emotion. I remember the short, round garbage man, with rosy cheeks from the cold air yelling back, "You sure?"

Ned said nothing, walked back in the house, went in his room, and pounded on his drum set. I tried to go in his room, but he locked the door and wouldn't answer.

I'll never forget it because my dad had given Ned that board on his birthday, and surfing was my brother's life. Now, with my dad and mom not loving each other anymore, my mean brother's love of surfing left with my dad, despite my pop telling Ned he'd take him to the beach, anytime. But Ned said he hated surfing. I knew what he really meant. And I still wonder if that garbage man copped the surfboard from the garbage bin and gave it to his son. It was a really nice board. I'd like to know someone is still enjoying it.

THAT SUMMER BEFORE I STARTED SECOND GRADE at Third Street Elementary, before I had joined the Bluebirds, before I was told to stay in my seat, before my mom got married to David and David died and went to heaven, and before Lana came back from Mexico and Shelly was released from juvie for running away, something happened to me on Detroit Street that I'm going to tell you about. Promise you won't be a big fink like Parker and tell on me. Ok?

You're the only one I am going to tell, and I don't want to get in big trouble.

It was a really confusing time after we moved to Detroit Street. My mom and dad were getting a divorce, and my mom was dating David, and sometimes he'd sleep over. My dad came to get me on a Saturday morning to take me to Kiddieland because the new plan was that he'd get to see me every weekend on Saturdays.

I stood there in the doorway with my mom and David standing behind me, and my dad stood on the porch and wouldn't say a word. He'd just look at me with his hands in his pockets, looking like he was waiting to pay for my stuff at the Blue Chips Stamp store. I loved going there, to the blue chip store. My dad would give me the stamps, and I would paste them to this little book. Then, when I had enough, I could buy stuff. We'd go to the store on Pico Blvd, not far from my dad's new apartment, and I bought: a superball that bounced like crazy; Sucrets lozenges that I ate like candy; white Fruit of the Loom socks with two blue stripes like Parker's; a cassette tape recorder that I'd sing *I'm a Believer* by the Monkee's into because I loved the Monkee's, especially Peter; and I bought my favorite game, *Mystery Date*. When we played the game, all my Bluebird friends wanted the door to open to that guy in the white jacket, or the boy who skied, or bowled, or had beach clothes on. But I wanted 'the dud'. He was the cutest looking fellow of them all, and all he needed was his pants washed. I liked him way better than the boy in the waiter's jacket. But when you got the dud, you lost the game. I didn't care. He was still the cutest one. Shelly told me one time I was playing with her that I better change my tune, or I just might end up with a dud one day in real life at the rate I was losing the game.

There we were, the four of us just standing on the porch on Detroit Street saying nothing, like the cat had all our tongues. My tummy had butterflies in it. Not real ones. I felt like I swallowed a whole pomegranate, and it was stuck in my throat. I couldn't look back at my dad for very long. I felt very unsure of what was going to happen next.

My mom and dad hated each other because my mom said so, and scary stuff happened when they were mad at each other. There would be yelling; sometimes things would get broken, like kitchen plates or an alarm clock when she threw it like a pitcher and made a hole in the wall . . . and my Chatty Cathy doll.

My mom would say, "Have her home by four," and then she'd push me toward my dad. He'd take my hand and lead me to his car that he just washed. He always washed his car on Saturday mornings. Sometimes he waxed it too.

One time after she shut the front door, I remember he stopped on the sidewalk and turned to me and said, "Is he living there?! Tell me, or I'm going to give you a spanking!" My dad was so mad at me. I didn't know why. But I started crying. He was talking about David, see. He wanted to know if David was living in the duplex, in my mom's room.

"No, Daddy. He lives down by the beach, where the tide pools are," I told him.

I only ever saw my dad's eyes that black that time he caught me lying to him about taking my bike to Pierce College.

"You're not lying? You better not be lying."

"No, Daddy. I swear." I wasn't.

"Get in the car," he told me.

He grabbed me by the hand and dragged me to the car. I don't know why he was so mad at me. I told him the truth. I don't remember talking on the drive to Kiddieland. It wasn't that far from where we lived on Detroit Street. It seemed like forever. I was hoping once we got to Kiddieland, that he would be happy and talk to me again, but I remember he was so quiet that day. I went on all the rides alone. Even the bumper cars. When we went to Pink's, he said he wasn't hungry. I wasn't hungry either and only had one hot dog without any chili and only ate half. My tummy was upset. The butterflies were back.

My dad was always happy when he was with me. He'd tell me jokes like, "Did you hear about the man who ran over himself?" I'd say, "No." But he had told me the same joke a hundred times, and I knew how it ended. He'd tell it again, pretending I never heard it.

"Well, this man was driving, and he pulled over to the curb and said to some kid on the sidewalk, 'Hey, Kid, if I give you a nickel, will you go across the street and buy me a newspaper?' And the kid said 'No', so the man ran over himself." Then my dad would start laughing and say how funny he thought that joke was. He told me it was Jewish humor. I didn't get it. Maybe because I was only half Jewish.

He had another joke that made him crack up.

"What's red and green and goes a thousand miles an hour?"

"What Daddy?" Of course, I knew because he told me this joke a thousand million times.

"A frog in a blender."

That was grody. I didn't like that joke because I loved frogs. Next to cats, dogs, chickens, sheep, horses, birds, and lions, they were my most favorite animal. I'd catch frogs in the creek by our house all the time when we moved to Grand Avenue. I let them go, of course. They love their home in the soggy grass.

We'd often drive past Rocketdyne in Canoga Park, where they make the rocket jets. Sometimes, you'd hear a big sonic BOOM! when you were playing outside, or even swimming underwater in the pool. It wasn't scary. We knew it wasn't the Atom bomb, just some guys starting an engine or something. It happened all the time. They were flying rockets to the moon and needed to be sure they could get there.

One time, my dad was driving and smoking a cigar; he took it out of his mouth and started saying weird things to me like, "Audrey Friedman! Audrey Friedman!" I had no idea why he was calling me that, but he would smile when he said it then take a puff on his cigar.

"Why are you calling me that, Daddy?"

"Because . . . it's your name."

"I thought my name is Audrey Franklin."

"Not really," he said.

"I don't get it, Dad. What's my last name?"

"Franklin."

"So why are you calling me that other name?" I was confused – as confused as a kid could be.

"I can't tell you why right now," he told me.

"Is it a secret?" I asked.

"For now, kiddo. I'll tell you the story when you're older."

I have no idea what he was talking about and why I couldn't know right then. He just started whistling, like it was no big deal. So many secrets.

On that morning he came to get me, when we lived on Detroit Street, it was like he had a cloud over his head, and it was making him sad; it was like he had a tummy ache and wanted to go to bed because he didn't feel well.

"Dad, do you want to ask me how much you love me? Because I have a new answer for you." I thought that would cheer him up.

"Not right now, Audrey," he barely said loud enough that I could hear him.

"Are you sure? Because I thinks it's a good one."

I waited for him to reply. He was so quiet. I'd never seen him like this, and I wasn't sure if I should spoil the surprise or if it would make him mad that I didn't wait.

"Well, I was going to tell you the universe the next time you asked me. There's something bigger than the world and it's called the universe. And I was hoping you loved me that much, more than the world, because it's a more bigger place."

My dad didn't say a peep. He just drove the car until we got to Kiddieland, pulled in the gravel parking lot like he always did, found a spot on the end, cut the engine, got out, and walked toward the ticket booth. He didn't even wait for me to get out of the car.

That's the problem with being in the middle of a divorce with a mom and a dad who hate each other. Sometimes, they hate you too.

My sister, Lana, had come back from Mexico and was living with us on Detroit Street. It was shortly after we moved there, when my parents were in the middle of their divorce and my mom was already dating David. Lana said that she wouldn't be there for long, 'cuz she was moving in with her boyfriend's parents in the Valley. She had a boyfriend named Thad. She had met him when we were living on Kittridge Street, right before he had gone to the war for a while; he wasn't killed and he was back. She said she loved him and they'd probably get married. We were having dinner in the dining hutch, and she told me and my mom and Ned about it.

"Yuck," I told her.

"You're going to like him, Porky. He's tall, dark and handsome, and he's in the Air Force."

"Does he fly airplanes that bomb palm trees and light them on fire?" I'd seen that on TV too many times. These planes would fly and drop bombs. There were so many bombs coming out of the plane, it looked like they were pooping (just like my mice did). I could see explosions and the palm trees catching fire, choppers with big propellers on top like Beanie had on his hat, and teeth on the front like a monster; they had guns that would shoot people below in the garden and kill them. I saw. All of it. War. Real war – not playing war – is bad. I sometimes have nightmares about the war, and palm trees burning, and boys and innocent people dying. When Mean Ned gets done with college, he'll have to pick a number in the draft lottery. Ned may be a butt to me and not take me with him when I want to go somewhere that he's going, but I don't want my brother to die in Vietnam.

"No. Thad was never in Nam. He was in the Philippines," my sister said.

"Where's the pillapeens?"

"Philippines," my mom corrected me.

"Over there somewhere by Nam," she said. "Now he's stationed down in San Diego, but you'll still think he's the cat's meow," she gushed and giggled like a weirdo.

"I don't know what that means, but I do like cats," I said. Then, she told my mom that she was walking home that afternoon and spotted my dad parked on the street, sitting in his car. She said she just passed by my dad's car, never making eye contact with him, waved,

"Hi, Dad," and just kept on walking. It made me feel good to know my dad was staked out on the street like a detective, watching us. My mom wasn't happy. "Are you serious?" She shook her head in disgust and rolled her eyes like when your favorite wrestler, Gorilla Monsoon, loses.

She said she couldn't wait until the divorce was final. I asked her what would happen after she and my dad got divorced.

"I'm going to marry David."

My brother was going into the eleventh grade. That's a grade for teenagers. They drive, listen to the record player until they wear it out, lock the door to their room when they're in it, and go steady. Ned had lots of friends, and one of his friends, Ross, lived in a house on our block, up the street – near Beverly Blvd. His dad drove a Rolls Royce like the movie stars drove. I would see it parked out front in the driveway. It was white with big wheels and a silver angel on the hood, who looked like she was running into the wind or the speed was blowing her off the hood.

I had just joined Bluebirds and Shelly had come home from juvenile hall. That's the place they send you when you've been a bad kid and made your mom mad. But I don't think Shelly was a bad kid. I think she ran away before Christmas, not because she didn't want to get me a present but because she was sad about what happened that night when we lived on Kittridge Street – when everything changed. It was a terrible night that is still hard to talk about. I'll tell you soon enough. That terrible night is why Shelly snuck out of the house a few months later, with some boy, and never came back to Kittridge Street.

Want to know the truth? I should have been the one put in juvenile hall. If I hadn't asked Shelly if I could spend the night at Parker's house, none of it would have happened, and she would never have run away. So, I was the bad kid. I made her leave. Just like I made my dad leave.

8 FORD MUSTANG

ROSS SAID I WAS HIS SPECIAL FRIEND. HE ASKED ME A VERY IMPORTANT QUESTION one day when I was seven, before I started second grade at Third Street Elementary and after I became a Bluebird.

I remember him folding my hand in his and whispering in my ear: "Can you keep a secret, Audrey?"

A year had passed from when we slipped and slid on Parker's front lawn on Kittridge Street, before my mom and dad divorced, before second grade, and before David died. Summer was coming around again, as it did the year before. I struggled to escape another hot day, although Detroit Street sidewalks didn't get hot enough to cook an egg like they would on a sizzling summer day in the Valley. See, the heat feels too hot and the cold feels too cold. I know. I've been to Yosemite with my family in the winter when it looked like a Christmas card, before my mom and dad divorced; my brother broke his ankle skiing, and Shelly lured a deer into our cabin with some bread. My mom was so irritated that Shelly coaxed the deer through the back door of the cabin. "Get it out of here!" You could hear a vibrato in her voice hitting a fear note. My mom looked frightened of the deer, imagining it would be a bull in a china shop and destroy the cabin and trample us. Shelly loved animals and didn't mind that it was a wild deer. She had a way with animals of every kind; it was really cute like Bambi and seemed to enjoy Wonder bread and trusted my sister.

You know what? Thinking about that trip to Yosemite, I don't think my brother and sisters knew how to ski. I think they just went down the hill as fast as they could and stopped when they ran into a tree, or something else, or just fell down in the snow. After Ned broke his ankle, it cut our vacation short, and we had to drive back to Canoga Park. The small mountain hospital put his leg in a cast that had a rubber heal set in the plaster so he wouldn't crack the mold if he tried to hobble. They gave him wooden crutches because he couldn't walk on his cast. I could tell it hurt, and I didn't want to bug him or tell him he was a spaz. I didn't want to hurt his feelings, even though he was mean to me and would knock me down with his pillow when I tried to wake him up or tell me he wish I had been born a brother.

I remember driving down this snowy road and everything was white, with the snow piled high on each side of the road and lights from the cabins reflecting off the snowflakes that kept falling and sticking to the ones that had floated down before them. The big redwood pine trees held little piles of snow on their branches; I could see into the passing cabins, all lit up by fires burning in the stone fireplaces, looking like something out of a Bing Crosby movie when families would be inside keeping warm, smiling and drinking hot chocolate.

Even Shelly was singing that winter wonderland song that Bing Crosby sings at Christmas. It was snowing really hard, and my dad was driving really slow. I remember the headlights on the icy winding road that went between the big redwood trees. My mom kept telling him to go slow and he'd say, "I am going as slow as I can, Sophia." I think he spoke too soon. Suddenly, on a steeper corner, the station wagon started to slide sideways because the tires couldn't stay straight. My dad had put on chains, but they didn't make a difference. Too much snow fell hiding the ice. Shelly stopped singing and we all became quiet, tensing up, waiting for the station wagon to stop turning, but it didn't. I watched my dad try to control the car, and my mom, of course, was scared, like on that road to Ojai. "Lee, Lee!" she shouted . . . *again*. My mom carried herself like Catwoman, Kung Fu-like, except when she was in the car sitting next to my dad when he was driving. Then she became Nell from *Bullwinkle*, like a damsel in distress tied to the train tracks, helpless. That's what you call a lady tied to train tracks. You'd see it in Charlie Chaplin movies or other silent movies while you eat your pizza at Shakey's. There were a lot of damsels in distress tied to train tracks back then. But they were always untied before the train came because the man knew how to untie knots.

The station wagon felt like The Scrambler ride in slow motion. There's one at POP, the pier at the end of Ocean Park in Santa Monica. I could feel myself pressing up against Shelly, who squished up against Lana as it slid and spun; then, going in the opposite direction, I was pressing up against Ned who was too distracted to say, "Get off me." Up ahead, through the wiper blades that were struggling to push the heavy falling snow off the glass, I could see cars gathered together like match box cars; they were piled up at the end of the track because they'd slipped on the ice too. We all felt the station wagon continue to spin in slow motion as if we were never stopping, ice skating on the ice, about to spin off the side of the road, down the rocky cliff . . . until the thud. The front chrome bumper bumped into the car ahead that had hit the pile-up and finally brought us to a dead stop; it kept us from tipping off the ledge into the redwood treetops and whatever hell was below. It was a close call, I tell you.

That particular day on Detroit Street had happened after my mom started me in ballet school on La Brea. It was down the street from the seventy-six gas station, where drivers could put a tiger in their tank and a little orange ball on top of their car antennas. Except, my days of ballet didn't last very long. The teacher kicked me out. Well, my mom said they politely asked me to leave. The ballet lady said I thought everything was a competition and that was not how ballet worked.

I loved ballet and thought it was fun. I felt pretty, Tinker Bell-like, in my ballet clothes. My mom bought me a pink leotard, pink tights, and pink ballet slippers that didn't feel like slippers at all – more like cardboard boxes. They felt stiff and kept your feet straight. The ballet studio was a big room with dark wooden floors and mirrors on the walls. We would do these exercises at a round bar, like a handrail when you walk down the stairs. We all turned to the side and hung on with one hand so we wouldn't fall down.

The teacher would ask us to do pliés, which is a weird word for squatting with your heels together and with your toes pointed out like a 'V.' You have to keep your feet and heels on the ground and try to touch your butt to the floor without falling, or bending forward, or moving your heels. It's hard. Your heels have a mind of their own, and they want to pop up. When you plié, you have to stand up really straight with your chest out and your chin down. It's a lot to remember, especially for a kid. The teacher would say, "Heels on the floor, girls." I would try, but it wasn't easy.

That's not why I got kicked out.

My third lesson on a Thursday afternoon, when I didn't have a Bluebird meeting, we were told to do pirouettes across the floor, spinning like a Mini Tin Top. No problem for me. I was super-duper good and fast. I knew how to twirl for a few years. Sometimes, it got me in trouble, like that day Parker was grounded, sitting in his front yard. And that Thursday, when my days of ballet dried up. Yet twirling made me disappear in a magical way, feeling freedom. I felt the feeling of floating – a dizzy glee, like my feet weren't touching the ground, and I could fly. Fly away.

We had all lined up on one side of the studio, and the ballet teacher would say, "Go!" Oh boy, would I. I would be across the floor to the windows that looked out on La Brea before anyone else left the other side of the room. I spun as fast as a tornado, kicking up dust like the Road Runner and blowing across the wooden floor, cleaning it as I went. I'd twirl across that floor as fast as a bowling ball being shot out of a cannon, spinning down the lane at warp speed. Twirling, you see, was in my blood.

Well, the ballet lady did not think that was groovy at all. She had a look of surprise. Not the kind of happy surprise look you have when you get a present you didn't expect; it was more like the look of surprise from when you step in dog poop. She told my mom I had too much energy and maybe I should do something else, like swimming. But I already knew how to swim. I had been swimming since I was not even two years old. I didn't want to swim. I wanted to be a ballet dancer because all the actresses I loved, like Debbie Reynolds and Nanette Fabray (my favorite actresses), knew how to dance. Watch *Singing in the Rain* or *The Band Wagon*. You'll get my drift. Actresses needed to know how to dance, and I wanted to be an actress – not Esther Williams.

My announcement that I wanted to be an actress left my lips one day at the dinner table when I was four after visiting my grandma at Judy's brick house; it was in a neighborhood that had lawns the size of a pasture and where I played with her little girl and little boy, who were older than I was. This Judy lady sang and danced too. I loved her, but Nanette Fabray was still my favorite. Judy wore lipstick and tap shoes. She had brown eyes, and she liked dogs and lions, like me. I had never met a scarecrow or a tin man, but I bet I would like them like Judy did when she was in that movie; it was about her being lost and wanting the Wizard of Oz to help her get back home to her Auntie Em. They were nice, the Scarecrow and Tin Man, and they had a good sense of direction, helping her find her way on the yellow brick road when she needed to get back home to Kansas – kind of like when I would help Lana find her way back to our old house.

I have had many people tell me, "You look like a young Judy Garland." I hope so. Something about my brown eyes. But I don't want to grow up to be like her. My grandma says she was sad and spent too much time in her bedroom with the curtains drawn and didn't eat. Yet when I watch her movies, I want to be an actress like she is and do the kind of musicals she does. So, I needed to know how to dance if I was going to be an actress like Judy or Nanette Fabray.

My ballet career ended after it started. The ballet lady told my mom that her studio 'was not a good fit for someone with my talents.' I think that was a nice way of saying I was too fast at pirouettes and made the other little girls look slow. At least that's what my mom told me.

I'm dragging my heels. I know you're wondering what happened on Detroit Street that summer of 1967. Nineteen sixty-seven adds up to eighty-six, if you were wondering. I know . . . I'm avoiding the subject. I feel like how I do when I wouldn't want to take a bath. Okay . . . here goes.

I can't remember what day it was when it first happened. I know it was in August because I had joined the Bluebirds and got my uniform, cap, and socks with the little blue birds on them. I met some other little girls that were starting second grade at Third Street. We all were excited to be Bluebirds, knowing that one day, when we were in fourth grade, we'd be Campfire Girls. Although it was only two more grades, it seemed like a hundred years away.

After the meeting (getting all my Bluebird stuff), we got home, and I put on my whole uniform from cap to socks because I was so excited to try it out. Dressed from head to toe in Bluebird majesty, I asked my mom if I could go show Mrs. Porter, and she said yes. I bolted out the kitchen door, and I walked down to her house and knocked on her door. She didn't answer. I put my ear up to the door like I'd do when I was trying to listen in on Mean Ned's room when he'd shut the door and lock it, telling me to stay out. "Don't even knock," he would tell me. I would anyway. He'd get so mad. I love to bug him.

I listened at Mrs. Porter's door. I didn't hear the television or the soap opera on in the living room, so I left thinking she must have gone out to get some milk, butter, bread, and eggs at the store – because I loved French toast for dinner when she'd look after me in the afternoon.

I walked down the street, searching the sidewalks and lawns for someone to show my uniform to. I decided the Clampetts were my next stop to show off my initiation into the Bluebirds and point out the detail of the birds on my socks. That's when I saw Ross coming out of our driveway. He was on a bike, wearing jeans with a white t-shirt, and he had a cancer stick tucked behind his ear. He came across the street and blocked the sidewalk with his bike.

"Stop. You have to pay a toll," he told me.

"What's a toll?" I asked.

"It's when you have to give me some money," Ross said.

"But I don't have any money."

"Then how are you going to pass?" he asked.

I thought a moment.

"Can I go across the street and walk on that sidewalk?"

"No. You have to pay to walk on that sidewalk too." He took the cancer stick from behind his ear, pulled a metal lighter from his pocket, and lit it, blowing the smoke in my face. I fanned it away, hating the smell.

"But how can I pay you if I don't have money? My mom didn't give me any," I said.

"You're Ned's kid sister, right?"

"Yes. You're Ross."

"I was just at your house, hanging out with your brother." Then he took another drag and stared at me. "What's that thing you're wearing?" He pointed to my uniform.

"I'm a Bluebird," I told him.

"Is that like a Girl Scout?"

"No," I said. "It's like a Camp Fire Girl, but we're littler than them and have birds on our socks."

"Groovy. "

He took two more long drags on his cancer stick and chucked it into the street, flicking it with his fingers; he blew out the smoke, missing my face, but I could smell the stink of the burnt tobacco.

"Ok. You can pass," he decided.

"Really?" I was excited.

"Yeah. Bluebirds are righteous. You're a nice kid."

"Thank you, Ross. I like your bike."

"You want to see something really bitchin'?"

"Okay," I told.

He got off his bike and started wheeling it down the street toward the corner. "Follow me."

I followed him down about seven houses, as far as where the parking lot began for the Ford dealership. He crossed the grass lining the curb and rolled his bike across the street. I stepped up to the curb and looked left, then right, then left again. No cars. I crossed the street. I walked up to where he was standing in his driveway, in front of a big white car.

"This is my dad's Rolls Royce. What do you think?" he asked me.

I gave it a once-over.

"I think it's bitchin'," I told him. Parker and I would call really groovy things "bitchin'".

"Come here." He stood at the front of the car. "Look at this hood ornament."

I walked over to it and took a look at this lady stuck on the front of this car hood. She looked like an angel.

"That looks like an angel," I said.

"Yeah. She's a beautiful girl with a pretty little nose, just like you."

I touched my nose, feeling it, seeing if it felt like what hers looked like.

"Really?"

"Sure. No one ever told you you were pretty?" He asked.

"Never," I said. I didn't feel pretty. I was called a tomboy a lot; I had short hair because Lana would practice haircutting on me and cut all my hair off. I liked to climb trees, catch tarantula spiders on Tarantula hill, and do cannonballs in the pool. Boys do that and so can girls. Because I was scrawny and had short hair (still do) and didn't wear dresses much (usually jeans), sometimes I was mistaken for a boy. "Excuse me, son," a man once said when he tried to get by me when I was deciding which candy bar I wanted at the candy rack at Market Basket. I felt weird for a second. I just looked up at him and said, "I'm a girl." I chose a Butterfinger and ate it before I got home.

Ross saying I was pretty when I was seven entered my imagination like a frog turning into a Prince.

"Listen, I got to go in. See you later, Audrey."

"Ok."

He rolled his bike to the gate and opened it.

"Thanks for not making me pay a toll!" I shouted after.

"I was just kidding, Audrey. Don't let anybody tell you you have to pay a toll."

I started walking up the street back to my house when I heard Ross's voice call me.

"Hey, Audrey, come here for a sec."

I turned, and he was standing on the sidewalk. I walked back to him.

"Do you want to see something else?"

"What?" I asked.

He pointed. "It's across the street, in that parking lot," he told me.

"At Ford?"

"Yeah."

"Is it another hood thing?" I wondered

"Yeah. It's really groovy. Want to see? It will just take a sec."

"Okay," I said.

I followed him across the street, looking both ways; we walked down the street toward Beverly Blvd and around the wall that lined the parking lot filled with all the Ford cars parked bumper to bumper. He kept walking, zig-zagging in between and around the cars until we got to the end of the wall in the corner.

"Here. Look at this car. It's a Mustang."

I knew Mustangs. Parker's dad had one.

"I like Mustangs. They're bitchin'," I told him.

He sat on the ground, in front of the car.

"Come sit and look at this grill."

I didn't want to get my new Bluebird uniform dirty. I squatted next to him to get a better view.

"Look at this horse on the grill. Isn't it bitchin'?"

"Yeah, bitchin'," I said under my breath. I love horses. I loved riding them at the pony ride next to Kiddieland. I love riding them in

Ojai. I love Mustangs. The horse *and* the car.

"Can you see it okay? Here, sit on my lap. You can see it better," Ross said.

I thought that was a good idea, as I wouldn't get my new uniform dirty. I moved closer to him and turned. He was sitting Indian style on the ground, and he helped me as I sat between his legs.

"Look. See how the horse is running, Audrey?"

"Bitchin'," I said.

"Right on."

He pushed my hair to the side. "Your hair is really shiny," he said. "You're blinding me."

I was sandy blonde, and my hair looked like the sun, on a clear day. In the summer, my hair got more blonde.

"I use Breck shampoo," I told him.

"Groovy. It smells nice too."

"That's the shampoo smell. You can use it if you want. It's not just for girls," I let him know.

"Maybe I will. Then I can smell nice like you."

We looked at the Mustang for another sec, and then he told me to get up.

"We got to get going. I have homework. But that was groovy, right . . . that new Mustang?"

"I really liked it," I told him.

We both stood up. He dusted off his pants, removing the little rocks and dirt stuck to his jeans.

"Yeah? Well, we both have something in common."

"What?"

"We like cars," he said. I did like cars, even though one time I was driving with my dad on Kittridge Street and a car ran a stop sign; my dad slammed on the breaks, and I went crashing into the dashboard, cutting my eye just below my eyebrow. He didn't have time to put his arm across my chest to stop me.

He was so upset. "Are you alright, Audrey?!" I was shaken up and bleeding from my eye cut. He grabbed his handkerchief from his back pocket and put it on my cut to stop the bleeding. He pressed hard against the cut and it hurt. "Stop, Daddy! It hurts!" I screamed.

"Hold this on your eye." I held the handkerchief tightly against my face. My dad turned the car around and took me to Dr. Kudrow's house right away because he was just up the block. Dr. Kudrow and his wife were my parents' friends. They would have cocktail hour together with my mom and dad, Pam and Big Ned, and some other people from the neighborhood. They'd drink martinis, eat weird stuff on crackers, and dip meat in a pot that had a flame keeping it warm. They called that fondue.

Dr. Kudrow is a headache doctor for when you get pain in your head. Sometimes, I would get a headache when I ate a snow cone or frosty freeze too fast. But I didn't usually go see Dr. Kudrow because he is for adults. I remember my mom would. She'd get migraines. That's what she called a really bad headache. I would go into her room and find her in bed in the dark with the curtains pulled and her eyes tightly shut, with a washcloth on her forehead. She would tell me to leave the room – that she didn't feel well. That happened a lot when she was married to my dad.

My sisters and Mean Ned were friends with Dr. and Mrs. Kudrow's son and daughter, who were the same ages. They also had a little girl named Lisa, who was three years old; Lana would babysit her when Dr. and Mrs. Kudrow would go out to dinner, or to a game, or the movies, or a party.

Dr. Kudrow had a bag of doctor things at his house. He cleaned off the blood from my eye with some alcohol that stung like when you get a rope burn or stub your toe; he looked at my cut and said that I was going to live, and all I needed was a butterfly Band-Aid, and that was it. It's not really a butterfly. Just the shape. He put the Band-Aid on my eye and told my dad not to worry. "Don't worry, Lee. She'll be fine." My dad wiped his face. He looked relieved. Dr. Kudrow was right. Eventually, it healed, but I have a scar.

Ross and I wove through the cars, back out of the parking lot. He took my hand as we crossed the street.

"Thanks, Ross. That was fun," I said.

"Do you want to do it again sometime?" he asked.

"Okay."

"Can you keep a secret, Audrey?"

"Yes," I told him.

"You're positive? Because it's really important." Sometimes I could be a fink, but not with the important stuff.

"I won't fink, Ross."

He leaned down and whispered in my ear.

"I like you. You're my special friend."

"Really?" I was surprised. I had never been someone's special friend. I was Parker's bestest friend. He never called me special; he called me a dork.

Yet, Ross thought I was special.

"I don't want you to tell anybody, okay? Not Ned, or your mom, or your sisters, or your dad, or your friends – because they will be jealous. Get it?" he said.

"I get it. I won't."

"You promise?"

"Cross my heart, Ross." I crossed my heart in front of him, so he knew I was serious.

"Good girl. See you 'round."

I watched Ross walk to his back gate. I turned and skipped home, forgetting to stop by and show the Clampetts my new Bluebird uniform. That's what being someone's special friend does to you. You forget.

9 SPIDER'S WEB

W HEN YOUR PARENTS DIVORCE, YOUR FAMILY
DISAPPEARS.
I can't remember when Lana came back home from
Mexico. I think it was around the same time Shelly came home from
juvenile hall. It was before summer and before I started second grade
because Lana already had a diploma from Canoga High, and we had
already moved to Detroit Street. Lana was lucky. She wouldn't have to
go to class anymore and sit through boring stuff and listen to the
teacher say, "Sit down! Stop talking! Pay attention!"

Lana already knew how to read really well. Sometimes, she would
help me read *Charlotte's Web* when I got stuck on a word, which didn't
happen very often. I love *Charlotte's Web*. My imagination ran away with
me and I would go live in the barn with Wilbur, 'cuz in my life, when
I was seven back then, it felt like being in a barn was a better place to
be than at my house. At my house, no one wanted me around. But in
the barn, all the animals loved each other. They even loved a spider;
she wasn't even an animal, had twice as many legs, and lived in a web
inside of a barn. It's my favorite book next to *Charlie and the Chocolate
Factory*. I just read that one. Sometimes, I feel like Charlie – that I need
a golden ticket to change my life and make my family happy. Besides,
I love candy. What's better than living in a chocolate factory with all
the candy a kid can eat, with Willy Wonka and his little oompa

loompas, who can roll you to a special room and squeeze you like orange juice if you eat the wrong thing and blow up like a blister? I wish I could've found a golden ticket; it would have changed everything.

I remember going with my mom and Shelly to enroll her as a senior at Fairfax High School, a few days after she came back from being away at Juvenile hall for six months. My parents said the police made her go to juvie for running away to be a hippie. She'd ditched a few weeks after I saw her leaving the house; I asked her where she was going and she said "Far from here." It was the same day that later I saw all of my dad's clothes on the front lawn, and a few months after that terrible night (that was my fault).

Finally, Shelly was back home. Lana came to stay too. Then, later, she moved in with Thad's parents until they got married. Having my sisters and mean brother under one roof for a while felt like we were a family again. My mom smiled more. I felt whole. We went on a Friday, two days before *Snow White and the Seven Dwarfs* came out. I remember because the movie theater was down from Fairfax High on Beverly Blvd, eight blocks from Kiddieland and seven blocks from our house. I saw it on the marquis as we turned right, and I screamed in happiness. "Mom . . . Snow White is coming out! Can we go see it?"

"It's not out until Sunday, Audrey."

"Well, can we see it on Sunday?"

"I can't. David and I have a date," she told me.

I did the next best thing a kid can do when they're thinking fast. The minute we got home, I called my dad.

"Dad . . . Snow White is coming out! Can we go see it?"

My dad agreed to not take me to Kiddieland and Pink's on Saturday and he took me on that Sunday to see *Snow White and the Seven Dwarfs*. Dads are good like that.

Shelly, my mom, and Ned walked the campus at Fairfax High and saw the big football field in the back. Ned too, because he was going to go to school there and carpooled with my sister. When we stood on the track field, where runners ran like lightning bolts, I asked my sister if she was going to be a cheerleader. She said, "Nah. It's not my bag. I'd rather join band." My brother was excited about the new gymnasium though. He likes to shoot hoops. Lew Alcindor is his favorite player. He played for the UCLA Bruins, Ned's favorite college team. Lew was the NBA number one draft pick and is going to play in Milwaukee – that's some place they make beer – for the Bucks. He has the best hook in the universe. That's why they chose him. I know basketball too. I told Ned that if he ever met Lew Alcindor, he'd look like a shrimp because Lew's as tall as a building.

My sister, Shelly, is very sensitive. I've seen her cry. She's gentle and kind and has a heart the size of a Volkswagen Beetle. She couldn't hurt a fly, even though they land on your food after they've landed on dog poop (my mom says they can carry disease). I still eat my food, even after they've landed on it. I'll take my chances.

Shelly's always loved all animals and knows how to train them. Our hair color is almost the same, and she is really pretty. I hope I grow up to look like her and Lana and not Mean Ned. I want to look like a girl and not a boy. Shelly is ten years older than me and, when I am her age, I want to be like her – except I don't want to run away and go to juvie. And you know what? She loves me. I know it. Like I told you before when we lived on Kittridge Street, I'd accidentally pee the bed, and she didn't yell at me or make me feel bad or ashamed; she didn't call me names or tell me to beat it and go play on the freeway. No. She moved over to the edge of the bed, on her side, and pulled me close to her so I wouldn't be sleeping in a wet spot. That's love.

After months away, she was so happy to be home. Shelly hated juvenile hall. I went to visit her one time with my mom, and I can see why. It felt really empty and lonely. She said it was the worst time she ever had being in there, like a prisoner in a jail, not allowed to go anywhere. She said she couldn't even go to the bathroom sometimes without having to ask permission. I'd have been afraid I would have peed my pants because when I have to go, I have to go. My mom hates it when I hold myself. I can't help it. Sometimes, I'm just too busy; I wait too long to go to the bathroom, and I do that to hold the pee in, otherwise, I just might pee my pants – and I'm too old to do that.

The duplex only had three bedrooms instead of four like we had on Kittridge Street. I shared a room with my two sisters, my two mice, and my ant farm. Shelly didn't have any animals since she went to juvie. She was sad her garden snake, Charlie, and her two rats, Ringo and Dennis, were given away. My dad hated those rats. He said that they stunk to all high heaven. I thought heaven smelled good.

Scooter went to live with another family because she was a poodle, and my mom didn't trust poodles (even though we had hardwood floors and no carpet); anyway, the people who owned the duplex didn't allow dogs to live there. Maybe they heard about Jacques. That made Shelly's heart very sad. She loved Scooter and was very attached to her, like I am to our cat, Migo, who was David's cat first. To make Shelly happy, I kept up the tradition of having smaller animals that I could keep on a table, like my mice and ants.

Since I was little, all I can remember is having animals. There were dogs, cats, rats, snakes, birds, chickens, turtles, goldfish, and kittens. But we never had ants – apart from the ones that weren't supposed to be in the house. My ant farm was in this thin, clear-green plastic box; it was a kit that I got at Sears one day with my dad. I put it together and filled it up with soil myself. I could watch the ants tunnel in the dirt, making this really bitchin' design. One time, in second grade, I brought it to show and tell. I had to be very careful not to drop it. I told my class about ants. It was really interesting, about how ants farm and get along in their colonies, which is what you call their town. They speed along and bump into each other sometimes, but they don't get mad. They are in a hurry and have somewhere to go, like when my dad drives on the 101 freeway. They zoom along and the other ants understand if they have an accident and run into them. They have a purpose, to help the soil, which I really thought was boss. Ants have two stomachs, one for themselves and one for sharing. They can carry up to fifty times their weight, which makes them super strong like a weightlifter. Also, they don't have ears, so if another ant says something mean about them, they can't hear it. They're not like turtles that just lay around or take forever to move. Though, I love turtles. I had two little water turtles that my mom and dad had brought back from a trip to San Francisco. They died. Shelly thought they would like to be out in the sun and get a tan, putting them out on the picnic table in my old backyard in their little plastic water bowl that had a plastic palm tree to sunbathe under; they dried up. I came home and found them stuck to the wooden table. I cried, but I forgave Shelly. She didn't do it on purpose.

Next to my sisters' double bed that they shared on Detroit Street, I had a cage with my two mice in it. One day, my mouse had thirteen babies. Thirteen. She ate eleven of them. Then she ate her husband. I don't think mice should get married if they're going to do that.

My mom didn't eat my dad or any of us. She was mad a lot when she lived with my dad and us kids on Kittridge Street but much less after we moved to Detroit Street. I wonder why. I wasn't bad all the time. I made her cupcakes in my easy bake oven and painted her pictures. One time, I made a box out of popsicle sticks for her birthday. I don't remember her ever being that happy on Kittridge Street. It was only really when they had cocktail parties, and she would entertain my friends' parents on my street, or when we were hiking in Ojai and she was outside in nature, in the town she grew up in. Or, when she was fishing in the rivers. Or when she was painting and making woman's heads out of clay. Or playing the piano. She plays the piano like no one I ever heard before. My grandma made her practice all the time for hours when she was a kid. My mom can play anything on the piano – classical, jazz, and even boogie woogie: "If you've got the beat and rhyme that's hard, then fry me chicken with a can of lard." Isn't that funny? I say it with her when she plays the boogie woogie song, and we laugh.

She plays this other song, by Chopin, called *Berceuse,* that I love. I'm not sure what that name means, but I think it's a beautiful word and so is the music. It makes my heart swell like a water balloon about to burst if you fill it too much. I flutter like Tinker Bell, as if I'm in a storybook magical land where there are no worries, or anger, or sadness, or people yelling at each other. You can float, standing in place, not feeling weighed down, because your wings are flapping so fast that you can't see it, and you're floating, softly, like a bubble before it pops.

When I was five and she was playing it, I sat beside her on the piano bench listening and told her "It's of rainbows and sunshine." She even wrote it on the music sheet. *Audrey – 1965.*

Oh . . . and she was really happy that one time we shared the trout that she caught for breakfast. I felt like she liked me and wanted me around. Other than that, I don't remember my mom being really happy until my dad left, and she fell in love with David.

Lana didn't stay long on Detroit Street. After a few months, she moved in with Thad's parents in the Valley. When she left, I was really sad. I think I was definitely restless in an unsettled way, anticipating more change that I wasn't ready for. Lana said that I was sleepwalking and talking in my sleep, sitting on the end of my bed babbling about my mom and my dad. I don't remember sleepwalking. I was asleep. But I did that sometimes when things became upside down and they weren't supposed to be – except if it's an hourglass and sand is running out.

After Lana left, Shelly met a boy named Joel, who liked to take pictures with his camera. They took me to the Pan Pacific Park on Gardner and I played on the merry-go-ground and swings. Pan Pacific has a big auditorium where I saw Billy Mummy. He's the little boy on *Lost in Space*. My dad took me to see him; I think he's cute, and I want to be an actress one day and be on a TV show, like *Lost in Space*, or *Gilligan's Island*. I want to make kids and grown-ups laugh.

Joel took pictures of me on the merry-go-round, which doesn't have horses like the one at the pier; it's a round metal ride that just spins fast like a dreidel. Gravity tries to pull you off the edge, spitting you into the dirt. Even if you're in the middle, you can still feel the pull, like if a bronco cowboy took his lasso and threw it around you, pulling you down like they do to a calf. They don't hurt it. It's just for fun. I saw it at the fair once. When you ride the merry-go-round, you have to hang on tight, or stand with your feet against the metal bars if you want to look like a big shot and not grab the bar to steady yourself.

Joel took pictures of me spinning. I was hanging off the side, smiling, showing off my new front teeth that grew back. Shelly would make me go faster, grabbing the metal bars and pulling and pushing as hard as she could. Sometimes, I would lay down on the round, metal platform and stare up at the sky and watch it spin by, wishing it were a time machine; I could travel to a different place where families lived together and I felt more like I was a part of it all.

Joel took a gob of pictures. He snapped pictures of me with Shelly too. She was hugging me, holding me tight against her, because she said she liked her kid sister and that she had missed me when she was away. I missed her too. She made me feel like I belonged.

On Detroit Street, my mean brother always kept his door closed and locked when he was inside. I hardly saw him. Between working for Colonel Sanders and doing stuff with his friends, I felt like he was never around. And when he was, he didn't want anything to do with me.

But his friend, Ross, did.

About a week after that first time I saw Ross on the sidewalk (and didn't have to pay a toll), I was playing tag with the Clampett kids on their front lawn. It was up by the Ford Dealership wall that I saw Ross again, standing on the sidewalk. He saw me too and waved me to come. I stopped the game and said I'd be right back. I walked up the sidewalk to where he was standing, puffing on a cancer stick.

"Want a drag?"

"I'm too young to smoke," I told him.

"No, you're not. Anyone can smoke. I think you're old enough to handle it," he said.

"Well, I tried it with the Meets kids when I was five, and I didn't like it," I replied. It was the truth. Cancer sticks are grody.

"Right on." He threw the cigarette on the pavement and stomped it out.

"I like your outfit. Where did you get it?"

I was wearing my favorite lemon drop outfit. That's what my dad called it. It was a yellow and blue striped shirt, with matching solid yellow shorts.

"I don't know. My mom got it for me."

"Groovy. Hey . . . come with me a sec. I want to show you something."

"Where are we going? I'm not supposed to go far," I let him know.

"Just in the parking lot. There's another bitchin' car I want to show you," he told me.

"Groovy," I said.

I followed him down the sidewalk, around the wall, and into the Ford dealership parking lot, weaving through the cars to the back corner where we were a few days before.

He sat down in front of the same Mustang, leaning against the wall. "Come look at the grill from here. You can see more of it," he told me.

I sat down beside him and stared at the Mustang rearing on the chrome grill.

"Bitchin'," I said under my breath.

He turned and smiled at me. Then he stroked my head. I think he was happy I liked the Mustang like he did. Then he said . . ., and I will never forget this . . .

"Hey, Audrey . . ."

"Yeah?"

"Can I show you something and you promise not to tell?"

"Ok."

"Promise?" he said.

"I swear, Ross. Cross my heart," I told him.

He took my hand and put it in his with his other hand on top of it, like a sandwich. "Do you know what a penis is?" he asked me.

"Yeah." I did, because Parker and I would check each other out sometimes when we'd have sleepovers. We'd take a flashlight under the covers and look at each other's privates, comparing them. Parker had a penis. I didn't. We were different that way. Boys and girls have different private parts.

"Have you ever seen one?"

"Um . . ."

"Audrey? You can tell me," he said.

"Yes," I said. "I saw my best friend Parker's, like . . . a couple times."

"When?"

"At his house, at a sleepover. I saw it another time when we made a fort out of blankets in his living room."

"Right on. Did you touch it?" he asked.

"No. I just looked at it with a flashlight. It was no big deal." I said.

"Did he see yours?" he asked me

"Yes."

"Were you supposed to do that?"

"I don't know," I told him.

"Had you ever done that with anyone else?"

"Done what?" I asked.

"Seen someone's privates?" he said.

I thought real hard. I remembered being at the Meets' house when I was five, almost six, years old. It was the day we smoked a cancer stick in their kitchen. It was me, Bobby Meets, who was thirteen, Ginny Meets, who was five too (but my birthday was first), and Heidi Meets, who was eleven, and Parker. Joanne Meets wasn't there. Neither were their mom and dad. We were all in their living room playing, and Bobby took off his clothes and started running around the living room naked. Then, Heidi took off her clothes . . . we all got naked. All of us were running around the living room, throwing pillows and having fun. Heidi grabbed my hand and said, "Come with me to my room."

I followed her to her room down the hall. We went into her room, and she closed the door. She climbed on her bed and was jumping up and down, bouncing, so I did too. After a few more bounces, she stopped and laid down on the bed. She told me to lay down too. I did. She pulled the sheet over our heads so I was under the covers lying next to her. I was further down with my head near her stomach. I could see it going up and down as she breathed.

"What are we doing?" I asked.

She told me we were playing doctor and to look at her *coochie*. That was her privates. I looked, and I noticed there was some black hair on it, just above where you go potty from. She told me to touch it. I hesitated. "Go ahead. I won't tell," she said. I took my finger and quickly touched it – afraid it might bite. "Not like that, silly. Don't be such a fraidy cat. Do it again."

I felt kind of scared. "Do I have to?" I asked.

"If you want to be my friend, you do." Suddenly, she heard something, threw the sheet down, and jumped up.

"My parents are home! Get in the closet!" I scrambled up, slid out of her bed and got in the closet; she shut the door. I wasn't sure if I had done something wrong. I don't know how long I was in there, but it felt like forever. I thought she was mad at me. Maybe I wasn't supposed to do that.

Ross told me that because Parker was my best friend, it was okay that I saw his penis, but my mom and dad would probably have not liked it because Parker was only my best friend and not my special friend. Special friends are different. Only special friends should see or touch your vagina or penis, he said. He used those words.

"So, can I see yours if I show you mine?" Ross asked.

"Because you're my special friend?" I said.

"Yes."

"Okay."

"Let me see yours, first," he said.

The feeling that went through my brain, for a sec, was that I shouldn't show him. I don't know why.

"Audrey . . . you're my special friend, right? And when you have a special friend, you show them," he told me.

"I guess so," I said.

"It's true. Cross my heart."

A weird feeling started to make me buzz like a bee. I could feel my body feeling different, tingly . . . energized, like when I'm waiting in line for the Matterhorn. I was nervous but not scared.

"Ok then. If you say so," I said.

"Hey . . . before you show me, come here. Sit on my lap."

I felt a little shy . . . unsure, still.

"Come here, Audrey. I'm not going to hurt you. I really, really like you. You're so pretty and sweet," he told me.

He put out his hand, and I took it. I inched closer to Ross, bent down, and he put me on his lap.

"I'm not going to hurt you. I'm just going to look." He laid me back in his lap like when you cradle your doll.

"Are you okay?" he asked.

"Yeah." I remember looking up at him, unsure of what was going to happen next. Then, I felt his hand go up my leg and under my shorts. I had these butterflies in my stomach, but not in a scary way. I wasn't going to throw up. I was just thinking hard about what was happening. Then, I felt his fingers go in my underpants, and he started touching my private parts.

"You feel so soft," he said. "Am I hurting you?"

"No." I could just feel his fingers and hand touching me, like the way you pet your dog, or cat, or a tiny little frog.

"Remember, this is a secret, Audrey. Don't tell anyone. They may not understand, and I don't want you to get into trouble. Get it?"

I couldn't speak. I just laid there. It didn't hurt. If you want to know the truth, it felt good in a weird way because he was gentle. I know the difference.

I don't know how many times Ross took me to see the Mustang running on the grill in the same corner of the Ford dealership. I can probably count it on my two hands – maybe my right foot too. The same thing would happen. He'd find me on the street riding my bike or playing alone, and I'd follow him to the parking lot across the street from his house. He'd sit on the pavement, leaning against the wall, and I'd lay in his lap; he would gently pull down my shorts and underpants, or if I was wearing my Bluebird uniform, he'd just pull down my underpants, and he would gently touch and look at me, telling me how sweet I was and that he liked me. I'd just lay there. I felt loved and happy in that moment – with my special friend, Ross.

Afterward, he'd remind me that it was a secret and to tell no one because he didn't want me to get in trouble. One time, maybe after the third time, I asked him, "What kind of trouble?" I wanted to know because I kind of got scolded a lot by my mom when I wouldn't take the orange pill, or when I ran between two parked cars into the street, or when my dad dropped me off and she wanted to know what he said. And that was just at home. School was a different matter.

"BIG trouble. The biggest trouble you could think of," he said.

"I could get a spanking with a belt?"

"Worse."

I thought about it. What could be worse than a spanking with a belt? "I could get grounded for a week?"

That's the most I had ever been grounded, after I wiped out and lied about taking my bike to Pierce College. What felt like a life sentence behind a wooden fence, I could only play in my backyard or go places with my mom and dad. I couldn't go play with any of my friends on Kittridge Street. It was super boring. I counted the days. It took forever.

"Worse than being grounded," he replied.

What could be worse than being grounded, I thought. Then, it hit me.

"Could I go to juvenile hall?" I asked.

"Yes. You definitely would, Audrey. You'd go to juvie *forever*. You wouldn't like that, would you?"

"No. It would be scary," I told him. "Forever would really seem like forever."

"Really scary. You'd never get out. You wouldn't see your family.

We wouldn't see each other anymore either. You don't want that to happen, right?" he asked me.

"No, Ross," I told him.

"So, NEVER tell anyone. Okay?" he said.

"Even when we are in school and we make new friends?" I asked.

"No one else will ever be yours or my special friend, Audrey. Promise."

I kept the secret because I never wanted to go to juvenile hall, and I really liked Ross. I liked being with him. He was really nice to me. He was out of sight. We both liked cars. I was his special friend, and he wanted me around because he loved me. That's what he told me.

Until the pool party.

10 LEO CARRILLO

MY DAD PULLED INTO THE DRIVEWAY, IN THE STATION WAGON. I HEARD THE brakes squeal, the engine come to a stop and the car door shut. After a moment, he came through the front door and stopped in the entry hall. It was a Saturday. I had just come back from Parker's house; I finished watching the *Flintstones* on the boob tube, and I was in the living room playing tug-o-war with Scooter using one of the dish towels I took from the kitchen.

He looked back at the driveway, shut the front door, and walked into the living room.

"Lana's not home?" He asked me.

"I haven't seen her," I said.

He looked frazzled – like he'd seen a ghost.

"Lana!" he shouted. He waited for her to answer.

I looked down the hall and could see her door open.

"Dad . . . she's not in her room. I can see it's open," I told him.

He walked back to the front door and opened it, stepping out onto the stoop, looking outside again. Then he stepped back in, shut the door, and walked through the living room to the kitchen. I could hear his wingtips on the linoleum. I heard the freezer door open and a cabinet door snap open, then close. I heard ice cubes drop into a glass and something being set down on the counter. He came back into the living room, sat on the couch, and took a sip of his drink. It looked like tea, but I think it wasn't because it wasn't in a mug. I think it was a cocktail. I'd seen him drink that kind of drink before, when we were at the Nevins' house, or when my mom and dad had people over.

It was so quiet. He didn't say anything, and I didn't say anything. Time ticked by. I'm not sure how much. I couldn't see a clock. I just did it in my mind. I knew how to count time.

When Lana burst through the door, she looked frazzled – as if she had seen five ghosts or had been on the roller coaster too many times.

"Where've you been?" my dad asked.

"I got lost," she said.

Of course, I thought to myself. She didn't have me to direct her home. She had a lousy sense of direction. I guess she drove the Thunderbird home from somewhere and took a wrong turn. My dad took a long drink, almost finishing it in one gulp. He set the glass down on the coffee table. It made a clink, glass to glass. My sister stood there for a moment rocking from side to side, holding herself like she was cold – kind of like I did when I got out of the pool and didn't have a towel. Lana loved to rock. I'd like to sleep with her because she would rock the bed and rock me to sleep.

My dad spilled this nervous chuckle. Biting his lip, he said, "I think your mom is going to be a little shocked when she finds out her car is gone." Lana was silent. At that moment, she looked really frosted.

"Why did you take Mom's car?" I asked.

"You're too young to know, Audrey," Lana told me.

"She left it where she wasn't supposed to, so I had Lana bring it back," my dad said.

"Like when I leave my bike on the sidewalk in front of the driveway and you can't get your T-Bird out?" I asked.

"Sort of. Or when you lie about where you've ridden your bike or who you were with." My dad folded his arms.

I got quiet. I think he was talking about when I took my bike to Pierce College with Parker and some other kids and lied about it.

"I'm going to my room," Lana said quietly. She cut out of the living room, down the hall, and I heard her slam her bedroom door.

"Why is she so uptight, Dad?"

"She got lost for an hour, driving home," he said. "Don't worry about it."

I wasn't worried. I was just asking a question, is all. I got up, walked down the hall to Lana's bedroom door, which she had closed. I knocked.

"Who is it?" I heard coming through the door.

"It's me, Lana."

"Not now, Porky. I'm busy."

"Doing what?" I asked.

The door abruptly opened and she stood there, staring at me.

"What do you want?" she snapped at me.

"What's wrong with you?" I asked.

"You're too young to understand," she said.

"But I'm ALWAYS too young to know stuff!" I told her.

"Not now." Then she slammed the door in my face.

"You don't have to have a cow!" I shouted through the door.

Then, I heard Mean Ned's door open and he poked his head out.

"Don't be such a twerp and bug us. Why don't you go play on the freeway and get out of our hair?" I stared at him a moment then did what any kid would do when they were six.

"*Dad*! Ned is being mean to me!"

A few hours later, my mom came home. I was in my brother's room because he'd cut out and went somewhere. He said I was taking up his air. I don't know where he went to get more air. I didn't mind. I liked to snoop through his stuff when he wasn't there, even though he still told me to "Never go in my room, Audrey, or I'll pound you." I knew he wouldn't. He'd get in trouble for doing that if I told on him. I didn't snoop in his room when we lived in Ojai because I had to go outside to his garage room, and it wasn't so convenient. There was no lookout window to know when he was coming so I was able to book it and he couldn't pound me. At my new house, I can hear him coming, and I just skip across the hall, ducking into my room. It works every time.

His room smell, on Kittridge Street, smelled like sweat. He had all sorts of boss stuff, like his drum set which I liked to bang on, books with pictures of bugs in them, pennies and other change on his dresser, a hat that looked like a pirate wore it, pens and pencils, some baseball cards, and a harmonica. There were Hershey kisses on his desk. I took one, hoping he hadn't counted them like I do. One thing I can say for my mean brother Ned is that he always makes his bed. He's weird that way.

I was doing a good job snooping when, through the shades of his room, I saw a yellow car slowly make its turn and pull into the driveway. The car sat there for a minute blocking the sidewalk, idling. It had a little yellow sign on top of its roof that was lit up, like a siren when a policeman is chasing a bad guy. But this wasn't a police car. They're black and white. Not yellow.

The back door opened, and I saw my mom get out. I watched her come up the driveway to the walkway that led to our front door. I came out of Ned's room, shut the door so he wouldn't know I had been snooping, and wandered into the living room to see what was up. My mom walked in and stood between the front door and my parents' bedroom door, which was to the right when you walked in the house.

She just stood there, holding her purse and her coat. She stared at my dad, who was sitting on the couch looking at the paper and whistling to himself. My mom breathed hard. I can still see her chest going up and down in her blouse. Her nostrils flaring, she looked like a bull ready to charge. Good thing my dad wasn't wearing red.

"You had NO right," she finally said.

My dad turned the page and readjusted his newspaper, folding it in half like he often did. He never looked up at her, using the paper as a shield.

"I'm surprised he didn't give you a ride home." Then, he started to whistle.

"Do you even care, Lee?" She asked him.

That silence again. Sometimes, it was scarier than the yelling. They didn't say anything more to each other; there was just the sound of his whistling and ruffling the paper. She looked at me. I said nothing. Then, she went into their bedroom and slammed the door. The house shook a little.

All I know, because no one tells me anything, is that night my dad slept on the couch.

The worst thing about my parents divorcing, besides the yelling and throwing stuff and slamming of doors, is that we didn't take the trailer to go camping in Yosemite or to Leo Carrillo beach anymore. Sure, I went and saw the tide pools when we lived on Detroit Street, and I still played on my raft in the ocean when I'd visit my dad, or go to Ventura with my mom and her sweetheart when he was in town and she wasn't working.

Before my parents divorced and really started yelling at each other all of the time, and before my dad sold the trailer to some people that lived in Thousand Oaks and he left for good, we had some fun days as a family.

I didn't always sleepwalk or wake up from a dream thinking no one was at home. There was a time when we camped, or opened Christmas presents on Christmas morning, or went for picnics in Chatsworth near the train tunnel, or ate dinner at the dinner table all together. But camping is one of my favorite memories, from before everyone moved away . . . before we moved to Ojai. When we went camping, everyone unfolded, relaxed, and seemed happy.

Lana surfed like Gidget. She'd learned from going to Malibu, which was on the ocean and a long winding drive through Topanga Canyon from Canoga Park. She loved riding the waves at Surfrider Beach; that's next to the pier, where all the surfers go. It was the hip scene, she said, with big teenagers surfing and dancing the twist to rock and roll. But her board got stolen when we went to Leo Carrillo. It was under the trailer and somebody lifted it in the middle of the night. That ended her surfing days.

Summer at the beach felt warm and cozy, like the sun itself when it shines on you and makes your skin hot. Camping at Leo Carrillo was groovy. I loved the smell of the wildflowers, sea salt and seaweed blowing in from the pacific. My dad pulled the camper behind the station wagon and would park the trailer under a tree in the campground, so if it got too hot, the tree would be shady. At Leo Carrillo, the beach is sandy and has big rocks you can climb on. In the rocks, there are tide pools too that have urchins and crabs. There's even a cave carved out that you can walk inside, and water washes in over your feet. The sound of the waves crashing, skimming over the sand, and hearing seagulls singing, calling after their friends to wait up, made the beach feel like you were a million miles away from the San Fernando Valley, in an isolated shipwrecked paradise.

Sometimes, I stood on the rocks, and big sets of waves would crash over them, splattering water ten times the size of me, and I'd get soaked. I'd laugh, covered in saltwater, wiping my eyes to see. I had a blue, yellow, and red striped beach towel that I would carefully lay next to my mom's and bake in the sun as if I were a chocolate chip cookie in the oven getting crispy. It was hard to keep the sand off the towel. It bugged me having sand on my towel. It felt like sandpaper. I'm neat that way.

My skin became more golden, and my hair got blonder the more the sun kissed it, with strands turning almost white. I was called a toe-head back when I was five or six because my hair was blonde – not because my head looked like a toe.

The first thing I wanted to do when we arrived at Leo Carrillo was go to the camping grounds' general store and buy candy. I had to wait for my dad to unhitch the trailer and secure it. I'd wait patiently, my mouth watering just thinking about it. When my dad did finally give me a quarter, I'd run to the tiny store and buy twenty-five pieces of red licorice. I'd walk down to the beach, sit on the sand, and would eat every whip all myself. One time, some boy asked if he could have a piece because I had so many, and I said "No." I loved licorice. Still do. I wouldn't even give my mom a piece either. I can't share it because I am selfish with it.

When we camped at Leo Carrillo, my two sisters and brother slept outside in sleeping bags. I would sleep in the trailer with my mom and dad on a big bed, at their feet, in a sleeping bag squished up against the side. I was little, so I fit as snug as a bug in a rug. There was a tiny kitchen that my mom would prepare food to barbecue; it had a stove and a little refrigerator the size of me. The table you ate at turned into another bed.

We all sat around a campfire my dad made, and we would eat barbecued hot dogs or hamburgers and potato salad and beans. Everyone in the campground did the same with their families. Sometimes, campers would stop by and say, "How you doing? Where you from?" After stuffing my face with food, I'd put marshmallows on a stick and put them in the fire. They'd catch fire and burn up like a fireball. I'd blow it out then stuff it in my mouth. The outside was black, burnt, and crunchy – and the inside was gooey and soft. The more burnt the marshmallow was, the more I thought it was delicious. Ned said I was a weirdo. I didn't care. It tasted good, and that's all that mattered.

One night, after we sat on the beach watching the sun sink into the ocean and disappear into the water, Shelly, Ned, and I were walking back to the trailer. It was a long sandy path, carved between the sage scrub bushes that stretched from the beach to the campground. With no light and little moon, it was pitch dark. Shelly led with a flashlight; I was following her, and Ned was following me. We couldn't see anything in the dark and needed to stay on the path. As we were walking along minding our own business, we heard some rustling in the bushes. Shelly turned the light on a bush to see if she could see anything. All of a sudden, Mean Ned grabs the flashlight out of Shelly's hand and starts running down the path, ditching us! She starts running after him, and I started running after her. Ned has long legs, and he is running fast. I can't keep up. I begin crying, screaming, "Wait up!" because I was just five, and little; it was dark and scary, and I realized there must be something probably as terrifying as a tiger in those bushes. I didn't want the tiger to get me. I've never run that fast or for that long thinking something may be chasing me. Shelly was so mad at Ned; by the time we got back to the trailer, she slugged him in the arm and said he was a jerk.

That's why Ned is mean. He wanted that tiger in the bushes to swallow me in one bite. He still does. He's hated me since I was born and wants nothing to do with me, especially when we lived in Ojai. He'll be going somewhere, like the park or to the mini market at the end of Grand Avenue, and I'll ask him if I can go with; he'll say "No, Audrey. Get lost."

I can't get lost. I have a good sense of direction.

"Please, Ned, can I go?"

"No," he'd say.

"I hate you! I hate you!" I was hurt that he wouldn't take me with him, because I wasn't always a pain, and I didn't want to be left alone. I'd try another approach.

"Please, pretty please, Ned. Can I go?"

"No, Audrey."

"I hate you! I hate you! Please, please, Ned, can I go?" One more time.

"I said no, Audrey," he'd remind me.

"I HATE YOU!"

I didn't really hate him. I felt brushed off. I felt like he thought I had cooties. I was lonely, always having to play alone. So, I learned to just do my own thing. I didn't need my mean brother to have a gas, though sometimes I'd still get lonely – until everything changed, and we moved again.

I can't remember the last time we went camping at Leo Carrillo. After my dad sold the trailer, everything started to be different. Maybe if they hadn't sold the trailer, they never would have gotten divorced. Mostly, if I had just been a better little kid and not asked Shelly if I could spend the night at Parker's, we'd still be living on Kittridge Street; then my brain wouldn't be filled with all this guilt, and my heart wouldn't feel like a hippo was sitting on it.

11 POOL PARTY

I WAS RAISED WITH CHRISTMAS AND HANUKKAH AND EASTER AND PASSOVER because my dad is Jewish and my mom is Catholic. My dad says he's only been to temple twice, but he still says he's Jewish. It's in his jeans, he'd tell me. I asked him if it were in my jeans too, and he said, "Half of your jeans." I still wonder which half because I have two pairs of jeans.

I like having a dad who is Jewish. I am one lucky kid because, for eight days, when it's Hanukkah, I get one present each day. It's neat. I've gotten a plastic horse and colt, a perfume set, a slinky, Liddle Kiddles in lime and grape, an Archie lunch box, a necklace and earrings set (with fake rubies, but I lost one of the earrings), an outfit for my Barbie, and different stuffed animals. Oh, SO many stuffed animals, I can't even begin to tell you their names and what they are.

During Hanukkah, besides getting presents, you light a candle every day and let it burn until it goes out. I don't know why. My mom is always afraid the house is going to burn down. One time, I was at my aunt's house on the last day of Hanukkah and all eight candles were burning really super-duper low. There were a bunch of people there, family and friends, and Sylvia and Babe – who I really like a lot. Babe is Sylvia's husband's name. Isn't that funny? A man name babe? I think of that as a girl's name, not a boy's name. But that's what people call him. My pop says it's not his real name.

Everyone was there eating brisket with vegetables, and potatoes and pastrami sandwiches with pickles and coleslaw; I had finished my sandwich and was carrying my plate to the kitchen, past the table where I saw the menorah, the candle holder, holding the eight candles burning almost to the bottom. They were like burning stumps and almost done burning. Thinking nothing of it and only trying to be helpful to my Aunt Ru I asked, "Do you want me to blow these out?" I'm telling you, you would have thought I had been about to walk in front of a speeding train filled with eggs, and they were more concerned with the eggs breaking. The whole room, filled with all Jewish relatives and friends, stopped and screamed, "*NO!*" I stood frozen, not sure what I had done – the force of the screaming feeling like dragon's fire. The whole room stared at me a moment. I felt like an actress in a scary movie. I took in each twisted face, one by one, until I got to Sylvia, who grabbed her chest like she was having a heart attack. She looked over at my dad with this scorn of disapproval. He shrugged, like he didn't know what I was doing or that I was even his kid at that moment. I wondered what was the big deal. I was just trying to be helpful and careful, remembering what my mom said about burning the house down. Hanukkah is still fun, even if you can't blow out the candles when you should.

On Christmas, which is only one day, I get eight or more presents. It's like the opposite of Hanukkah and you don't light candles (except for fun), and you can blow them out whenever you want. Instead of eight candles, you open a calendar your mom puts on the wall in the kitchen. Then, you stare at the picture inside, wishing you were already at the end of the calendar because that means Santa would be coming down the chimney on that day. We'd put up a Christmas tree, and it's usually dry by the time Christmas Day arrives. My mom says not to leave the lights on when we're not at home. She doesn't want to burn the house down.

Hanukkah doesn't have a Christmas tree, but the Siegels, who lived on Kittridge Street, put one up at Christmas time and call it a

Hanukkah bush because their kids wanted a tree like us. They decorated it with blue and white dradles and matzo crackers that they'd poke holes through and tie some string to. It was the first tree I ever saw that you could eat the ornaments. At Christmas, you also sing a song about the twelve days of Christmas even though it's only one day. I wish it were twelve. Can you imagine that? Boy, would that be groovy – having twelve days of Christmas. That's more than Hanukkah. By the way, twelve times eight equals ninety-six. That's a really easy one. I could do that in my sleep.

Getting a bunch of presents on the one day works out really well. I get one from Lana, one from Shelly, one from Mean Ned, one from my dad, one from my mom, one from my aunt and uncle in Queens, New York, one from my grandma, and whatever Santa puts under the tree. He's really generous. This year, before we moved, I got a Tricky Tommy the Turtle (which I love), a Barbie doll with a bitchin' wardrobe and pink Go-Go boots, and a new stingray bicycle! My new bike is a special blue. Teal is what they call it (it's like if blue and green colored each other, they'd make teal), and it has a matching banana seat in the same color. It's so boss. I ride it like a motorcycle. I gave my old bicycle away because another child might need it, and I hope it's bringing as much joy and road adventure that that old bike brought me.

I love Christmas. I have never seen so much candy and cookies to eat. Passover is boring. You sit at a table and have to eat parsley dipped in saltwater, an egg, something really bitter that you have to spit out, and these crackers called 'matzo', which taste like saltines without the salt. There's this fish called *kafeltafish*, which I'm not sure is even fish because it looks like a blob on a plate and nothing like the trout my mom cooked, that my aunt makes me eat every time I go to Passover. I don't like it. I like the horseradish with nuts, so I smear it on the fake-looking fish just so I can get it down when it's time to eat it. At Passover, you have to follow the rules. You can't just dig in. You have to wait to be told what to eat. There is an instruction book that each person who knows how to read reads from. They pass it from one person to the next so everyone has a chance to practice their reading.

There is a long table in the middle of the living room that's set really pretty with the "good stuff" (as my Aunt Chickie calls it). It's full of silver and crystal that you have to be really careful with. I help set the table sometimes if we get to Chickie's early. There are some candles at the end that Chickie lights at the beginning while she says a prayer in Jewish, and there's some bread and a bone on the table. I have no idea what that bone is for. Maybe it's to hit somebody over the head if they put their elbows on the table or pick at the food and eat it before they're supposed to. I got whapped in the head a few times by my mom for doing that. At Passover, men wear a suit and tie and little beanies to cover their bald spots; the women don't because they just went to the beauty salon and had their hair curled.

We all read from this particular book (I told you about) that tells the story of some angel of death that passed over a house and took the first baby born in that house. That's a mean angel, stealing a baby. Storks don't do that. They deliver them in their beaks and go get another baby after they're done. They don't have time for pickups – Just deliveries.

The Jewish people were very clever, I tell you. In order to fool this angel of death, the trick was to put some lamb's blood on your door, and the wicked angel *passes over* your house and leaves you alone. I wonder if it knew the difference between lamb's blood and red paint. That's where this dinner party gets its name. The angel is flying over your house, passing over. Pass-over. Get it?

I don't like the fact that this angel of death wanted to take someone's little child. The only time I would have approved this angel thing is if Mean Ned had been the first one born, instead of Lana, and he got stolen. Well, not really. But sometimes I think that, because Ned can be a butt, as I've said.

I get to see my aunt and uncle and my Aunt Chickie and Uncle Bert (who are not really my aunt and uncle but my dad and Aunt Ru's good friends, like Parker is mine) at Passover, as well as all of their families and my cousins and ladies I don't know, who squeeze my cheek and say, "Lee, she's delicious!" like they're going to eat me up before dinner starts. But the best thing about Passover is a game called *hide the matzo*. This is MY kind of game. They wrap that big stale cracker that tastes like paste in a napkin and put it somewhere in the living room. Usually, it's behind the curtains or under the couch (thinking I wouldn't look there), but it's really the first place to look.

The game goes like this: the youngest child at the party, that's usually me, has to go find the matzo, kind of like an Easter egg hunt but without the eggs and basket. The living room isn't as big as a park and I pretty much know where to look. But I like to act like I don't and keep the room in suspense, drawing it out, so they get their money's worth. I pretend I'm in a movie, and I am acting like I can't find something. I get these looks on my face like I'm frustrated or puzzled. Except, I know exactly where to look. Who's kidding who?

They all watch me, sipping on their drinks or coffee, and they laugh, watching me search. Their eyes get big as saucers when I get close to the place where it's hidden. I can tell when I'm getting warm. They blab to each other about how adorable I am, saying things like, "Such a bubbalah, Lee," then gush that I have "pretty, long legs" and that I've "gotten so tall" since they saw me last. I feel like I'm the same size. Mean Ned still calls me squirt. Actually, finding the matzo is really fun. I enjoy watching the adults enjoying watching me. When I finally find the stash, I then go and collect. See, the men pay me money when I find it. That's why Passover is so good, and I go every year. I make almost fifty dollars every time! Do you know how much candy that buys? A LOT. It's the best part of Passover. I never want to grow up.

My grandma, who lives in Ojai, and my grandpa (who I've never met), are both from Italy. They came here like my dad's parents did, through an island in New York. My Grandpa Chirelli lives far away on the other side of the United States. I can't talk to him though because he can't speak English. He speaks Italian and eats a dozen eggs for breakfast. My mom calls him Pa and hasn't seen him since she was a little girl – when my grandma moved to California to marry another man.

I never met my dad's mom and papa because they died before I was born. My daddy's mom died when he was at Berkeley. I don't know where that is, but I don't want to go there (so my mom won't die). His dad died six months before the stork dropped me at the doorstep. My mom just told me the other day that she's going to tell me the truth about the stork, whatever that means. Maybe the stork is really a pelican in a cap.

My dad said his Pop was a character and sold things. My grandpa once had a grocery store on Third Street, a few blocks from the Farmers' Market where I like to go for hot dogs and candy. He was from Austria and my grandma was from Russia. Her name was Bella. That means beautiful in Italian. Isn't that interesting?

They took a boat to New York then went to Nebraska. My dad was born in Omaha. That's somewhere where an insurance company is. I see the commercials, but my dad didn't work there. He works at The Times, like I said. My mom's parents came from Italy and moved to Danbury. That's where my mom lived with her sister and my uncle before she went to live in Ojai.

You want to hear something? My dad has lived in Los Angeles since he was three years old. They moved to Pomona. That's on the way to Disneyland but you take a freeway the other way. He told me a story when we were driving to Kiddieland (before I moved to Ojai) that, when he was a little boy, he'd get up really early before the sun shined, grab a bunch of bananas from the kitchen, go sit on the curb, and watch the milkman deliver milk and eggs. The milkman had a horse and cart – not a truck – that he would lead by the reins down the street. With the morning hardly lit up by the sunshine, he'd stop in front of each house, pour milk from a big metal milk can into bottles, and put them on people's doorstep for their cereal in the morning. My dad told me he'd sit there for a while and he'd eat five bananas because he loved them like I love ice cream. My Aunt Ru was mad that he ate them all. She thought it was stingy.

When we drive around Los Angeles, he always points to buildings or something and says, "I remember when that was a field, and that was a field, and that was a field, and I remember when that was an oil well, and that was an orange grove . . . and that was a field . . . and that was a field . . . and that was an orange grove." He always says that. It can go on for blocks and blocks. Everything was fields, orange groves and oil fields when my dad was my age.

Los Angeles must have looked really different back then if everything was like that – with no Kiddieland or Pink's. There's an oil field behind Kiddieland. I've seen the pump pumping the oil. It seems different than all the oil pumps near my aunt and uncle's house. It's the only one around, like it was in a herd of dinosaur pumps and it went to drink some oil and got left behind because no one noticed. Or, maybe it went to explore and didn't have a sense of direction, like Lana, and got lost. Whatever happened to that oil pump behind Kiddieland, I hope it's not lonely being by itself.

My dad said there were lots of dirt roads, little houses and no buildings (except in downtown Los Angeles) when he was a kid. They moved to Pomona from near the Farmers' Market when he was eight. That's one year younger than me. My dad said that Wilshire Blvd ended where the La Brea tar pits are, and there were only dirt roads from there to the beach. He also said dinosaurs were found in the tar of the La Brea tar pits. Dinosaurs. That's neato.

My dad knows all of this because he's old and remembers. Before he married my mom, and before he went to fight in World War Two, he went to Carthay Elementary School next to the Carthay movie theatre; he was eight years old, his dad owned the grocery store on 3rd Street, and they lived in a duplex on 4th Street. I know that school because my dad lives in his apartment way down the street in Century City, and we went and saw a really strange movie at Carthay theatre (next to his old school) when I went to spend the weekend with him last month. It was called *2001: A space Odyssey*. Did you see it? It was scary! There were these cavemen frightened by a big, grey square (called a monolith) that was the size of a building. The cavemen tried to touch it, but it looked like it felt hot, and they didn't like it. There was a lot of space and stars, with beautiful music like the kind my mom plays on the piano or the record player. A head guy named Dave was leaving his family to go on a trip; he had a little boy. When they were flying through space, this stewardess in the spaceship walked up a wall, then turned upside down on the ceiling, went through a door, and gave Dave his coffee or something. It was surprising she could do that. They talked to their families on TV's, where they can see each other like the Jetsons do. There was this computer robot named Hal who could talk and answer questions – and even make decisions. I didn't like his voice though. He reminded me of my mom when she's really, really calm and tells me to talk in my regular voice when I'm upset, like that's going to help make me stop. It just makes me more upset, until she yells at me; then I know she means business.

I'm not sure why Dave couldn't just turn Hal off or pull out his battery like George Jetson could do to Rosie when she gave too much lip. But Hal was bad and needed to be unplugged. Hal wouldn't do what he was told, and Dave couldn't punish him. Hal was like the robot in *Lost in Space* when he talks back to the professor. Or when Rosie would break down and start smoking, like she caught fire. What's wrong with robots?

Hal had 'a listening problem'. That's what my aunt would call it when you didn't do what you were told. One time at my aunt's school, a little boy said a bad word. Shit. That's what he said. Mildred told my aunt, and she took the kid in the office. I was standing outside and could hear her tell him that she had told him not to say that word; she said he had a listening problem. Then she told him that the next time he wanted to say the bad word, he could come inside and say it in the office – but not in the play area. Then she let him go outside again. The next day, I was outside at the Play-Doh table (the same day another kid ate the Play-Doh thinking it was cake), and the little boy who said the bad word was at the table with his little friend who he was playing with the day before. THAT little boy said . . . a bad word. Shit. That's the word. I didn't say it. SO, the little kid who was sent to the office the day before, and who my aunt told had a listening problem, said to his friend, "Hey . . . there's no shitting out here. If you want to shit, shit in the office." I'm not sure he listened. But that's a listening problem.

So, in the movie, Dave was locked outside of the spaceship in space, and Hal wouldn't open the door. Dave told him to open the door. Hal would say things like, "I'm sorry Dave, I can't do that," and Hal worked for Dave. After that, Dave was in this fancy room with a white floor and weird furniture; he got old, and a giant baby appeared in the sky. The end. It was like a bad dream. I think my dad was sorry he took me to see it. I liked the music and the space though. To be perfectly honest, I had no idea what was going on in that movie. I like Dr Dolittle way better. He talks to animals, and they don't talk back.

The valley still has orange groves way up near the hills. I had a babysitter who lives in Northridge on a farm. 'Ma,' I'd call her. She has a son named Shorty. He's a man, but he thinks like a boy. He's different, he talks slow, and he's very sweet. He wouldn't hurt an ant. He steps around them every time he sees one. I think that's nice. I liked to go to their house because they had chickens and a garden where I could pick corn and drive on a tractor.

In Ojai, there are so many orange groves you sometimes can't see anything else. There are orange trees everywhere. Also, oak trees. In Ojai, they love the oak trees so much, they build the street around them and paint white stripes on the trunks so cars can see them and don't run into them.

I love oranges. I can eat a ton. We'd walk down the street and pick the oranges off the trees in people's yards and eat them. They didn't mind. There are so many oranges everywhere and they are delicious. At my house on Grand Avenue, we had a walnut tree, an avocado tree, and an apricot tree. The apricot tree was in the back yard; I'd climb the trunk to the bottom branches, pick the apricots, and eat them like when we'd walk the walls on Kittridge Street and steal the neighbors' plums. I wasn't stealing the apricots, because my mom owned the tree in our backyard. Shelly climbed the tree to pick some apricots when she came to visit us in Ojai one weekend with her boyfriend, Joel, and her little dog, Bosco (that looked like a black mop).

That summer, two days after I went to Pan Pacific Park with Shelly and Joel, when he took my pictures on the merry-go-round, something happened that I still don't know why. I didn't do anything. I just went to Ross's house because I thought he forgot to invite me to his pool party.

Ned was in his room, dressed in a t-shirt, shorts and thongs, so I asked him where he was going. He told me he was going to Ross's for a pool party; he said that summer was ending, and all the kids were going. Well, first he told me to buzz off because it was none of my business what he was doing, THEN, he told me he was going to the pool party.

"All the kids?" I asked.

"Yeah," he said.

Then he told me to get out of his room and to quit bugging him. He shut his door, locked it and left through his other door that went outside. He was on to me and always locked his room on Detroit Street.

Moping, I went to my room and stared at my ant farm for a while, watching an ant carry another ant like it was too tired to walk itself. After that, I went over and petted my mice and gave them some fresh water. I left my bedroom, went into the kitchen, and poured myself a glass of milk. I only drank half. No one was home, and I was bored. I went back into my room, picked up my etch-a-sketch, and drew some squiggles. I couldn't think. My mind was racing. I felt like when I can't stay in my seat at school, and I'm bothered by something but I don't know what. Or when I would wake up in the middle of the night and think no one was at home.

Mostly, I couldn't understand why Ross didn't invite me to his pool party. I knew how to swim. I've been swimming since I was three, without a life jacket. I had a bathing suit. I was his special friend. I did

things with him that I have never done with anyone. It was our secret
. . . like he asked. I even crossed my heart and hoped to die, stick a
needle in my eye.

I decided to go to Ross's house to find out why he invited all the
kids – and my mean brother – but didn't invite me. I went in my room
and changed into my swimsuit. It was a red bikini and had two starfish
on the top. I changed into my favorite Lemon drop shirt and shorts,
laced up my blue Keds, went into the kitchen, finished my glass of
milk, and left through the kitchen door.

I walked down the driveway toward the sidewalk and saw the
Clampett kids playing with hula hoops on their front lawn with Bodhi,
the neighbor kid who lived in the next-door duplex; he had long hair
for a boy because his parents said he was free to make his own
decisions. Bodhi decided not to cut his hair. He also called his mom
and dad by their first names, Sunshine and Revolution, who liked to
make cardboard signs and go join the hippies and protest the war. They
liked flowers and the wilderness and named Bodhi after some tree.

Before stepping off the curb, I looked both ways and crossed the
street. I wondered if they were invited to the pool party.

"You wanna hula hoop with us?"

"No," I said. "Are you going to the pool party?"

They didn't know what I was talking about.

"The one at Ross's house."

"Who's Ross? Is he a hippie?" Bodhi asked.

"I don't think so. He lives down the street, across from the Ford
dealership parking lot. His dad drives that white Rolls Royce. He's my
friend," I explained.

"Rich people send the poor man to war," Bodhi told us. "I don't
know him. Is he in our grade?" Bodhi asked me.

"No. He's in my brother's grade."

The Clampetts weren't interested. They were now fighting over the
blue hula hoop because it went faster than the pink and yellow one.

"I don't know big people like that," Bodhi said.

"Ok." I started to walk down the street.

"Where you going?" Bodhi called after me.

"To the pool party," I said.

I walked down to the Ford parking lot where Ross had taken me more times I could count on my hands and right foot, and I crossed the street, looking both ways. I walked past the white Rolls Royce on his driveway and up to the gate that led back to the pool. It had no slats, and you couldn't see through it. I heard the music *Windy* by The Association coming from the backyard; there were loud voices talking and laughing.

I was too short to reach the latch at the top of the fence. I guess Ned was right: I was still a squirt.

I knocked on the gate. No one came. I waited.

After a little while, a teenager came out of the gate and shut it. He was as tall as Ned, and he was carrying a skateboard.

"Is Ross here?" I asked him.

"Yeah. He's in the back."

"Could you tell him I'm here?"

"Who are you? Does he know you?" he asked me.

"I'm Audrey," I told him. "He forgot to invite me to the party, but I know he'd like to know I'm here," I explained. That could be the only explanation. Sometimes people forget things when they are rushing.

He looked at me like he didn't believe me. "You sure?" he asked.

"Yes. I'm super sure," I told him.

"Okey-dokey. Wait here. I'll go tell him." The teenager went back through the gate, closing it behind. I was certain he would tell Ross. I looked up and felt the sun on my face, feeling a kind of happiness that felt warm. After about ninety-seven seconds (I can remember exactly), the boy came back through the gate with his skateboard and told me that Ross would be out in a second, which had already passed. But I knew what he meant. Then he skateboarded down the sidewalk.

I smiled because I knew Ross would be happy to see me; he must have just forgotten to invite me, being distracted by getting all the pool party favors, the cake, the piñata, and having so many friends who like to swim. I waited a little while longer and heard the metal move. I saw the gate unlatch, and Ross poked his head out. I remember his hair was wet and slicked back and he had a striped towel around his neck. He wasn't wearing a shirt.

"Hi, Ross," I said. I was cheerful.

He didn't smile. His eyes looked black. He stared at me like he didn't know me. He wiped his forehead with his towel, then looked back over his shoulder and back at me; through his gritted teeth, like when my brother is furious with me and yells at me but doesn't want my mom or dad to hear, Ross said, "WHAT ARE YOU DOING HERE?!"

He said it just like that.

I wasn't sure what to say. My heart was pounding because I could see that he was mad. I know what mad looks like. I had seen it on the faces of the people I loved and who I thought loved me. And I'd seen it many times.

"I . . . I wanted to come to the pool party," I told him.

"What?"

"I wore my bathing suit under my lemon drop outfit," I said. I came prepared like a good Bluebird, ready to swim.

Ross practically ripped his hair out when he ran his hand through his wet hair.

"You thought you could come to my pool party? You're a twerp! A child! What the hell is wrong with you?!"

"But . . ." The cat had my tongue.

"GET OUT OF HERE!" he shouted at me.

Then, he slammed the gate in my face.

I wasn't sure what to do. I stood there. I was shaking. My knees felt like spaghetti. I shivered, but I wasn't cold. It was summer and hot. I backed away from the gate. Struggling to get my feet to move, I slowly walked down the driveway to the sidewalk. I looked back one more time at the gate to see if I was dreaming or that maybe he'd come back out again and tell me he was teasing me. I waited for the metal latch to move. It didn't. And he didn't.

I walked home, my heart pounding, my heart hurting, with a lump in my throat, wondering what I did wrong. Mostly, I was scared he'd tell on me, and I would be in big trouble.

Ross stopped being my friend that day at the pool party. He never took me back to the Ford Dealership parking lot to see the Mustang on the grill, and I don't remember him ever coming to our house after that day. I saw him a few times on the street when I was playing, and he walked past me like he didn't know me. I still don't know what I did wrong to make Ross hate me, just like I don't know why Sonya put that tack in my tire.

I felt like when the teacher writes on the chalkboard and she points at what she wrote, saying, "Did you write that down, boys and girls? I'll wait." And she does. When all the kids are done writing it down on their piece of paper, she takes the eraser and wipes away everything she just wrote on the board. And the chalkboard is black, like nothing was ever there.

That's what I felt like. Like the words on the chalkboard that were once there, weren't anymore.

Erased.

12 CHATTY CATHY

ICE CREAM DOESN'T ALWAYS MAKE EVERYTHING BETTER. I LEARNED THAT.

It couldn't make David better when he got sick and died in the hospital, and not even a push-up could make it better when my tire got a tack in it (even though my dad wasn't mad and the ice cream truck came just in time to melt away some of my sadness). Ice cream is not medicine or a rabbit hole you go down and end up at some strange tea party that takes you on an adventure. It's only good for one thing: eating and putting on cake, at a birthday party, for double treating. I know this now. You know how? The same day I got a flat, that night my Chatty Cathy doll that I loved was broken into pieces.

I didn't break my doll. My sister, Shelly, didn't either. My dad didn't accidentally run it over in the driveway or step on her head with his shoe.

My mom broke it.

I'm not sure what happened that night before my mom and dad came to Parker's house to pick me up. My mom was more furious than I had ever seen her. She was even more angry than when I lied about going to Pierce College – and every other time I got in trouble. This anger was worse than when she broke stuff or ranted she was going to kill my dad because she was fuming, like a small flame that turns into a raging fire and burns everything to the ground.

All I know is, after that night, when my Chatty Cathy was broken, nothing was ever the same again. Nothing. That's when everything I loved broke. Everything. My family would no longer be a family. I would no longer feel safe, ever again. Because if what happened that night could happen to Shelly, what could happen to me?

"Cannonball!" That's what I'd shout as I ran off the diving board and wad up into a ball, grabbing both my knees at once, pulling them to my chest and trying to make a big splash. Cannonballs did way more splashing than jack knives. With jack knives, you only wad up one knee and not two. It's a baby cannonball.

I loved spending time at Parker's. It was like my second home, and Pam was so nice to me. Big Ned, Parker's dad, was super-duper nice too. Big Ned was funny and would make me laugh, pretending he was Herman Munster or Frankenstein. He went as Herman Munster for Halloween that year and wore really big boots that almost made his head hit the ceiling. Big Ned has the same name as my mean brother, but he was way taller and had a job. He makes record covers. Sometimes, I would go to his work on Ventura Blvd, down near Barham, where the Batmobile is parked. That Batmobile is so cool. It's still parked there.

Big Ned was friends with Herb Alpert and the Tijuana's Brass. Herb came to their house once, and I met him. He didn't have his brass with him. I loved listening to the Tijuana Brass and Brazil '66 too. It's called Bossa Nova. It might seem strange that a kid my age likes Bossa Nova music, that I'm not listening to Jungle Book records, or Cinderella, or The Beatles all the time. I liked the beat of Bossa Nova, the way it made my bones want to move and my fingers want to snap to its rhythm. I learned to dance the Bossa nova too. Pam and Big Ned would play it on their record player and showed me the steps. They're hard steps. I had to dance backward, which wasn't fair. Plus, you have to hold hands with your dance partner, and Parker wouldn't hold hands with me. So, I was just doing the Bossa and no Nova, I guess. I can hum the music. Do you want to hear it? *Hum . . . hum . . . . . . hum,*

hum . . . hum, hum, hum . . . Hum . . . hum . . . . . . hum, hum . . . hum, hum, hum . . . Snappy! I love the brass because it has its own special sound. It would be like if a parking lot of cars started honking their horns to music. Something like that.

Did you know that the lady who sings in the Brazil '66 group is married to Herb Alpert? Lani. It's spelled like Lana but with an *i* instead of an *a* at the end. They are a musical family because Herb plays music and Lani sings it. I like her voice a lot. I want to sing like her when I grow up. Maybe if my dad was musical like my mom, and he played the guitar or banjo or bongos, they would have liked each other more, stopped yelling at one another, and stayed together.

I love music. It makes me feel good when I feel bad. Sure, The Beatles, The Byrds, The Turtles, The Rascals, The Monkees, The Rolling Stones, The Beach Boys, The Mamas and the Papas, The Association, (I knew all the words to "Cherish", and it still reminds me of Shelly for some reason), The Doors, The Who and The Band are all groovy groups with groovy songs. But I like all sorts of music, including folk. "Puff, the Magic Dragon" is a folk song, and "Like a Rolling Stone" – not the band but the song – is folk too. Sometimes, I listen to music, and I go somewhere that isn't here, using my imagination to build another world (like Disneyland). It's a magical place, and no one is ever sad, or mad, or stingy with their toys. It's like how Henry Monowski described to me his secret world that he was the President of when I went over to his house to visit. He was my friend who lived across the street from us on Grand Avenue. He also liked to dance to music. Sometimes, Henry got really wild and did moves like Tom Jones or Elvis, swinging his hips and arms like he was being swarmed by bees and they were trying to sting him. Henry was a really good dancer like that.

Besides what Nanette Fabray sings, I like flower power music too. My brother plays it. He puts Jefferson Airplane on the record player and gets on his drums and keeps along, as if he's the drummer in the band. My brother isn't as cute as Ringo or Mickey. He's a dork that can't grow a mustache. Hippies act and dress weird with flowers in

their hair and lots of frilly, fringy bright clothing that looks torn up –
like they got attacked by a bear and then it gets caught in the car door
when they shut it. I got my finger caught in the car door once and I'm
not a hippie. Boy, that smarts. Shelly wanted to be a hippie, and my
mom said, "Over my dead body." That meant NO.

I don't think Shelly ran away because my mom said she couldn't be
a hippie. I think she ran away because my mom did something that no
mom should ever do to their child, even when they are really angry or
didn't mean to.

My mom came into the living room, all dressed up. She was
wearing green shoes with a buckle, black pants, a silk blouse, a green
scarf, and pearls. Her hair was done, and she looked beautiful. My
mom always knows how to dress and comb her hair. My dad sat on
the couch, waiting. He was in slacks, a turtleneck, and loafers. They
were going out to a party.

"Have you seen my purse?" my mom asked my dad.

"No," he said.

My mom went back in her room. A few minutes later, she returned
with a green and white purse. My mom always says your shoes should
match your purse.

"Found it. Let's go."

My dad got up off the couch and walked to the front door, pulling
his keys from his pocket. They were taking the T-Bird.

"Shelly!" my mom shouted.

Shelly was in her room. I heard the door open. "Yeah?" She could
be heard down the hall.

"We're leaving!"

"Okay, Mom!" Shelly shut her door.

"Mom, can I go to Parker's?" I asked.

"Not tonight," my mom said.

"Please, please, Mom?" I pleaded.

"No, Audrey. We won't be late. There's meat loaf in the fridge. No
pop tonight – it'll get you too wound up." She gave me a kiss on my

cheek and left out the door.

I waited for the car to leave the driveway, and then I ran down the hall and knocked on Shelly's door.

"Shelly . . . can I come in?"

"Open, sesame," she said. I walked in. "What do you want?" She was laying on her bed looking at pictures in a magazine.

"Can I go to Parker's? Just for a little while. Paul is there with him and they're watching *The Wizard of Oz*," I told her.

"You've seen it."

"Yeah. So what? I want to see it again," I said.

She turned a page, not answering.

"Pretty please, Shelly?" I asked nicely.

"Okay."

"Thank you!" I jumped up and down. "I love you!" I did. I charged over to her bed and grabbed her by the arm and started pulling her off the bed; I was so excited to go.

"Hold your horses and go put on your shoes, squirt."

I ran out of her room into mine, found my white go-go boots, and put them on without socks – which made it hard to squeeze my feet in. I grabbed my Chatty Cathy and bolted out my bedroom door, charging down the hall, turning right into the living room, past the wheat bale end table that scratches you, out the front door, and down the driveway. I think I was halfway down the block before she ever left the house. I arrived out of breath and in a good mood, letting myself in and plopping on the couch as if Parker's house was Disneyland and their couch was the boat in *It's A Small World*. I was ready for adventure and wonder.

I don't want to tell you the rest of the story. I'm scared. You won't be my friend anymore because it was all my fault. All of it.

When you're six, almost seven, all you think about is candy, toys, watching tv, playing, and having fun. You don't want to take a bath or put on clean underwear because they'll just get dirty. I didn't have time for naps. I was too busy doing stuff. From the minute I got up, to

when I was dragged to bed, I didn't stop moving. That's what my mom
and dad would tell me. I was like a wind-up toy, they'd say. Still am.
But I don't cry now when I have to go to bed. No one has to tell me
when it's time to hit the sack. I go to bed when I'm tired, and I take a
shower every day, believe it or not.

Back when I was a little kid and it was time for bed, I didn't feel like
going; they'd have to make me. I'd be lying on the couch, watching TV
with my eyes closed, listening. My mom would tell me, "Time for bed."

"Why? I'm not tired," I'd protest.

"You're falling asleep, sweetheart," my dad would say.

"I'm watching with my ears, not my eyes," I'd tell them.

"We can see you're tired." I guess my cheeks got rosy when the
clock got past eight p.m. They were a dead giveaway, tattle-telling on
myself because my cheeks couldn't be quiet.

"Go on," my mom would say.

I'd start crying, "I'm not tired."

"Yes, you are, Audrey," my mom would quietly say.

"No, I'm not," I blubbered. To be honest, I could barely keep my
eyes open.

"Go on to bed," my mom would say.

I'd slide off the couch and drag myself to bed, walking at a snail's
pace, still blubbering and saying, "I'm not tired". I'd climb under the
covers, still blubbering, because I was just a kid and kids do that. I'd
lay my head on my pillow and . . . I don't remember anything after that,
except waking up the next morning and doing it all over again.

Parker's mom and dad were at the same cocktail party as my mom
and dad. No one else was home at Parker's except Paul. He hadn't left
for Vietnam yet, and his hair was still long because his dad said he'd
buzz it off for the Army when the time came. Paul said it would never
happen. He said his hair was his mane and no lion lets anyone get near
him with dog clippers.

Shelly finally showed up at Parker's a little while after I did. She
and Paul strolled out by the pool, smoking cancer sticks and shooting
the breeze. There was a bucket of Kentucky Fried Chicken on the

dining room table with rolls and gravy. Parker sat on the couch with a bowl of popcorn in his lap and wouldn't share, telling me to get my own. It wasn't that late because my cheeks weren't rosy yet.

The day cruised by and it was now officially night. Maybe 7 pm. The nights were still light, not getting dark. Unlike Halloween, when it gets dark before dinner, so you can trick and treat. The sun was going down because I remember hearing the birds chirping. They did that when they were getting ready for bed. They do that when they get up too.

Parker and I were on the couch in front of the tube. From the couch, facing the sliding door that went out to the terrace, I could see Shelly and Paul lying in lounge chairs under the pool cabana that had a sign posted: *We don't swim in your toilet, so please don't pee in our pool.* To be frank – I did. A lot. I didn't want to get out of the pool when I was having so much fun. I'd pee, then swim away from it to pretend it wasn't me; it's warm when you pee in a pool, and if someone swims near you, they will know.

While watching *The Wizard of Oz*, the story was at the part when the Tin Man gets rusty and Dorothy has to put oil on him so he can move; they're off to see the Wizard because Dorothy wants to go home to Kansas. Only the Wizard knows how to get there because it's far from Oz and there are no buses . . . it was right then that my mom and dad busted through the front door like it was a raid.

I remember looking over my left shoulder at the door as it hit against the wall, startling me. My mom marched in and said to me with her teeth gritted, "Get – up – *NOW.*"

I scrambled up, grabbed my Chatty Cathy doll, walked around the couch and stood near the dining room table. I put some distance between my mom and me, like Ali would do in the ring before he punched someone in the face or knocked him to the floor; the steam was coming out of everywhere in her head, explosive-like. She looked so angry. I looked at my dad and he just looked down, knowing there was nothing he could say to calm the storm about to hit. Parker just ate his popcorn, still glued to the tube, like if my mom had become a part of the movie as one of the flying monkeys or the Wicked Witch of the West.

"Where's Shelly?" she scolded at me. Before I could open my mouth, right then, Shelly came through the sliding door. She stopped, sensing my mom's fury.

"Hi, Mom," Shelly said.

"Who told you that you could come here?"

Shelly looked at me.

"No one. I just thought it would be fun for Audrey . . ." Shelly tried to explain but my mom wouldn't let her.

"I told Audrey she was to stay home tonight," she said. "You had no right to let her come here."

"What's the big deal, Mom? She's always here. I didn't think it would be so heavy," Shelly told her.

"Sophia . . . Let's just go home," my dad said.

"Stay out of this, Lee," she said to my dad. She turned to Shelly and told her to, "Get home, NOW!"

Shelly walked over to me, took my left hand, and slowly walked me to the door. Passing my mom, we walked out the door onto the front walkway. My mom started to follow, and my dad calmly shut the front door behind him. I didn't even say goodbye to Parker or see the end of the movie when the good witch lands in Oz and tells Dorothy all she has to do is click her ruby red heels and say, "There's no place like home . . . there's no place like home . . . ." Shelly then snapped, "She didn't do anything, and neither did I, Mom. You're overreacting."

I'm not sure what happened next, but all I know is that my mom ripped my Chatty Cathy out of my hand and started hitting Shelly over the head with it.

"DON'T YOU DARE TALK BACK TO ME!" my mom screamed.

Shelly started running down the walkway to the sidewalk as my mom ran after her, beating her with my doll.

My dad ran after my mom, telling her to "Stop it, Sophia! STOP!"

I ran after my dad, trying to keep up. We were this train of people.

All I could see was my sister running, my mom hitting my sister with my Chatty Cathy, and my dad running after my mom down the sidewalk on Kittridge Street. I noticed the last rays of sunlight gleaming through the trees at the top of the street, before the sun went completely down.

I was the last one in the house, not even closing the door behind me. Out of breath, I ran into the living room and saw my Chatty Cathy laying on the floor, broken; her head was hanging on by a shred of plastic and she had an arm missing. My mom and Shelly were standing in the living room. Shelly was in front of my mom, not even an arm's length away, and my dad was closer to the kitchen behind my mom. I could see fire coming out of her nose like a dragon – her eyes red from the heat of her fury.

"Mommy!" I tried to get her attention like the rodeo clown does to distract the angry bull when the Bronco rider falls in the arena and has nowhere to go.

Shelly and my mom just stared at each other for a minute. I could see tears had rolled down Shelly's cheeks, but she looked mad too. Breathing. Breathing. Quiet and only the sound of breathing, before these three words came out of Shelly's mouth and nothing was ever the same again.

"I hate you," she said quietly to my mom.

It happened so fast – swinging a bat, hitting the baseball on the sweet spot, and sending it flying to left field, into the stands.

My mom pulled back her right arm back and backhanded Shelly, knocking her down to the floor. I remember my mom looking at Shelly, then the ring on her finger – a big brass-looking ring – then looking down again at Shelly, who wasn't moving. I saw my mom's bottom lip quiver and a realization paint her face; it was like a clown drawing their smile like a frown, looking like they're about to cry and covering every hurt line in their face with make-up.

It's like the room spun backward and all the air was sucked out. Everything became as small as it could be, shrinking like an atom you can't see and going into blackness.

"Oh my God . . . Lee! Lee!" my mom called out in that same panic I had heard before on that drive to Ojai. "Oh my God! Do something!" she shouted.

My dad ran over to Shelly and knelt down to her; he was brushing her hair back and stroking her head. I could see a red spot near her temple. I watched for a second, waiting for her to get up, but she didn't.

"Is she dead?" I asked.

Is she dead? See, I thought my mom killed my sister, right then.

My dad gently rocked her, "Shelly . . . honey?"

Then Shelly's left hand moved, and she rolled onto her back, letting out a sigh. She blinked a few times. Then sat up. She rubbed her cheek. My dad helped her to her feet. He asked her if she was okay, steadying her for a sec. She pushed the hair out of her eyes and looked at my mom. She didn't say a word, turned, and walked down the hallway to her room, quietly shutting the door.

I watched my mom and dad not move from their spots. My mom still looked shaken, as if she were in a trance. She looked down at her hand one more time, straightening out the ring on her finger. My dad wiped his brow, stepped away from her, and shook his head in confusion; it was as if his favorite player, Sandy Koufax, threw a hanging pitch with the bases loaded – and lost the game.

I wanted to check on Shelly and began to walk down the hall. I heard my dad say, "You forgot your doll." Maybe he couldn't see how broken she was, how her face was shattered – how she no longer looked the same.

"I don't want it anymore," I said. I never touched my Chatty Cathy again. I'm not sure what my dad did with her. I don't care. I never wanted to see that doll again.

Shelly was standing in front of her opened closet when I peeked into her room. I gently opened the door, tiptoed in, sat on her bed as quiet as a mouse, and watched her sort through her clothes.

"What are you doing?" I asked.

"I'm running away," she said.

And she did.

And it was all my fault. I never should have gone to Parker's like I was told.

I made her leave. I was the one who changed everything because I had a listening problem.

13 COMMON SENSE

WHEN YOU'RE A KID, YOU DON'T HAVE TO HELP PACK WHEN YOU'RE moving. You just have to put all of your toys and books in a box and take things to the trash when your mom asks you to. I know. We moved to Seattle a few months ago. That's where the bluest skies are. Perry Como sings that song. It's also the theme song to *Here Comes the Brides*. There are blue skies, and lots of trees, and girls who want to get married in Seattle. My mom isn't a girl, like Candy Pruitt. She's a grown-up. And, guess what? She got married again to a really nice man, who lived in Seattle.

His initials spell SET. Stephen Eugene Thompson. That's his name. He showed me his initials on his briefcase when I first met him, after we moved from Detroit Street to Ojai last year. He came to Ojai to take my mom to dinner at the Valley Oaks. They have good food like Papino's Pizza Place, out on the road to Santa Paula, but the Valley Oaks doesn't have pizza. They have steak. My mom worked there when she was sixteen. She told me a story about how all the big shots from Hollywood would come to Ojai for the weekend. She would play tennis with Angela Lansbury, who is close to her age. Do you know who Angela Lansbury is? I know she's an actress, is all. One time when my mom was waiting tables, these men were sitting in a booth, and they yelled to my mom across the restaurant, "Clean our table." They didn't say please. She hates when I don't say please after I ask for something.

She went over to their table and asked them, "You want your table cleaned?"

"Yeah," one of the men said. I think he was smoking a cigar, or maybe I just think he was because I saw it in a movie when a mean man didn't say please. She said a lot of people were like that, and she didn't like it – that it got sour like curdled milk. I drank curdled milk once, by accident. Don't ever do that. You'll be sorry.

My mom said, "Ok."

Then, she told me in order to clean the men's table like they'd asked, she pulled the entire tablecloth off the table like a magician – except she wasn't one! All the plates and silverware flew onto the floor with a crash. I guess she had her fill of cigar-smoking mean men who didn't say please. She told me she didn't say another word. She turned, took off her apron, walked past her manger, and said, "You can't fire me because I quit." She left and went to Wheeler Hot Springs for a swim.

She got her job back. Customers liked her spunk. She was good at bringing food out and other waitress stuff, and her boss thought those men didn't have manners and had it coming to them.

Beanie has this big briefcase that weighs as much as a car; I can hardly lift it. It's so heavy with papers. Oh . . . you're probably wondering who Beanie is. Well, he's my new stepfather who I live in Seattle with. My mom got married again. That's what I call him. Beanie. It's not his real name. I guess his little brother called him that when they were tykes because he couldn't pronounce Gene, Beanie's middle name, which is what they call him as his first name. So, Bean was Gene. Get it?

When I first met him, after we moved to Grand Avenue in Ojai and he came to visit my mom, I tried to lift his briefcase. "What do you have in there, a tree?" I asked him. He was from Seattle, after all. They have lots of trees. "Paper comes from trees, you know?" I let him know in case he didn't study that in school. He went to some place called Princeton. It's far away and for really big kids who like to wrestle;

he said he was the champion of all the college wrestlers, but not like the guys on television. He told me that's fake and for show.

He thought that was funny, what I said that about having a tree in his briefcase; he flashed a really sweet smile, showing his pearly whites. Those are his teeth. And they're straight. My mom's are a little crooked in the front, but she's so pretty anyhow, and I like her teeth a little crooked.

Beanie pointed to the leather bag with some letter blazed near the handles, "Do you know what that spells?" he asked me, sitting on the blue velvet couch in our living room on Grand Avenue; it was the couch that was on Kittridge Street and Detroit Street and, now, in our house on Broadmoor Drive where we live in Seattle. I get to that part soon.

See, Beanie's house is four houses down the street from my Aunt Roma and Uncle Ken, who live in Seattle too. My mom is living on the same block as her big sister. That's how my mom met Beanie. She met him at a dinner party at my aunt's when she went to visit her after David died. When my mom came back home to Grand Avenue, her sister said, "Gene (that's Beanie), next time you're in Los Angeles, you should look up my sister, Sophia." And he did. His wife died of cancer like David did. They had dinner one night in Los Angeles and decided they liked each other and started kissing and playing tennis. That's how it works.

His briefcase is big, like a magician could hide a rabbit in it – as well as a table to put the hat on to pull the rabbit out of. I took a look at the letters he was pointing at. "Yes, I know what they spell," I told him. "SET." I got an A in spelling at Topa Topa, my third-grade school, and that one was a no brainer. Give me a harder one to spell and I can do it. I am really good at the spelling bee. Either me or Grant won – every time. That and the math bee too.

"That's right, kiddo," he told me. He smiled at me like I was the smartest person in the world, which made me feel good (even though SET is not a hard word to spell or read). He got a kick out of it I think, knowing his initials spell a word. It's nice to be called smart. I remember my mom said that David was the first person to make her feel real smart. She told me that, after he died. He'd say to her that she was smarter than he was because she had something he didn't have: common sense. It made an impression because no one had ever told her that she was smart before.

"I think you're smart, Mom." She knows how to do so many things I don't, like play the piano, paint, fish – and then cook it, decorate the living room, dress groovy, go to a job, do her hair, ride a horse on the street, and shoot a rifle. Yes, my mom knows how to shoot a rifle. Parker's dad taught her when he came up to visit us when we first moved to Ojai and he brought her a rifle. I was never allowed to touch the rifle or ride our horse, Lady, on the street like the other kids could. She said I was too young to take Lady along the roads and I'd have to wait until I was bigger; it was a bummer because it looked so fun to go from your house to the park on your horse instead of your bike. And that's not going to happen now, since we moved away from Ojai, and they don't allow horses on the street in Seattle like they do in *Here Comes the Brides*.

She never really talked about David again after he died, except for one day when she was talking to me about how important common sense is to have so you know what to do when you really don't. I had never heard of common sense before she told me. We were having lunch at the Farmers' Market, at one of the green metal and wood tables near the ice cream shop that has lots of flavors (but not thirty-one flavors, like Basket Robinson). Before we moved to Ojai, and after she bought me a small bag of black licorice buttons, she explained that David was an engineer for the defense department. "Do you know what that is?"

I didn't know what an engineer was or the defense department. My teacher never talked about that stuff in second grade, but it sounded really smart and complicated.

"No," I told her.

"He would design secret things for the military, for war," she told me.

"Secret things? Like secret rocket ships?" I asked.

"No. For war," she told me. "That's all I know."

"Like planes and bombs?" I still would see all the war on the boob tube. Terrifying stuff no kid should have to see and should only be in the movies.

"I don't know exactly what he designed. It was a secret. He could never talk about his work with me."

"Did he cross his heart?"

"I'm sure he did," she said.

"Well, if it was secret, how did the military know what he was making if he couldn't tell anyone?" I wondered.

"They gave him the secret job, so he had to tell them."

"So, he could only tell the people who gave him the job and not his mom or dad?"

"No. No one. Not even me. Only his boss," she said.

"He must've been really good if he could make stuff like that and keep it secret. "'Cept, I don't like all the war, Mom. It's scary." I said.

"I know, sweetheart. Neither do I," she assured me. "David didn't either. He was a smart and kind man who did his job. And you know what he told me?"

"What?" I asked. I didn't want to guess. That seemed too hard.

"He told me that I was much smarter than he was because I had common sense," she said. "Isn't that something? Remember that, Audrey. Common sense is trusting your gut . . . the feelings in your tummy . . . and it goes a long way."

"Like butterflies in your tummy?"

"Something like that. It's more of a knowing what is right and what is wrong." She took her finger and poked my tummy, but not hard like Ned would when he was trying to tease me. She gently poked my stomach the way a mom does.

"Trust it. Trust your feelings. It's important to have common sense. You wouldn't jump off a cliff if your friends did, would you?" she asked.

I thought about it for a second. Would I jump off a cliff if Parker, or Grant, or Rosie, or Emily, or Roger (who's a boy I have a crush on and kissed on the way to school), did? Hmmm. I don't think it was a trick question. I think she was serious.

"I don't think so, Mom. That seems dumb. Unless there's a big gallon of melted Rocky Road chocolate ice cream and the marshmallows break your fall." I mean, I'd jump into that. Who wouldn't?

"Well . . . good. You understand. I think. So, use your common sense when you're not sure or something feels funny," she told me.

I wish she had told me about common sense before David died.

I think common sense is knowing that you're going to get into big trouble if you do something that you're not supposed to do. Or common sense is when you can't stop somebody from doing something you don't want them to do and you know they shouldn't be doing it, but you can't stop them and they do it anyway, even though you know they shouldn't. That's common sense . . . I think.

I know that funny feeling in my tummy. I should have used common sense more. Especially that day when Gabriel came up to Ojai to help my mom with the yard.

14 HAUNTED HOUSE

WE HAD MOVED TO GRAND AVENUE ON JUNE 11, 1968, AFTER I FINISHED second grade and Ned finished eleventh. I never made it into Camp Fire Girls. My time in the Bluebirds was cut short because my mom decided to move us to Ojai, after David died, and when school was all finished. I had some good times and still have my Bluebird pin, to remember. My mom decided to wait until I was done with second grade before we moved because she wasn't going to drive me from Ojai to Third Street Elementary near Detroit Street every day. They had done that when we moved on my birthday in first grade; I'd be driven to Fullbright Elementary in Canoga Park from L.A., which she said was a pain in the neck and that she'd never do it again. And she didn't. Mostly, my mom wasn't going to let me live with my dad, no matter what.

She bought a house on Grand Avenue, just up the street and around the bend from my grandma's house. She lived on Oak Street, off of Signal and down the street from an old oak tree that the road went around; it's trunk was painted white so the cars would see it at night (and not run into it). Ojai loves its oak trees like I love ice cream, root beer, and French fries.

Signal Street turned into Grand Avenue, near where the old haunted house sat in the middle of a grassy field. I went there once

142

with Grant and Rosie and some other kid that I didn't know (whose name I can't remember). The haunted house legend is that a jar of blood was found in the old house and no one knows how it got there. It was a mystery.

Ned said, "Someone put it there," and told me I was dumb.

I told him to use his common sense, because I knew what it was, since Detroit Street.

"How can a ghost hold a jar of blood when his hands are like clouds and it would slip through?" You can walk through a ghost like a plane can fly through a cloud, so it was a mystery how a ghost could hold a jar of blood.

"Because a ghost didn't put it there in the first place, stupid. Someone else did," he said.

"Like who, if the house is haunted and no one lived there except ghosts?" I asked.

Then Ned put his hands up like he was a monster. He started tiptoeing toward me and – while rolling his eyes back – said in a deep voice, "A creepy man who's going to . . . GET YOU! BLAH!" Then chased me down the driveway.

"Stop it, you butt!" He laughed at that. He always thinks it's funny when he scares me.

I asked him one more time about who could have put the jar of blood in the haunted house, if it wasn't a ghost, because I wanted to make sure there wasn't some creepy man lurking around the neighborhood, leaving jars of blood. It was summer, and I'd leave my window open at night because of the heat. What if he came through my window and left a jar of blood on my bed? Ned just shook his head and said he wasn't going to explain, that I'm just a kid and didn't know anything.

"Can I still leave my window open?" I asked.

"No stranger is going to hurt you, you twerp." That's what he told me.

I only went to that house once when we were playing in the brook near it. I never went back again, only looking from the distance when

I walked by or rode past it on my bike. I knew I wasn't supposed to take candy from a stranger – or a ghost, for that matter.

Ned was right. It wasn't a ghost or stranger that would hurt me. He was as real as you are. And I'd known him since I was five.

Before we started packing up the duplex to move to Ojai, Shelly graduated from Fairfax High, and we all went to her graduation. It took place in the big field behind the school. My mom, grandma, Lana, her fiancé, Thad (who she was engaged to), Mean Ned, and I went to see her get her diploma, along with all the other kids from her class. Shelly was dressed in this white robe and a white square hat with a tassel hanging from it that looked more like she was balancing a plate on her head. When the graduation was done, all the teenagers threw their hat plates into the air. It looked like a swarm of frisbees. They were happy high school was over, I guess.

The day was really sunny, and I wore a bright, paisley dress and my black Mary Janes. I have a picture of all of us. Thad took it. We all look really happy, smiling. Except, Ned. he looked mad.

My dad wasn't in the picture. I don't know where he was that day. He said he was there, but I never saw him. My mom and my dad try not to see or talk to each other whenever they can. Kind of like how I'd avoid Rebecca Watkins who I saw a few months ago before we moved to Seattle when I went to visit Parker on Kittridge Street. I was standing across the street from Parker's, talking to Ginny Meet when Rebecca walked up. It had been a few years since I'd seen her and she beat me up last. She was nice at first, barging into our conservation, asking me where I lived and stuff. I told Rebecca I had a horse in Ojai named Lady. That's what started it.

"You do not," she said.

"Do too," I said.

"DO NOT!" She shouted.

"I do too have a horse!" I shouted back.

Then it happened. I snapped. I didn't care that Rebecca Watkins was a foot taller than me and could sit on me, or that she beat me and other kids up more times than I could count. I bent down, picked up a newspaper that was lying in the Howards' driveway, and started hitting her with it. I couldn't take it anymore. She bullied me too many times before, and everything was coming out, with each swat. She recoiled in shock, defending my incoming newspaper strikes with her hands; finally, she turned and bolted down the street toward her house. She was bigger and a faster runner than me, so I couldn't keep up as I ran after her, screaming, "I DO TOO HAVE A HORSE!" Then, I stopped and threw the paper at her like a paperboy, hitting her in the head. I walked back to Ginny, out of breath, and she looked at me in shock – then burst out laughing. I surprised both of us, I guess, with my anger bubbling to the surface like the gas in the La Brea tar pits, trapping millions of years of history.

Shelly didn't move to Grand Avenue. She stayed in Los Angeles and moved to her own apartment in North Hollywood – and got a spider monkey. My mom thought she was nuts to do that. The spider monkey part. But Shelly loved animals, and she never had a monkey. Of course, my mom was right. It would climb the drapes, swing from the curtain rods, knock over lamps, and destroy everything, so she had to get rid of it.

Before her graduation, I asked Shelly why she wasn't coming to Ojai with us. She told me that I was too young to understand and that it was better if she didn't live with our mom anymore because they got along better when they weren't under the same roof. I told her she could live out in the garage with Ned and then she wouldn't be under the same roof as Mom. She said she didn't want to be in the same room as Ned and it would be better if she stayed back.

I didn't believe her. I knew it was something else.

"Shelly . . . is it because you don't love me anymore?" I asked her.

"Of course I do. I love you more than anything," she told me.

"You're not mad at me for making you run away?"

"Never. You NEVER made me run away, Audrey. Don't ever think that," she said. I couldn't not think that. It was my fault. If I had just listened and minded my mom and stayed home like she told me, none of it would have happened.

"But I'll never see you anymore," I told her. Honest, I felt like everyone was leaving again. I loved Shelly. She made me feel safe.

"Yes, you will see me. I'll come up and see you all the time," she told me.

"You swear? Stick a needle in your eye?" I had to ask.

"I'm not going to do that. You're just going to have to believe me, squirt," she said. Then, she hugged me. I was going to miss her.

Since then, I've only seen her a few times. Once, when she came up with Joel and they found Harvey, my tortoise, trying to cross the road on Highway 150, near Lake Casitas, and brought him home to me. I love Harvey. Joel drilled a hole in the edge of his shell and hooked him to the clothes line in the backyard so he could go anywhere he wanted to in the backyard – but couldn't run away. Joel said the drilling didn't hurt him because it was on the edge of his shell, away from his flesh, and that he attached him to the line because tortoises are good diggers. Did you know that? They can dig under fences and stuff. They could dig to China if they wanted to. I dug a hole in the flower bed near the fence and put a board over it with the dirt on top for him to go inside and sleep when he was tired (or hide in at night for safety); it was like he had his very own cave.

The other times Shelly came up was to plan Lana's wedding to Thad. It took place in a church, not far from my grandma's house. Oh, boy, was that a fiasco. Mean Ned really did it that time.

I decided before we moved to Ojai that I wasn't going to miss Detroit Street. Of course, I was going to miss the Clampetts and the picture of Cecil painted on the bottom of their pool. But that was it. Too much confusion happened when we lived in the duplex, from my mouse eating her family, to fights between my mom and dad before he picked me up on Saturdays, to David dying. David promised my mom in the Rabbi's office that he would love her forever and ever and ever, like Prince Charming; once he found Cinderella, he said that he would never leave because she was pretty, a good dancer, she knew how to wash floors, had a small foot, and had a magical fairy godmother who could turn anything into something wonderful. Personally, I think it would just be easier to be Samantha and twinkle your nose like you have an itch to make stuff appear and disappear and not have to deal with two mean stepsisters – just a few pesky warlocks that like to make mischief. I know what you're thinking. Yes . . . if I could, I'd wiggle my nose and make Mean Ned disappear for a week or two, or turn him into a poly wog to teach him a lesson, or until my mom asked, "What happened to Ned? I haven't seen him in days." I'd twinkle my nose a lot when it came to Ned.

I was looking forward to moving to Ojai, where I only had good memories with my family; also, I was going to be closer to my grandma. I love my grandma. Whenever she would come over to our house, she always brought me See's lollipops, in chocolate and butterscotch. She knows I love candy.

My grandma moved to Ojai the first time when my mom was thirteen. That's four years older than I am now. Before she worked for the people in Beverly Hills, she had a restaurant in Oxnard with her husband named Benny, who I never knew. My mom said I wouldn't want to have known him. That he was mean.

"Was he mean like Ned, Mom?" I asked her.

"No. He was a very cruel man." That's all she said. She didn't want to talk about him. He died a long time ago. Years later, I guess, my grandma moved to Los Angeles to work for Mr. Robert Stack and his wife in Beverly Hills. They are the ones who gave me my little lamb when I was born that's sitting on my bed with all my other stuffed animals. That was before she worked for Judy and Judy wouldn't come out of her room.

My grandma drives a pink car. It's called a Studebaker, but the 'baker' part doesn't make cookies. That would be neato if you opened the trunk and it was full of cookies or they came out of the exhaust pipe when you drove, like if her car was at Willy Wonka's factory and had special powers. She does keep a box of candy in the front seat called AYDS. They're brown and square and look like caramels. She tells me they're not candy and not to eat them. But I like to sneak them when she's not in the car or if the car's parked in the driveway and she's inside the house. Heck, they taste like candy to me, so why wouldn't I?

Shelly says Grandma drives bad. She does drive funny. She puts her foot on the gas, then takes it off, puts it on the gas, and takes it off – over and over again. You go back and forth in your seat because the force of the car pulls you forward when she takes her foot off the gas and then the car forces you back when she gasses it. How would I describe it to you exactly? A roller coaster rocking chair going up and over a bump comes to mind. Except, a Studebaker is not as fun as a roller coaster or a rocking chair. It's just a car.

One time, before we moved, we were driving down Santa Monica Blvd in Beverly Hills because my grandma worked for Mrs. Williams; this was before she moved back to her house in Ojai for good. Shelly was in the car too. I do have to admit, it's so annoying when my grandma drives because one minute you think you're going to hit the dashboard with your head, then when she puts her foot on the gas, your head hits the seat behind you. It's like she can't make up her mind what to do. Who taught her to drive, the Mad Hatter? Finally, Shelly huffily said, "Grandma, just keep your foot on the gas." Shelly knows because she has her driver's license and knows how to drive; she doesn't get lost like Lana.

I think Shelly was sorry she said anything because my grandma floored it. Suddenly, we're bookin' down Santa Monica Blvd and Shelly starts yelling, "Take your foot off the gas, Grandma! Take your foot off the gas!" Finally, she did.

I think it taught us all a lesson that, when you drive with Grandma, you keep your trap shut.

My dad wasn't happy we were moving to Ojai. He called one day and I answered the phone. My mom and I were in the kitchen. She was making me a Charlie the Tuna sandwich. I answered and my dad didn't even say hello. "Where's your Mother?" he barked at me, like the Tyler's mean dog would do, back on Kittridge Street. It was on a chain and would growl and bark when you walked by their front yard, which was loaded with broken cars with no wheels and junk piled to the sky. They were the only house on the block that looked like an eyesore and my dad hated it, saying they didn't know how to respect their things and take care of them. Their lawn was filled with weeds – and loads of dog poop.

I told my dad to hold on, and I handed the phone to my mom. She put her hand over the phone so he couldn't hear and told me to go in the other room. There were a few rooms to choose from, and I didn't know which one I should go in. So, I went into the living room and sat on the couch.

I heard her on the phone saying, "It's ninety miles away! It's not like I'm taking her out of the state, Lee." Well it's funny she said that because, I have to tell you, when he found out my mom was marrying Beanie, he was really mad that I was moving to Seattle. It's super-duper far and out of the state of California, in another state called Washington. You have to take a big plane. I had never been on a big plane. I guess there were more 'visitation rules' when he finally agreed I could go with my mom and Ned to Seattle. Then, there was more yelling on the phone – like that day, before I left Grand Avenue for good.

I remember when my mom said we were moving to Grand Avenue. It felt like it would be far, and I wasn't sure how I would feel about it. I only heard my mom on the phone with my dad, but I could tell they were yelling at each other. I could hear my mom's voice screaming down the hall and around the corner into the living room; it was coming like a train around the bend, choo-chooing her anger with the steam coming out of the smokestack – all because *I* was riding with the engineer, shoveling the coal and making it all happen; I was the one they were *always* fighting about.

"Don't threaten me now that you're in law school . . .." My dad had started taking law classes at night in West L.A. to become a lawyer, right after my parents divorced. He studies all the time. When I go down to visit him, he takes me ice skating at the Culver City ice skating rink on Sepulveda Blvd. I skate and twirl on the ice while he's in the bleachers, reading law books, highlighting pages with a fat, yellow marker. He wants to become a lawyer and still work for The Times.

I guess his lawyer-studying really frosted my mom. I could hear the combat continue, echoing from the kitchen. "Oh, really? . . . I don't care what the judge said! . . . Well, you do what you want!" Then I heard the phone slam on the cradle so hard, I thought maybe she broke it. My heart pounds just thinking about it. I felt like the war was exploding in our house, wondering if it would ever be over, just like Vietnam. Before I walked back to my room, I peeked into the kitchen to see if the phone was still on the wall, hoping it would still be there in the cradle and she didn't break it.

Over a Pink's hot dog that Saturday, my dad said that he would come visit me in Ojai on the weekends, and I could come see him any time I wanted (even though there were 'visitation rules'). I guess a judge told my mom and dad what they could do. I had no say. I couldn't go see my dad whenever I wanted, even if I wanted to. I would be starting in a new school. My mom would tell him that he could come see me, but she wanted me in Ojai getting settled and making friends.

One time, Ned and I took the bus to Santa Monica; my dad came and got us, and we stayed with him for the weekend in his studio apartment. There were two beds. I'd sleep with my dad, and Ned slept in his own bed. I loved to sleep with my dad. He'd put his hands behind his head and cradle my head in the corner of his elbow. He started wearing Old Spice, so his armpits smelled like an old pirate ship, which I liked because *Pirates of the Caribbean* was my favorite ride at Disneyland. ALL the eTicket rides are my favorite. I even like the General Electric ride when you go around and look at all the kitchen appliances. The Matterhorn is fun, except you feel like you can get whiplash, which is where your head snaps back like mine did when my grandmother was driving and the bumps in the tracks hurt my bottom.

I think they could improve the experience with cushions on the seat. Who says bobsleds have to be cushion-less? The Jungle Cruise is fun too. I drove the boat a bunch of times. I'm a good skipper, like the Skipper on *Gilligan's Island*. But that hippo peeking out of the water that you have to shoot scares me every time, and I've been on the ride more than most kids.

Mostly, my dad drives up to Ojai to see me because I can't drive like Ned can. If Ned asked nicely, my mom would let him take her car to Century City when she was gone visiting Beanie or she said she didn't need the car for the weekend. Before we moved, and before I started third grade at Topa Topa Elementary, my dad told me that for every A I got, he would give me a dollar. I think he was sorry he told me that. I'd gotten all A's and made a haul. A 'no hitter' third grade. That's a GOOD thing. It means the pitcher pitched a perfect game with no players on base. I decided that the reason why I got all A's is because Ojai was really fun; also, my mom and dad hardly saw each other. There was no more fighting (that I could see). Even when he'd come up for his weekend visit, I'd just go out to the car, get in and we'd go to eat at the Mighty Bite, or we'd go to the park, or do something else that was fun. They never saw each other. Never ever.

After we moved to Grand Avenue, my mom wanted to fix up the house and the yard. The garage had been turned into a bedroom for Ned to sleep in. That was it. The yard looked like a jungle, and my mom hired Gabriel to garden it.

Why? Why him? Were there no gardeners in Ojai? Who did the neighbors' yards? Why did she have to hire Gabriel? I'm still asking myself that question.

All I know is that haunted houses don't have to have a jar of blood. Sometimes, the scariest things that haunt you can be in your own front yard.

15 YELLOW CANARY

BEANIE'S DIFFERENT FROM DAVID. HE DOESN'T DRIVE WITH ONE FINGER OR have a grey, short crew cut, but a pile of hair like Elvis Presley. I don't know many grown-up old men that do, seeing there's lots of shiny heads around. Beanie doesn't weed the lawn either, like my dad would like to do; he has a gardener to do it. I asked him if he's good at math. He told me he was because he has to talk about math problems in his job. He says he has to decide if the risk is worth it. He helps insure things, whatever that means. I asked him what kind of things he helps insure. He said stuff like buildings and spaceships . . . things that cost a lot of money and are hard to replace. Not a skateboard or a pogo stick. Sometimes, a building can tip over in an earthquake or a rocket ship can get lost in space. He doesn't want that to happen. He says it's bad for his customers. Anyway, he's good at math. I added fourteen hundred and fifty-three plus two thousand and thirty-seven for him, carrying the one, and he told me I was good at math too, because I got it right. I'm not going to tell you the answer. Go ahead and add it yourself. I'll tell you if you get it right.

I asked SET if his son and daughter were good at math, and he told me they were. They're older than I am. They're closer to Ned and my big sisters' ages. Ron, Beanie's son, is a couple of years younger than Ned and not as tall. I'd only met his kids once; it was the day before the wedding, before we all got on a plane and went to live together in Seattle. I'd never done that before . . . been on a plane, or met someone and then went to live in their house. There was a bedroom just for me.

I remember being excited about flying on a big jet airplane, but at the same time, I was a little nervous. They aren't birds or balloons. They're not little planes that can glide if they have to. I'm still not sure exactly how they fly because I've never taken one apart. People take it for granted that a plane can fly. It's magic, really, if you think about it – that a plane or a rocket can sail through the air and get from one place to the other without falling out of the sky. Do you ever think about that, that you can fly like a bird and you're a person? I think it's the grooviest thing ever.

Beanie goes to a lot of places for his work on airplanes. He likes to fly. He told me I'd like it too because there's free soda pop and peanuts – as much as a kid could want! I want a lot, I tell you, and ask for extra when I fly. Beanie was right. Flying is fun. I like Beanie more than I liked David because I've known him longer; I feel like he likes me just as much as I like him, and he's really nice and hasn't died.

My mom says she's really happy for the first time in her life. My dad didn't make her happy. Maybe it's because she and Beanie would go out to dinner and eat steak and played tennis together at the Ojai Valley Inn. It's a big hotel and country club with a golf course and swimming pool that I'd swim in all the time. That's where they had their married party after they get hitched. My mom had been planning the wedding for a few months, and Lana had been helping. It was small, not like Lana's, and no one passed out or made a scene like what happened at Lana's wedding.

Lana and Thad got married in Ojai in a church. There were a lot of people I knew from Lana's dance parties. Some of the girls were bridesmaids. Thad's parents were there too. The whole church was filled, right to the nosebleed seats. Well, all the way to the back of the church, where your view wasn't as good. I was the flower girl and Shelly was the maid of honor (that's the sister's oldest sister or best friend). That's what they told me. I asked. There were four bridesmaids and four groomsmen. That's the boys' side. Ned was one of the groomsmen and ruined the whole wedding.

Lana and Thad were standing in front of the man marrying them, with their backs to the audience. The man was talking about how a woman should do what her husband tells her and that she still has to like him if he gets sick and stuff. I remember looking over at my brother and he was rocking, toe to heel. He didn't look so good. He closed his eyes and the next thing you know, out of nowhere, Ned went over like a tree, hitting the floor with a big thud. He passed out.

My grandma stood up and cried, "Oh my God, he's dead!"

Now I know where my mom gets it.

Ned was laying on the floor, out cold, as if Mohamed Ali clocked him a good one. Lana and Thad looked over their shoulder and saw Ned laying at their heels, not realizing he was passed out. They could have stepped on him if they weren't looking. The good thing is that he turned his head at the last minute, so he didn't break his nose. That would have been smarts, and bloody – and would have gotten Lana's dress all dirty.

The wedding stopped. My mom hauled out of the pew and ran up to the stage over to Ned. She was kneeling next to him, gently smacking his face to wake him up. I guess he wasn't feeling well that day and locked his knees and "Timber!"

I watched my mom gently say, "Ned . . . honey, wake up."

Concerned, I asked, "Is he dead yet?"

Finally, Ned came to. Some of the other groomsmen helped him up, and my mom took him to a room behind the stage to get him some water. The wedding continued and Lana and Thad were pronounced man and wife. They kissed in front of everyone. It was grody. The reception party was fun. It was at our house. The backyard looked really pretty. My mom really knows how to decorate and throw a party. We drank punch and ate cake. People danced and told stories. Then, it was time for Lana and Thad to leave and go on their honeymoon. I don't know what got into me.

The afternoon was beautiful, the sun hitting the faces of all the people lining the driveway, tossing rice at Lana and Thad as they ducked for their car. They were getting into their VW, saying goodbye to everyone, excited to go on their honeymoon. All I know is in one breath I went from laughing to crying, realizing what was really happening and what getting married really meant.

"Don't go! Take me with you!" Wailing, I wrapped my arms tightly around Lana and wouldn't let her go. It hit me. I didn't want to see her leave for good.

"Please take me with you, Lana! Please!"

"Oh, Porky . . ." she said.

"Please, Lana! Please!" I shouted.

Lana started crying and asked Thad if they could take me with them on their honeymoon.

"Absolutely NOT!" my mom said.

"Please don't go! Take me with you!" I begged, still hanging onto her for dear life.

I did that when I wanted to go or felt scared and lonely. I didn't like always being left.

"Audrey . . . let go of your sister, NOW! Do you want a spanking?!

She began to pry me off Lana, wrangling me. Then, my mom wrapped her arms around me and told me everything was going to be okay.

"I know this is a lot for you to handle, Audrey. But Lana is married now, and she needs to go on her honeymoon. You'll see her soon," she told me.

"No, I won't! We're moving to Seattle, and she's not coming!" I cried.

"But she'll see you at mine and Beanie's wedding in a few months."

"Yes, Audrey," Lana said. "I'll be up for the wedding and we'll spend some time."

Through tears, I muttered, "Promise?"

"I promise," she told me.

"Ok." I slowly stopped crying and let her get in the VW so she could go away on her honeymoon to Mexico. I knew my life would never be the same because she had left for good. I sang that rhyme in my head over and over again: *There were ten in the bed and the little one said roll over, roll over. So, they all rolled over and one fell out. There were nine in the bed . . ..* Pretty soon the bed would be empty, I thought to myself.

The car pulled out of the driveway, and we all waved goodbye. I watched the VW as far as I could, drive off into the distance, down Grand Avenue, until I couldn't see it anymore.

"You okay?" my mom asked. I nodded. "You want some more cake?" I nodded. I tried to smile. "Let's go get some," she said. She took my hand and led me into the house. Cake might not make my heart stop hurting, but it would at least make my tummy happy.

There's something really wonderful about S.E.T. that I can't describe. Sure, he knows math, and he has all of his hair. But it's something else. All I know is that my mom has this softness about her, like butter you leave on the table; it's easier to put on your toast than when it's been in the refrig and it's cold. She's warm like soft butter. I've never seen her quite like this before. She's hardly ever mad at me anymore. She's lovey-dovey with Beanie, kissing and laughing, holding hands, and all gooey about being married to him. That's why she decided not to buy the restaurant and stay in Ojai.

A little while after we moved to Grand Avenue, my mom found this cute little restaurant near Meiner's Oaks that looked like a house; she was going to call it the *Lemon Tree*. The door would be yellow, and there would be a lemon tree in a pot on the porch. She said Ned and I could work there. We talked about how we were going to wear jeans, white t-shirts, with red bandana's around our necks. My grandma said my mom was crazy to want to own a restaurant because they're hard work and customers complain about the cooking if it's not just right.

My mom decided not to buy it, not because of what my grandma said, but because Beanie proposed to her with a ring with a round diamond on it, the size of a pea. I'd never seen a ring like that. It has two more rings with little diamonds too. It looks like what a movie star would wear. When he gave her the ring and asked her if she wanted to get married, I guess she said, "Ok, I won't buy the restaurant." She came home and told Ned and I that we were going to move to Seattle to start a new life; she said that it would be different from any life me or Ned would ever know.

I wasn't sure what to expect. I'd never been to Seattle, but the singer who sings about it on *Here Comes the Brides* said that "the bluest skies are in Seattle." And it's true, I tell you. They're blue as blue can be, and there's a humongous snow-covered mountain that sticks out, on a clear day, called Mount Rainer.

All I know is, if my mom and Beanie ever need a new gardener, I hope they never have Gabriel come and do the yard.

After we moved from Detroit Street to Grand Avenue, I finished unpacking my room and took the empty boxes out to the trash can that was by the curb in front of our house. I stuffed the boxes into the tin can and put the lid on; that's the first time I saw Henry Monowski. Henry lived across the street, on the corner right across from our driveway. He was standing in his grandparents' (who he lived with) front yard, dressed in blue shorts, a blue jacket, white shirt, and striped tie. He was seven years old and going into the fourth grade. Can you believe that? He skipped two grades. He was smart as a whip. When I first saw Henry staring at me, I didn't know what to do. I tightly put the lid on the garbage can so the neighbor's dog couldn't get in it, and I continued to stare back. We hadn't gotten our beagle, Zachery, yet. If we had, garbage would have been all over the place.

We adopted Zachery after Migo ran away, which was the saddest day ever. Migo being gone was awful. We looked everywhere for her. My mom was so upset. Ned was upset. I was too because I loved her so much. I knew I didn't make her run away. I know she loved me because she likes to sleep with me. She still sleeps behind my knees or tucked in against my stomach, under the covers.

A few weeks after we thought Migo ran away, we got another cat named Snowball. We still have her, too. Her fur is pure white, except when she was out with Zachery all day. My mom called them borders because they were never home. Zachery got Snowball into all kinds of trouble. She'd come home covered in soot from them playing in the neighbors' incinerator or burnt leaves pile. Sometimes, Zachery brought home a bunch of dogs for dinner, like he finished little league and they built up an appetite. He was a character. He was either eating, or sleeping, or gone all day, or had a cold, and we would have to give him a pill hidden in a hot dog to make him feel better.

Months later, we got Migo back, but not without a fight. See, she didn't run away after all. Someone took her. She had been missing for almost six months. We thought she'd never ever come home and gave up ever seeing her again. Then one day, some man dropped off my mom's dry cleaning and said he had worked for the fire department. That was a few months before Migo ran away. He stood on the porch and told my mom about this beautiful Siamese cat that he rescued from a tree on Grand Avenue and that he and his family just loved her.

"Is it a Blue Point Siamese and has crossed blue eyes?" my mom asked.

"Yes," he said.

My mom looked at him hard and said, "You've got my cat."

He said, "No, I don't."

"You have my cat." She stood her ground.

My mom told him that if he didn't return Migo, she would go to the police or something. After a few weeks of arguing, the man finally brought Migo home. I remember when she arrived. I opened a can of sardines for her in celebration because she loved sardines. We were so happy to have her home. It was like when Shelly came home after juvenile hall. Everything felt normal again – back in place.

That was after we had already gotten knucklehead, Zachery, before all of this hoopla happened with Migo. My mom was reading the ad we put in the paper that Sunday about Migo being lost, and she saw an ad for Zachery. Ned thought it would be a good idea to get a dog because there had been someone who tried to break into his garage room, and the dog would bark if someone did try to rob the house.

Oh boy, was Ned right. I'm not sure if you've really heard barking until you get a beagle. Just the barking alone would irritate a robber. They'd have to skip your house just because they'd wouldn't be able to stand the howling. But we didn't know that until it was too late. My mom drove us to the people's house that couldn't keep Zachery anymore (in Meiners Oaks) to pick him up. I watched her knock on the front door, but no one answered. We went around to the back of the house to the white gate that fenced off the backyard from the driveway. Tied to a tree, there he was; this cute little Beagle was wagging his tail – so happy to see us.

On the way back to Ojai, my brother asked my mom why the people gave away such a cute dog.

"They didn't have room for him," my mom said.

Ned had a confused look. "Did you see the size of their backyard, Mom?"

"Yeah, Mom. It was the size of the neighbors' pasture, practically," I said.

Well, we learned really fast why Zachery got the boot. He was like Wiley Coyote. When he was at the house long enough, he was always into something or in trouble; usually, he was out and about most of the day. It's like we didn't have a dog, but we did. On top of that, he barked non-stop, always had a cold, and brought home a pack of dogs every night for dinner. Snowball joined him on his daily adventures, wherever he'd go. She was a troublemaker too. Snowball did something that I will never forgive her for, even though she's a cat and can't apologize.

I was with my friend, Roseanne, the daughter of Rose, who my mom knew in Ojai when she lived there before. Rose and my mom went to high school together. We were riding our bikes on North Montgomery and went past this pet store; we stopped our bikes in front of the store. Staring at all the birds through the window, I spotted this one yellow canary within a second, and I fell in love. I went home and asked my mom if I could get it. She said I had to save my allowance for it. The canary was five dollars and I would have to work for ten weeks to have enough money because I got fifty cents a week. Fifty cents goes into five dollars ten times.

Every day that summer, I rode my bike to visit my yellow canary. I loved it so much.

I did all sorts of chores. I worked very hard. And, just to show how responsible I could be, I washed my face, brushed my teeth, didn't put my hands on the wall, and remembered not to talk back. I played it safe. After about three weeks, my mom said that I had been such a hard worker and good girl that she would give me three dollars and fifty cents to buy the canary and she would pay for the cage and canary food. We drove to the pet store, I bought my yellow canary, took it home, and put it in my room.

About five minutes later – and I mean five minutes – I heard a crash. I was sitting in the living room talking to my mom, deciding what I was going to name my new pet, because my dream had come true and I'd got the canary. I was deciding between Roy or Joy because I didn't know if it was a boy or girl canary. The bellowing coming from my room sounded like the bookshelf fell over. I jumped from the couch, flung open the door, and bolted in, startled to see the cage was on the floor with bird seed scattered everywhere. And there she was – Snowball – with my canary in her mouth. She got home early, without Zachery and his pack of dogs, and came through my opened window.

"NO, SNOWBALL! MOM, SNOWBALL HAS MY CANARY! I screamed.

My mom rushed in and captured Snowball, holding her by the back of the neck because that's how you hold cats so they don't get away, and pried Roy or Joy out of Snowball's mouth – but it was too late; it was dead. Roy or Joy had died . . . of a heart attack, I think. I would have too if I was stuck in a cat's mouth. Maybe Tweety Bird can handle it, but not Roy or Joy. The waterworks came flooding. I cried and cried. I was SO mad at Snowball for killing my canary. My mom got a shoebox out of her closet and we buried Roy or Joy in the backyard, near where Harvey's house was dug; that way, my canary, that I only had for five minutes, would have company. That same day my two

Guppies committed suicide when they jumped out of their bowl. I think they thought Snowball might be back and they should make a run for it and forgot they were fish.

I told my mom it wasn't worth saving for anything if it's just going to die. But I still do. I had a box full of paper money that I saved. Tens, Fives, and ones, all turned in the same direction in a box like a cash register, totaling one hundred dollars. That was until Mean Ned turned it ALL into pennies that I found on my bed last week, piled the size of Mount Rainer. He's such a butt. I still save money in case I have to buy a train ticket for somewhere else.

Despite Snowball killing my canary, I still miss our tiny house on Grand Avenue. I could walk from my bedroom to the kitchen in thirty-four steps. It was a cute little house, and I loved that there were no sidewalks; people could ride their horses in the street along Grand Avenue, and I'd watch from my porch, dreaming of doing that one day too.

My mom had decorated the house really pretty. I relished the big backyard where my tortoise could explore the garden, with the apricot tree and walnut tree giving me something to eat when I was hungry. I miss the pasture where, if I stretch my head across the fence and look to the right, I could see Mrs. Rolston's backyard. I loved living in Ojai. I felt good there. I liked my friends. I liked school. I really hope I'll like Seattle just as much.

IT WAS MORNING, ABOUT 9 AM ON A SATURDAY, when our staring contest happened. I was standing on the curb next to the trash can, and across the other side of Grand Avenue on the corner lot in the grass, wearing oxfords and a blue suit with shorts and a tie, was Henry Monowski. He was standing real tall (even though he was shorter than me), staring at me like I was a hobo going through the trash. So, I stared back.

We looked at each other for about a minute before he waved his hand, gesturing for me to come over. I double-checked the lid on the can to make sure it was tight and walked into the street, looking both ways. I crossed over Grand Avenue to Henry and asked if I could come on the lawn. He told me I could.

Henry was a cute boy with blond hair that he combed into a nice shape over his head, like one of The Beach Boys, and he had blue eyes that looked like a swimming pool (if you don't do a cannonball in it). They were still. They stared super-duper good. He was an excellent eye starer.

I approached him, and he held out his hand like he was a businessman about to sell me something.

"I'm Henry Monowski, and I live here with my grandparents. Who are you?"

"I'm Audrey Franklin; I just moved here. I live with my mom and mean brother, Ned, and my cat, Migo, who has blue eyes like you," I said. Henry was very formal, like a king.

"Nice to meet you, Miss Franklin," he said.

"Can I call you Henry?" I asked.

"Of course," he told me.

Then I noticed it. Pinned to his jacket was a black and white button that read: MR. PRESIDENT.

"What's that?" I asked.

"That's my badge," he said.

"Why are you wearing that?" I was curious.

"Because I am the President," he told me.

"Oh."

"Do you want to come inside and meet everyone?" he asked me.

I wasn't sure who everyone was, but it sounded fine to me. "Okay," I told him; we walked across the grass to the driveway and through the side door into his grandmother's kitchen. We went past the dining room table and through the living room, where I saw his grandpa asleep in a recliner; his mouth was wide open like a fly trap, and he was snoring like Shuteye Popeye. We ended up in a tiny hallway, where we came to a door with a lock on it and all kinds of signs taped to it. "KEEP OUT!" "PRIVATE!" "OFFICE OF THE PRESIDENT."

He opened the door, and I went into his office; that's where I began to learn about Henry Monowski and his wonderful, wondrous world – and where I could forget parts of mine.

16 HENRY MONOWSKI

"CALL ME 'MR. PRESIDENT'." THAT'S WHAT HENRY SAID WHEN I WENT INTO his room. He pulled out the chair and sat at his dark, wooden desk that had scratches on it. The desk was small like him, and it was covered in school papers with math numbers and signs that looked like aliens made them for big kids. There was also a book about Harry Truman, who Henry said was the second-best president because no one ever believed he could be president when the newspaper made a goof and he felt kind of bad after dropping the A-bomb on all those people in Japan (even though they made him mad). Also, I spotted a Lite-Brite made into the Iron Giant robot – which was one of his favorite books about some metal, superhuman fighting a dragon in outer space – that leaned against a GI Joe in an astronaut suit. You couldn't really even see the top of his desk because it was cluttered with so much junk. It was boys' stuff, like super balls, a chuck wagon missing a wheel, pencils, a protractor, a space capsule, two Mattel cars, a giant slinky, Monopoly money, a half-eaten Butter Finger, and some dominos. Parker's desk was never covered with so much stuff. I don't even think he had a desk. Then, again, Parker wasn't Henry. Henry was a very special kind of boy. I never met anyone like him.

"I can't call you Henry, Henry?" I asked.

"Not when you're in my office," he said, "Only Mr. President."

"Ok," I said, "I can do that if you insist."

I decided to go along with it, even though I was older but a grade behind him. He went to a private school, St. Thomas, which was a Catholic school. That means he was taught by nuns, like Sister Betrille, but they couldn't fly like she could. Henry said they were very strict, never smiled, and acted like Colonel Klink. He started in the first grade when he was five because he's really smart. Then, they skipped him to the third grade. The summer when I met Henry, he was going into the fourth grade, and he was only seven years old. I was eight and going into the third grade, like normal kids with brains smaller than Henry's.

Now that I was in his room, I had to call him Mr. President. I never called a kid Mr. President before, and it seemed strange – but harmless.

"So, Mr. President, do you want to play Candy Cane Lane, or Barrel of Monkeys, or something else?" I spotted the games up on his shelf.

"Not right now. We have more important matters to attend to," he said. Henry got this super-serious look on his face. He leaned into me and said in a hushed voice that he was going to share something with me and I could never tell anyone. Another secret. I was collecting them like caterpillars. I told him I was good at keeping secrets; I said I had a few that I was managing and I could keep his too.

"That's excellent," he said.

He got up, went to his closet door, reached in, and took something out. I couldn't see what. He turned around slowly and was holding a cute little clown up to his face, covering his mouth and nose. Then, it happened.

"Hi, I'm Clownie. What's your name?" Henry asked in a high-pitched voice.

I wasn't sure what to say. I'd never seen a kid do this either. Not even at my Aunt Ru's school. Sure, we talked for our dolls and stuff, but Henry wasn't doing that. Clownie was supposed to be real.

"Um . . . I'm Audrey," I said. I went along with it. I knew Henry was talking but pretended that I didn't.

"It's nice to meet you," said . . . Clownie. "Where do you live?"

"I live across the street. We just moved here from Los Angeles a few weeks ago," I told Clownie.

"Do you like it?"

"Yes. My grandma lives down the street, and I like being in Ojai, making new friends," I told him.

"Why did you move to Ojai. Are you running from the law?"

"No. My mom and dad divorced. Then, David, my mom's new husband, died and she buried him here, under the oak trees over by Nordoff High, off of the 150," I said.

"Very interesting, Audrey. I'm sorry your mommy and daddy don't love each other anymore." I never thought about it that way. I was just happy all the yelling and other stuff had stopped.

"I know how that is. My parents divorced too." I wasn't sure if it was Clownie's or Henry's parents who had divorced.

"Is that why you live with Henry and his grandparents, Clownie?"

"Yes."

I didn't want to be a snoop and ask more questions, but I did.

"Where are your mom and dad?" I asked.

In a higher-pitched voice, Clownie said, "I don't want to talk about that."

Henry then lowered Clownie and chimed in. "Clownie's sensitive about that subject, Audrey. He doesn't know where his parents live."

"Oh. Maybe they live in space," I said. I saw that 2001 movie, and it was possible, I thought. Henry thought about that for a second. "I don't think so. They weren't astronauts." Then, he put Clownie back up to his face.

"Do you want to be my friend?" Clownie asked.

"Sure. And Henry's. I mean, I'd like to be Mr. President's friend too," I said.

Henry turned and put Clownie back in the closet. He shut the door.

"Clownie's tired and needs a nap," Henry said.

Who is Clownie, exactly?" I asked.

"He's my Secretary of State," Henry said.

"What's that?" I asked.

"He types my official letters to keep the peace," he said.

"Oh."

Henry sat at his desk and laced his fingers, putting them behind his head and leaning back; it was just like I'd seen my dad do at his desk when I would go with him to The Times. My pop would sit at his desk that was in a group of other desks on the eighth floor of The Times building, in display advertising; he'd lean back in a chair, smoking a cigar, watching me as I'd sit at another desk gluing paper with rubber cement, pretending I was my dad working.

"I have an important question to ask you, Audrey," Henry said.

"Yes, Mr. President?"

"How would you like to be my vice president?" Henry asked.

"Sure. What do I have to do?" I didn't know what a vice president did exactly, seeing I never met a president before.

"You have to run the office when I'm down in my secret room."

"Where's your secret room?" I asked. "Remember, I can keep a secret, Mr. President." I could.

Henry looked at me with approval, got up from his desk, and walked to a door (next to his closet) that opened into the front yard. He turned and said, "Follow me." We walked out into the front yard and around the side of the house. Henry stopped and pointed to a hole in the flower bed that looked as if a bush had been dug up.

"That's the entrance to my secret room."

"How do you get down there? It looks like a hole in the dirt," I said.

"That's the fake out. It looks like a hole, but it's not," he said.

"Ok," I said. "But how do you open the hole?"

"Magic."

I believed him because he wanted me to. I didn't see any harm in going along with his imagination. In fact, I liked it. I also knew that not many kids would understand Henry's imagination and would probably make fun of him. That happened a few months later, when Parker came to visit me with his dad, and when Big Ned brought my mom the rifle.

We were sitting outside on our back patio that day, at the picnic table that my mom had painted light blue (the same color as the kitchen). I didn't have Harvey yet, and I hadn't drunk that Fresca that made me sick to my stomach. It was mid-July and it was hot. Parker and I were sitting at the table. My mom had brought us out hot dogs, potato chips, and root beer. We were eating hot dogs when Henry came through the back kitchen door . . . with Clownie. He was dressed in his suit and tie with his Mr. President badge pinned to his blazer and his blond hair combed perfectly.

He walked up to the table and said, "Hi, I'm Henry."

Parker looked at him and made a face to me, like, "Who's this twerp?"

"This is my friend, Henry. Henry lives across the street. Henry, this is my friend Parker, who I told you about. He's visiting from Canoga Park."

Henry walked over to Parker and put his hand out to shake his hand. "I am very pleasantly happy to make your acquaintance, Parker." Parker just ate his hot dog and with a full mouth said, "What's with this kid?"

Henry looked at me. I took a deep breath and shrugged. "Do you want a root beer, Henry?"

"No, thank you, Vice President," Henry said.

"Vice President?" Parker asked.

"Never mind. It's just a thing he says," I replied.

Henry looked antsy, like he had an ant farm in his pants. I could tell he was uncomfortable, and I was hoping he wouldn't do it. I knew Parker wouldn't understand, but you can't stop a seven-year-old president with a mind of his own from doing whatever he wants. Then, my fear came true as I saw the head of Clownie, hidden behind Henry's back, peeking out. I closed my eyes for a second and, right as I opened them again, Henry put Clownie up to his face and started talking. I put my head down, knowing he was no longer safe, and there was nothing I could do to protect him.

"Hi, I'm Clownie. What's your name?"

I let out a sigh and looked at Parker because I knew what was going to happen next; I tried to coax him with my eyes to just pretend it wasn't happening, but Parker was a year older than I was and two years older than Henry – and he had a big mouth.

"What's with you? I can see you talking. Are you a weirdo or something?" Parker started to laugh.

I could see the look on Henry's face, wounded like he was punctured with an arrow or shot by a BB gun. His face was churning in expression, like mine did when I accidentally broke something and I was terrified.

"Parker, don't. He's just playing," I said.

Henry looked at me with this distressed look. Then, he screamed, "NO I'M NOT!" He turned and ran inside, through the kitchen door. A second after, I could hear the front door slam.

"Henry!" I called.

"That kid is weird. Who does that?"

"Don't be mean, Parker. He's my friend!"

I threw my hot dog down, pushed the bench out (tumbling it over), and ran out of my yard through the side gate on the other side of the house; I darted across the street, without looking both ways, to Henry's house. I opened up the front door to his room and looked inside. Henry was on his bed face down, crying. Clownie was on the floor, staring at the ceiling, looking like he had been hit by a Miller High Life beer truck and died.

"It's okay, Henry. I understand."

Henry continued to cry.

I picked up Clownie off the floor and laid him next to Henry. I put my hand on Henry's back and patted it like my dad would do to me when I was little and fell down or crashed my bike when I was first learning; it was how he'd tried to get me to stop crying.

"There, there, Mr. President. Please don't cry."

Henry had all of these toys that talked to me. Over the next few weeks after meeting Henry, I met all of his Cabinet. Henry said that a president had a Cabinet like dishes had a shelf. There was Clownie, who I'd already met, and Peaches – who was a bear that had been appointed Head of Bears. As far as I knew, Ojai didn't have any bears, so it seemed like an easy job for Peaches. There was Simon, who looked like Howdy Doody, and you always had to do what he said. I met Oscar, who was a plastic wiener on wheels and was head of making lunches and snacks. Mrs. Monowski usually made the snacks because Oscar didn't have any hands – just wheels. Lastly, there was Donald, who was a duck; he couldn't speak and only quacked, but I understood everything he said. I'm not sure what his job in the Cabinet was, but I was hoping it had something to do with Disneyland.

Even though I have met other kids, and have other friends, and play at their houses, there was something about going over to Henry's house that I loved. Someone was always home. My mom worked a lot, and my brother was always out with his friends, or in his garage room sleeping, or playing the drums. Henry's house was much bigger than ours and had a bigger front yard. It was on the corner and wrapped around from Grand Avenue to Fulton, having two front lawns. He didn't have a mean brother. He was the only kid that lived in the house. His grandmother always wore an apron and she had an accent, so it was hard to understand what she was saying to me. "Udrey, you want for eat?" She served sauerkraut with everything. I'd never had a peanut butter and jelly sandwich with a side of sauerkraut until I ate at Henry's house. He said she and Mr. Monowski were from Poland. That's across the ocean somewhere. That's where the polish jokes come from. They like to eat sauerkraut in Poland. A LOT.

Mrs. Monowski had rabbits and birds, and we could play with them whenever we wanted. She also kept chickens in a chicken coop, and we'd collect the fresh eggs. His grandpa was always asleep in front of the television in a lazy boy armchair that leaned back. He didn't talk much. When he did speak, it was things like: "Boy, get paper news." He had an accent too. I wondered if he didn't know Henry's name because he always called him 'boy'. But that was better than 'hey you', which is what Mr. Monowski called me when he needed something. I'd usually pass him on the way to Henry's room, and he'd open his eyes and say, "Hey you, get me drink water."

I would go over to Henry's a lot in the beginning, when I first met him – before the school year started. His room would come alive. It was like a puppet show. I think he was a lonely boy before he met me. I seemed to be his only real friend. Not everyone understood his imagination or played along. I didn't make fun of him, ever. I listened. I think that's how he got his feelings out.

For the first few months after school started, I'd only see Henry on the weekends. Then, suddenly, right before Thanksgiving, Henry got pulled out of school and sent away. He did something that you're not supposed to ever do, unless you want out of the nun school. During morning roll call, he climbed up on his desk, pulled his penis out, and peed in class – just missing Patsy Pliner; she lived around the corner and was in his class. The nuns made him put his penis back in his uniform, dragged him off his desk and straight to the head nun's office.

Before he was shipped off to somewhere back east to live with some other relatives, I asked him why he did that. "Why didn't you just go to the toilet like most kids?" He told me he didn't know exactly why. His legs just did what they wanted and climbed up on his desk.

"But then you peed, Henry," I said.

"I was mad," he said.

"Why? Who were you mad at?"

"I don't know. I guess it's because I was tired of kids making fun of me."

I was standing on my driveway when Henry finished putting his suitcase (and his Cabinet that were all stuffed in a box) in his grandma's car. He walked across the lawn and then across the street, holding Clownie.

"Did you come to say goodbye, Clownie?"

"Clownie doesn't feel like talking," Henry said.

"Well, I'm going to miss you, Clownie." I told him.

Henry put his hand out to shake mine. I didn't take it. Instead, I hugged him like Lana or Shelly would hug me to make the sadness disappear. I could hear a sniffle. I think Henry was fighting back some tears, not wanting to be a crybaby. I looked at him and smiled.

"You are a wonderful boy, Henry," I told him.

"It was very nice to know you, Audrey," he told me.

"Don't let Clownie talk to everyone, Henry. They may not understand how special he is," I told him.

He nodded, turned around, and crossed back over to his grandma's house. I watched him open the door of the car. Before he got in, I shouted, "I'll miss you, Mr. President!" He turned and looked at me, then sat in the back seat, shut the door, and his grandma drove away.

I never saw Henry Monowski again.

Maybe it's just as well. I'm not sure what he would have done if he knew I'd be moving to Seattle. Maybe he would have gone to the entrance of his secret room and thrown himself in that hole where some bush once was; I'd played along and pretended it led to some secret place that he was the president of, and he'd stay there forever and never come out. That's what you do for friends . . . you imagine with them, and you don't make fun of them, because it hurts their feelings and that's not nice.

Henry Monowski was a sensitive, sweet, and smart boy. I miss him. I miss his room coming alive. I miss being vice president. I miss talking to Clownie. Maybe if I told him what had happened when we first moved to Ojai, Clownie would have listened to me; maybe I would feel better getting it out and not carrying it around in the back of my mind like I do, wondering what I did to have something like that happen to me. I didn't take any candy. He wasn't a stranger.

I know I never should have gotten in his car. It was my fault. That's all I know.

17 ORANGE GROVES

SOMEONE HAD ASKED ME AT SCHOOL IF I WANTED MY MOM AND DAD TO get back together. I thought about it. If they got back together, the yelling would start again and we wouldn't have moved to Ojai – and I really loved it there. It was easy. I loved going to the creek near my house to catch frogs and pollywogs. Those are little fish that look like slugs and turn into frogs when they get bigger. I don't know where they got the name pollywog, but I think it's cute. It got hot in Ojai in the summer – *really* hot! One time, I drank Fresca on a really hot day, and it made my stomach hurt. I told my brother, and he said it was because it had grapefruit in it. What does that have to do with anything? Oranges don't make me sick on hot days, so why would grapefruit? I think it's because Fresca tastes bad, not because it's made of grapefruit.

Above our house, a few blocks up the street near where Roseanne lives, was Tarantula Hill. It's a dirt hill at the bottom of the Topa Topa mountains. I liked going to Tarantula Hill and catching tarantulas. It's not like they're running around like ants do. You have to look for them, but then you do have to be careful of the rattlesnakes. Once, I was playing with Roseanne near the creek up by Red Hill Road, and we heard rustling in the bushes. I walked over to take a look because it could have been a lizard, or a bunny, or a quail. Nope. Rattlesnake. I ran as fast as I could, just in case the rattlesnake was following me; if they bite you, then you have to go to the hospital. Who had time for that when it was summer, and there was so much other fun stuff to do?

Rule #1: Don't get bitten by a rattlesnake.

Rule #2: Don't step on a yellow jacket, which I learned the hard way.

Tarantulas are different. Roger, the boy I kissed on the mouth in the dry creek on the way to school, caught one and I let it climb up my leg. It wasn't scary. They're furry and cute, and they don't bite if you're gentle with them. I didn't tell my mom though. She'd probably scream, "Ned!" because there'd be no one else around unless Beanie had been in town. She would have had a heart attack and tell me I couldn't go do that anymore, which would make me unhappy because I like tarantulas and think they like me too. Not all scary-looking things or people are mean, and not all sugar and spice-looking things or people are nice.

I loved the smell of the orange groves when I rode through them on Lady. She was a black quarter horse with white between her eyes. My mom bought her a few months after we moved to Ojai. We didn't keep her in the backyard or in our neighbor's pasture. We kept her about five miles away, east, where the big dip in Grand Avenue is and where it floods it when it pours. That happened in January – before we moved to Seattle. We got the biggest rainstorm I'd ever seen. Sure, it'd rain in Canoga Park, the streets would flood up to the curb, and I'd go splashing through it in my rain boots. This was more rain than ever. Ojai flooded. Ventura flooded too. Grand Avenue, where the dip is, was washed out. After the rain finally stopped, some of the houses below Tarantula Hill had mud up to their roofs from the rain carrying it down the hill. It was a muddy mess.

I rode with my riding teacher, Edgar, through the groves. He's one hundred years old and has skin like Beanie's briefcase. He's the only man around Ojai that I've seen that looks like that. He says he's a black man because his skin isn't a rainbow of colors or looks like mine. But really, he's more brown. His skin looks like honey.

Once a week we'd ride through the groves. He wore a straw cowboy hat and had a big buckle on his belt which had a cow's head and horns. He told me that when he was younger, he was a cowboy and would herd cattle. Then, he went to the war in Germany. There were no palm trees there to catch fire (that's what Edgar said), but they blew up a lot of buildings and cities, turning them into rubble; apparently, it looked like the bottom of a dry riverbed after they were through.

My dad and Beanie went to the Germany war. I asked Edgar if he knew them. He said he didn't; he explained that he was older than my dad and Beanie, and he was in the First World War in Germany. I told Edgar that my dad and Beanie were both captains and told men what to do. "Turn the boat . . . drive the truck." He said captains told him what to do too.

Edgar explained to me that there was World War One and Two; he said that Germans were troublemakers back then. I guess Germany liked to go fight – as if one time wasn't enough. I don't get that. If I don't like something, I don't do it again unless someone makes me or dares me. Then, I do the dare; but that's it.

The men who fought in the war came from different parts, and they all went to different places, Edgar said. Some were on the ocean, like Beanie, some were flying in the sky, and some were on the ground, like my dad. My dad didn't fight. He directed missions on the ground. Edgar didn't fight either. He fixed planes when they broke. He said he was one of the few black men like him that did that. He said he wasn't allowed to fight in the war. I told him I had been in a little plane and steered it. He said he only fixed them and was never allowed to fly the planes.

I spilled that I heard Mean Ned saying he was afraid to graduate from high school because he didn't want to get drafted and go to Vietnam and die. Edgar understood. He said this Vietnam War was nothing like he'd ever seen. He said he didn't blame the hippies for protesting. I told Edgar that even though Ned was really mean to me, I didn't want him to go to Vietnam and be killed.

"Did men die in World War One and Two?" I asked.

"Yes. Too many. Millions," he said.

"Millions? I can't even count that high," I told him.

"Too many people have died for no good reason, Audrey. Too many."

"Why did people have to die in World War One and Two?" I asked.

"Hate, child. Fear and pure hate in men's hearts. And, if they don't kill because they hate you, they kill and make war because they want to steal something from you, like land, or precious things, or your self-worth," he said.

"Do they want to steal my tortoise?" I asked. I was worried because Harvey was precious to me.

"They don't want your tortoise, Audrey. Now, don't you worry. You just think about good things and school and being a girl who minds and does the right thing. That's all you have to worry about. Let the big folk worry about everything else, okay?" he said.

"Yes, Edgar. I will just try to be a good girl, not talk in class, or bug my mean brother for one day. But sometimes, I just can't help it."

Edgar talked a lot about growing up in the South, in Mississippi. I like to spell that word. It's fun. Edgar said he didn't like Mississippi. He said life was hard for him and his whole family; that they were treated like lepers. Lepers are people whose fingers fall off; people are afraid if they touch them, they'll get leper cooties and their fingers will fall off too. It's not true. Still, nobody trusts lepers or likes them because they can't shake their hand.

That's how Edgar and his family felt about white folks – that they treated them like they had cooties and they didn't belong. He said he couldn't drink from a water fountain, because the white people said no, or even buy ice cream because "money was hard to come by". I told him I would have given him my fifty cents to buy ice cream so he would have felt better.

Edgar told me on one of our rides that he didn't feel like a free man because "in the eyes of most white folks" he wasn't free. Working on a plantation, tending to the cattle while others did other chores, was hard, back-breaking work, he explained, as we rode through the orange groves, taking in the Topa Topa mountains and the smell of citrus.

"Why weren't you free? Were you grounded?" I asked.

"No. People like me were once slaves, Audrey. Do you know what a slave is?" I shook my head. I didn't know.

"My ancestors were stolen from our homes – way across the ocean in a different land called Africa – brought here to the United States, and sold to white men. They were shackled, like wolves caught in a trap, and made to do things against their will. Unspeakable things, child, that you're too young to know."

"That's not right, Edgar." That's what common sense told me. I hated it when Mean Ned would hold my head underwater or trap me in a sleeping bag.

"You're right. No one should ever be held down or be the property of another man." He told me all sorts of stuff that maybe a kid shouldn't know, but should too, because his heart hurt and it wasn't right or fair; he wanted to spit it out, like rattlesnake poison. I liked knowing what he had to say. It made me feel important because my family always kept things from me, telling me I wouldn't understand; he thought I was old enough to know and could understand.

"The south has been hell for the black man; hatred and fear burns across the land like a wildfire, keeping my folks' poor – treated less well than rabid dogs; it's just so hopeless, child. There's no hope in hate. After years and years, still we're feared and put down – and even killed." he said.

"Killed? Did you call the policeman?" I asked.

"No, child. The police don't help the black man. Sometimes, the police are the ones killing us," he said. "But you don't have to worry. No one's going to hurt you like they tried to hurt me," he said.

"I don't understand, Edgar." I didn't. "Why are they afraid of you and want to hurt you if you didn't do anything wrong or weren't bad?"

"Because . . . I'm different from them . . . I look different."

I thought a second. "Because you're a black man and your skin looks like honey?" I asked.

"Yes, because my skin doesn't look like yours, see?" He put his arm up against mine. "Their fear of my looking different is as vivid as a photograph, and it was passed down from parent to child to hate others for no good reason – only because we look different."

"Well, I don't look like Grant. He wears glasses, and I don't. He's my friend."

"You're not like them. You don't have it in your heart to not like someone who is different from you," he said. "Keep that, child. Keep that as you grow older."

"But I don't like that people were mean to you, just because you're old as a mummy and a black man," I told him. "I like you, Edgar. You're nice."

"It's a cruel world for some folks, Audrey. There's a lot of people angry for no good reason, except they need someone to be angry at," he told me.

"Like when my mom sometimes gets angry for no reason and yells at me?"

"Sometimes when people are unhappy, they take it out on other people," Edgar said. "What I'm talking about is different. It's flat out wrong . . . cruel . . . and taught. It's not born in the hearts of babies. This kind of folk, who hate for no reason, can't help themselves. The light has gone out in their soul. They've forgotten who they are."

"I'm Audrey and I'm never turning off the light in my soul, Edgar."

"That's a good girl. Don't let the worst of people dim your light, child," he told me.

"Cross my heart," I promised.

'Remember this that I'm gonna tell you because Dr. Martin Luther King, who was a great black man and was killed for trying to change how we treat people, said it best: *Don't judge a man by the color of his skin but by the content of his character.* Understand?"

"Just be nice to everyone that's nice to you, because it's nice to be nice," I said.

"Yes. You can start there."

Edgar told me that it wasn't until after the war, when he came west to California and eventually settled in Ojai, that he felt like he was home. We rode through the sea of orange trees as far as you could see, all planted in rows; he would tell me all sorts of stories of when my mom was a teenager and she was spirited. He knew my mom and grandma, back then, when my grandma and mom first moved to Ojai from the other side of the United States. After he had been a cowboy and herded cattle (after he came back from the war), Edgar worked as a short-order cook in my grandma's and Benny's restaurant in Oxnard.

He told me a story of how my mom once confided in him. She made him swear not to tell my grandma about how her friends loved to tease this police officer on Saturday nights and how they could get him to go ape. "Did she make you cross your heart and stick a needle in your eye, Edgar?"

"Nah. Just how Bernie would get so burned up." Edgar laughed as he told me what my mom would do; he thought it was funny and that it took some guts, seeing the police would never tolerate that where he came from.

"Your mama would get in a hot rod with a couple of her friends, and they would go down to the police station, stop in front, and honk the horn. Bernie would come to the station door, they'd rev the engine, and then peel out – burning rubber. Bernie would run out, jump in his squad car, and chase them all over town; it was like a game," he told me.

My eyes got so big. I couldn't believe my mom could be such a bad girl and do that.

"Did they get in trouble when he caught them?"

"No, 'cause he never did. They'd go down to the station the next Saturday night and do it all over again."

"Why didn't he go to their house and tell their moms and dads on them? Maybe, they would have been grounded. I know Grandma would have grounded my mom," I said.

"I think Bernie liked it. Nothing happened in Ojai, especially back then. I think maybe the man was bored, and it gave him something to do," he said. Then he laughed. "That mother of yours was a character and had a mind of her own. Still does."

I loved riding through the orange groves with Edgar, looking up at the Topa Topas on a clear day, smelling the smell of the rows of citrus, and being able to easily pick an orange right off the trees as you rode by. It was easier than climbing the tree or trying to jump high enough to snag one. I'm too little anyhow. There was nothing as delicious as a freshly picked orange. I loved riding through the orange groves and hearing all of his stories. Edgar didn't talk to me like a kid, but like someone he trusted. That made me feel good, like I meant something. And, Edgar never made me feel scared, ever. He was my friend and he protected me.

Henry Monowski had two orange trees in his front yard. We had two, too, until Gabriel cut one down that day he came to clean up our yard. My mom never should have let him do it. Maybe if she knew what would happen, she would have changed her mind, and that orange tree would still be growing – and I never would have gotten in the back seat of his car.

18 YELLOW JACKET

CHRISTMAS CAME AND WENT AS FAST AS SANTA HIMSELF, WHEN HE ZOOMS down your chimney, with a bag of toys, and up again, faster than you can blink an eye. That's why you never see Santa Claus. He's faster than a speeding bullet.

Vacation was still on for another week. My mom had gone to Los Angeles that Friday morning. Beanie was coming to town to visit, and they wanted the weekend together, with no kids, for some reason.

My mom appointed Ned in charge of me and offered Grandma as back up if something went wrong – which it did that Sunday. Until that morning, I didn't need him to be the boss of me. I knew how to make scrambled eggs; I add just a tad bit of milk and water and beat the crap out of them to make them fluffy. Mean Ned taught me that. I hate to admit it, but Ned makes really good scrambled eggs that are light and fluffy and taste really delicious. If I didn't want to make scrambled eggs, I could make Malt-O-Meal cereal. My grandma had taught me how to when she made it for me after I spent the night at her house. One time, I had a really bad flu and she took care of me, swabbing my forehand with alcohol to bring my 103-degree temperature down. That's what grandmas do. They pay attention to you and make you feel better in ways that your mom or dad can't.

I like cooking. I'm not a gourmet cook like my mom, but I know how to make a peanut butter and jelly sandwich, Kraft's macaroni and cheese, cinnamon toast, and hot dogs. To make hot dogs extra delicious, I stick potato chips inside the bun. It kills two birds with one stone, making the hot dog taste crunchy. Though I was prepared like a good 'used to be' Bluebird, I ended up not needing to cook that weekend my mom split.

Bored, early Saturday, I broke out my mom's oil paints, and I painted over a canvas of a woman my sister, Lana, had painted first. When Lana eventually saw the painting, months later, she wasn't happy I did that. I'm not sure if it was what I painted or that I used her painting as my canvas. But I liked the lady I painted. She was much more colorful than the one underneath the paints I used, spattered with orange, green and red, with a bigger smile. Mostly, I wanted to paint just like my mom, which she'd do often with my dad's cousin's wife, Leslie, and Sherry Segal when we lived on Kittridge Street. They'd paint canvases into pictures of boats, or naked people, or flowers in a vase, or fruit in a bowl, and they sculpted heads out of clay with their bare hands. One day, Sherry died. I remember when my mom hung up the phone call from Leslie. My mom stood there, staring. She looked lost for a second. Later, I overheard her tell Beanie that Sherry had told my mom that, once her children were graduated from school, she was going to take her own life and end it all. After her kids got out of school, she kept her promise. But she died before she could end all of it. Ned said I didn't get it. My mom didn't want him to explain it to me because she thought it would upset and confuse me. But I knew what it meant now. She killed herself. She killed herself because she was sad and couldn't take it anymore. Killing herself just ended her sadness. It didn't end all the stuff that caused it. That's what I meant. I just wish she had lived because I loved her paintings and all the colors she used. They're still hanging on the walls of our house.

My mom likes art, and she likes people who like art and make art. I do too. When we lived on Kittridge Street, I remember a cocktail party and liking this man who was dressed in bell-bottoms, a black turtle neck, and wearing a big necklace. He had blond hair and wore a top hat like the Penguin. He smoked cancer sticks too, but with his fingers and not out of a wand. He waved his hands when he talked like he was painting the air, or throwing an invisible baseball, or conducting an invisible band. He talked about art, and I showed him one of my drawings from my Aunt Ru's school; he told me it reminded him of a famous artist that liked to splatter paint. He talked about how the war was killing us all, which made me worried because I still had stuff to do. He drank two cocktails that looked like water with a green olive in them. I asked for a sip because I was thirsty and I liked olives; he told me it was poison for a kid and to go get some Kool-Aid or Tang. I just listened to him and watched his lips move and howl when he talked about some guy named Ginsberg, who was a beatnik and like to yell a lot. I said I like Nanette Fabray, and he said he liked Judy Garland. I told him my grandma worked for that Judy. "Stop!" he screamed at me. So, I did. I guess he didn't like me talking about Judy Garland. That man was very nice and I liked his outfit.

A few days later, my mom, dad, and me were having dinner at my second favorite restaurant, El Torrito, because I wanted enchiladas; also, my mom didn't feel like cooking and wanted an excuse to go out to eat.

"That's a great idea, Audrey. It's a good excuse to get out." I was glad that made her happy. She seemed stressed, and I could feel it, as if we were connected by two tin cans and a string.

The El Torrito place was packed. I didn't see anyone I knew. I looked really hard and there was not one person who I recognized from Kittridge Street. I had a Shirley Temple with four cherries and ate corn chips dipped in salsa. I was kind of uncomfortable. My mom and dad hardly were talking, just drinking their margaritas that they ordered from the Señor. I think their mouths might have been tired from all the yelling the night before. They yelled at each other almost every night. My mom's mouth was especially tired, I guess, because she hardly touched her enchilada and she loves enchiladas. After I ate my enchilada and had taken two bites out of my mom's enchilada that she didn't eat and gave to me, my stomach had no more room for Mexican food.

Sitting in that big booth, with me in the middle, my mom and dad just sipped their margaritas; they were so quiet, looking around the room – but not at each other. I looked at them back and forth, like I was watching a tennis match with nobody playing tennis, waiting for someone to serve the ball. I play tennis now. I know how the game works. You have to wait for someone to serve the ball before you can hit it back. So I decided to talk, seeing no one else said they wanted to talk, or stopped me, or that I was interrupting.

I told my dad that, when I got bigger, I wanted to marry that man Darby in the black turtle neck and top hat from the cocktail party they had because his hair cut was like mine and I could one day be big enough to wear his go-go boots. He told me that I should pick another guy because he was "light in the loafers."

"My God, Lee. No, he's not," my mom said.

"He was wearing white boots, Dad," I reminded him. "Loafers have pennies in them and are brown."

"I say he is." My dad didn't look at my mom when he said that. "Half of the guys there were."

"What exactly is it that you hate about my artist friends? Is it because you couldn't draw your way out of a paper bag?"

"I use paper bags to draw on. I'm going to try to draw from the inside and see if I can draw my way out. That should keep me out of everyone's hair," I told them.

"First off, I draw all my ads for Hardy Brothers." Hardy Brothers is a big lumber place in Canoga Park that my dad still places the ads for.

"That's not art, Lee. It's printing big letters with felt pens," she told him.

"Darby liked my drawing I did at Aunt Ru's school. He said it reminded him of a famous artist that likes to splatter paint all over the place."

"Jackson Pollock, Audrey. He's a wonderful contemporary artist," my mom told me, barely smiling.

"I don't hate Sherry or Leslie. Even Bob Eddy," my dad said. He was in World War number two with Bob Eddy, who liked to smoke cigars and eat ham sandwiches at the same time.

"That's because they're married to your best friend and cousin, while Bob is in produce and has no imagination. But Jacqueline does. Usually, the wives do." My mom stared at my dad when she said that. But my dad looked around the restaurant, like he wanted the Señor to come to our table again.

"No . . . I could still find them boring," my dad said. "Just because they're artists doesn't make them interesting." Then, he took a drink of his margarita, swirling the glass, clinking the ice, then trying to drink the last bit, kind of like when I try to suck the last of the ice cream out of the cone, not missing a lick.

"Is this a nice conversation? Because, you're sounding nice when you say your words," I noticed.

"No. It's not a nice conversation, Audrey. Your dad has no tolerance for people who are eccentric or creative."

"What's eccentric?" I asked.

"Eccentric? Bullshit." My dad set down his empty glass. "I don't like the guy because he voted for Goldwater, not because he's an artist or light in the damn loafers. What hipster, arty idiot votes for that numbskull? I told you I was in boot camp with that fraud."

Boot camp is where they first send boys and dress them in army clothes and teach them to kill other boys in war. It's kind of like war school. My dad was at a war school with an actor guy named Clark Gable; he was once a really big deal in the movies and had a thin mustache and would shout orders at the soldiers when they were lined up, waiting to be told what to do. My dad told me that Hitler, who was the mean man they were fighting against in World War Two, loved Clark Gable's movies and wanted to capture Clarke Gable like a pet monkey and make him his friend (or maybe it was because they both had mustaches and black hair).

"For your information, I voted for Goldwater," my mom spilled.

I remember my dad staring at my mom for a really long time, and I could see his jaw do that clenching thing. The silence was scary.

"Dad . . . you said a bad word. TWO." I remember starting to feel a little hot and queasy. Maybe I ate too much salsa or enchilada.

"He said more than that, Audrey," my mom told me.

"He said eccentric. What's that?" I asked again.

"Everything your Father deplores." She took one last sip of her margarita. "I so want to leave this place. I have to get out." My mom slid out of the booth and grabbed her purse. She walked out.

And I still don't know what eccentric means.

My dad drove up to Ojai and arrived later that Saturday morning. He took me and Ned to breakfast, to lunch too, and to see a movie. We saw *Chitty Chitty Bang Bang*. Ned thought it was dumb. He said he was too old to like it, like a small fry. I loved it. I thought it was boss that a car could fly. Ned said it didn't fly, that it was fake. I told him to shut up and shouted, "It could too fly!" My dad told me not to talk to Ned like that and that I wasn't to say 'shut up'. As my dad lectured me on manners, Mean Ned stood behind him, held his belly, pointed at me, and pretended to laugh so my dad couldn't see him teasing me. Every time I'd say, "Dad, Ned is teasing me!" my dad would turn to look and Ned would quickly stop, acting innocent. "No, I'm not, Dad." The minute my dad would turn back to me, Ned would do it again.

Ned can be such a butt like that. I didn't let him ruin my good time though. I ate popcorn and Milk Duds until my stomach hurt. I couldn't even think about dinner. Once my dad brought us home, I conked out on the couch. A while later, Ned woke me and made me go to bed. I was still half asleep and don't remember walking from the living room to my room.

I woke up in my clothes, which was perfect because that way I didn't have to get dressed. I brushed my teeth super quiet and tiptoed through the living room into the kitchen. Ned was sleeping in my mom's room because Zachery had brought six of his dog friends home the afternoon before and had gotten into Ned's garage room; he'd had a dog party, with all his friends, peeing and pooping all over everything, including Ned's bed. Ned thought there were burglars in his garage room when he got home and first heard the ruckus. He tried to open the door and couldn't get in. That's when he said his heart fell into his stomach, thinking there was a bad guy on the other side. But it was just Zachery. They had moved some furniture or something and Ned had to climb through the window to let them out. Zachary could be a pill, sometimes.

Ned made me swear that I wouldn't wake him up in the morning, otherwise he'd pound me. So, I tiptoed extra soft.

I grabbed an orange in the kitchen then tiptoed out the front door. It was a sunny morning; I opened the screen door, went out barefoot onto the front porch, sat down on the first step, and peeled my orange. All you could hear was quiet because no one was awake yet but me, and no cars were driving by on Grand Avenue like they would be on a week day or a Saturday.

The orange tasted sweet, reminding me of the summer that passed when we first moved to Ojai and before I was ambushed like those Indians do on *Gun Smoke*. I looked across the street at Henry's grandparents' house and wondered what he was doing on the other side of the United States (where he lived now). It had been a few months since I saw him last, and I missed him. I missed seeing him standing on his front lawn, looking at my house as a signal, gesturing for me to come out and play.

I finished the last section of my orange and walked into the front yard (onto the long grass that Ned needed to mow) to throw my peels in the flower bed. That's when it happened. I felt the blades of grass in my toes and under my feet . . . then, "OUCH!" I stepped on a yellow jacket and it stung me. I felt the burn. I looked down, and I saw the bee looking like he was doing the backstroke, flailing, crushed in the grass.

I screamed in pain. Guarding my foot, I hopped up the steps and limped inside the house. I stood in the living room calling for Ned, hoping he'd hear my wails. "NED!" I limped to the small kitchen table.

"Ned! Ned! Help me!" I sat and stared at my foot, which was quivering, the pain of the stinger stabbing me like a knife.

I heard the bedroom door open and footsteps on the wood floor.

"Audrey?"

"I'm in the kitchen, Ned!"

Ned, half asleep and his hair sticking up in every direction, came through the kitchen door. He looked too tired to be mad at me for waking him up.

"I tried to be quiet, Ned. Don't pound me," I whimpered.

"What's wrong?"

I began to cry. "I stepped on a yellow jacket! And it hurts, Ned. Please help me."

"It's okay. Let me look."

"Don't touch it, Ned. It hurts!" I cried.

"I have to look for the stinger, Audrey. Let me just look. I won't touch it."

Ned gently lifted up my foot and looked for the stinger. He was an expert stinger finder, I learned.

"I see it. Sit tight. Let me get some tweezers."

He hurried through the living room to the bathroom and, after a second, returned with my mom's tweezers.

"You're going to hurt me," I protested.

"No, I'm not. I'm just going to take the stinger out, okay? Trust me," he said.

I had never trusted Ned before. He was my mean brother and he didn't like me. He never wanted me to be born because he wanted a brother and cried when they brought me home. But I needed him to help me because I was just a kid; I didn't know what to do, and I was in a lot of pain.

"Okay, Ned," I said through my tears. "You promise you won't hurt me?"

"Promise," he said. There was no time to make him cross his heart and stick a needle (or the tweezers) in his eye. I needed him to get the stinger out, striking as fast as a lightning bolt, or as fast as Speed Racer.

"Here we go." He gently lifted up my foot. "Try to relax, Audrey," he asked. I remember it shaking like crazy and was hard to keep still. Ned steadied my foot with his hand and, within a few seconds, he showed me the tiny stinger in the grip of the tweezers. "There it is. All better."

I looked at Ned. I remember the way the front parts of his hair were swept to the side over his thick eyebrow, and his green-blue eyes were peering at me without malice. His face looked concerned. He didn't look mean. Looking at him, I felt real love for my big brother for the first time in my life.

He smiled at me. "You okay, twerp?"

"Yes, Ned," I said.

"It's probably going to be sore to walk on. Let me get a Band-Aid." Ned rummaged through the junk drawer (next to the silverware drawer) and pulled one out; he unwrapped it and stuck it on the bottom of my foot where the stinger stung me. He looked up at me, smiled, then squeezed my nose in a playful way. He didn't pretend to steal it and stick his thumb through his fingers, and say he had my nose. I think he knew I was too worn out for that game.

I'm allergic to yellow jackets. I discovered that about two hours later when my foot swelled up to the size of a football. Ned was nice not to make fun of me and call me football foot or any other names, mocking me for stepping on that bee.

My mom and Beanie drove home that afternoon from a weekend in Santa Barbara. They were going steady. Beanie came to town and my mom said she and Beanie wanted to be alone for the weekend because that's what grown-ups do. So, they drove to Santa Barbara. She came through the door, laughing, carrying her big beach hat and two wet striped towels because, I guess, they went to the beach too. Then, her laughing suddenly stopped, like she was frozen in her tracks or her feet got stuck in cement. Seeing the size of my foot, she pretended not to be shocked so she wouldn't scare me, but I could tell the sight of my foot was creepy. Because, before she left for Santa

Barbara, I had a regular kid's foot that I could do stuff with.

"It's okay, Mom. I know it looks like a Sasquatch foot," I told her.

Sasquatches are monsters that live in the woods, and their feet are the size of board games. My foot couldn't even fit in a shoe. It was the size of two foots. That night, as a treat, Beanie took us all out to dinner at the Ojai Valley Inn – but I only could wear one shoe. People stared, probably wondering if I was trying to start a trend or I'd stepped in dog poop and left the other shoe outside. While we were waiting for our table, a man noticed and asked me what happened to my foot, like I was deformed or something.

"I stepped on a yellow jacket and it stung me. My brother took the stinger out, but it still swelled up like the Goodyear Blimp," I told him.

I'm not sure he believed me. I think he thought I just had a funny fat foot. It hurt a lot – and itched. But I couldn't scratch it because it would hurt. I didn't like it one bit. I called my dad to tell him what happened. He said he didn't know why my foot swelled up the way it did. "I don't know, Audrey. You must get it from your mother," he said.

Whenever something bad happened or I had a bad habit, like biting my fingernails or an ear infection, both my mom and dad would say I must have gotten it from the other. I'm not sure where I got being allergic to yellow jackets came from, but it was good for getting to eat out, I tell you. The next night, Beanie took us to Papino's pizzeria, which is my favorite pizza in the whole wide world. I can still smell it cooking in the oven. Papino knows how to make a pizza. He's from Italy and speaks bad English, but his spaghetti and his pizza are good. My grandma would talk to him in Italian when she'd come with us. His restaurant sits on the triangle where the 150 and Reeves Road go their separate ways, at the edge of an orange grove. When you drive out there, you pass a big oak tree on the right side of the road that's painted white too so a car doesn't run into it. When we got out of the car, Beanie put me up on his shoulders so I didn't have to walk on my foot. He's strong and has broad shoulders for sitting on. He said I could order anything I wanted on the menu, as he often did. I ordered spaghetti with meatballs, and he ordered two pizzas with pepperoni so I could have some too. My mom loves pepperoni pizza. I think he really ordered it for her.

After dinner, he put me up on his shoulders again to walk to the car. He said he was still hungry and pretended to gnaw on my leg. I know he was teasing me. He makes me laugh. I really like Beanie. He's the nicest man I have ever met, and he loves my mom – and my mom really loves him. I can tell. She's soft, like I said. Softer than I've ever seen her before.

I wish Beanie had met my mom before Gabriel came to clean the yard. I know he would have used his muscles to protect me. Beanie wrestled in college; he was a champ and could have pinned him down and stopped him that day from hurting me.

That's what good guys do to bad guys.

19 OAK STREET

I'M ALMOST READY TO TELL YOU WHAT HAPPENED, ON THAT SATURDAY afternoon in Ojai, a few months after we moved to Grand Avenue when my mom asked Gabriel to come clean our yard. It's hard to talk about because I'm not sure what I did to have that happen to me. I know that it never should have happened, and I can't tell anyone because I don't want to get into trouble and go to juvenile hall.

Since we moved to Seattle, I've been better at behaving and following directions, doing what I'm told, and not making my mom have to ask me again. I make my bed every day, put my clothes where they belong, and keep my room clean. We have a lady that comes twice a week to clean the house, except, my mom doesn't always want her to clean my room every time. She wants to teach me good habits and responsibility so I will learn how to do things for myself when I'm big. I know how to do everything, including vacuum. Well, yesterday I took the vacuum cleaner apart. Don't worry, I put it back together again before the housekeeper showed up. I do stuff like that sometimes, so I know how it works.

We live in a storybook neighborhood, something Mary Poppins would like, surrounded by the golf course I like to use as a playground. The houses are all different in shapes and sizes, and the yards are kept like a castle's garden with everything looking magical and clean. My aunt, uncle, and two cousins live four houses up the street. Sometimes, I see my cousin washing his car in the driveway when I walk by. Our backyard has a stone terrace and a big lawn that melts into the golf course grass; it's hard to know where our lawn stops and the golf course starts because there's no fence. Sometimes, the golf balls land in our yard. One time, one hit the house. It's a terrible golf shot to hit the ball out of bounds and all the way into our house. Luckily, nothing was broken. I threw the ball back out on the course, letting that golfer think he hit a good shot.

We're on the twelfth fairway. I can watch the golfers teeing off and watch them all the way to putting on the green. There are two cherry blossom trees between the course and our lawn with delicate branches that reach for the ground like a ballerina. There's a cluster of tall redwood trees like the ones I saw in Yosemite that squirrels love to climb.

It's summer here, and it gets dark really late – way past my bedtime. Last night, I stayed up late and slept on the deck after watching an electrical storm in the north. The sky was filled with lightning veins. The storm went on for hours, yet there was no rain. It was boss to watch. I belong to the tennis club, not far from our house, at the bottom of the hill. I'm called a junior member, and I have a locker in the girls' locker room. I go swimming there and play in the lake. I'm running around the club from morning until late at night with all the other kids. There's a snack bar and I have a three-dollar punch card; I order whatever I want – hamburgers, hot dogs, French fries, ice cream – you name it. I've made friends with lots of kids. There are too many to name. Some of them are on the tennis club swim team I joined. I compete in the breaststroke. I'm fast like a frog. I win my meets a lot. I also swim breaststroke in the medley relay. The tennis club has a good team. Sometimes, my family comes to see me compete and they sit in the bleachers and cheer. I think they're proud I can swim so fast, seeing I'm a squirt still.

Beanie works with a man at his company who is the son of his boss, and he lives right down the street from us with his wife. The

Mulligans. They have four children around my age. Two girls. Sandy is one year older than me, and Lara is two years older than me. They took me under their wings (that's how my mom put it) when I first moved to Seattle to make sure I had a friend. I like them a lot. Sometimes, we have sleepovers and order pizza to be delivered to the house across the street; we watch the delivery man show up and then Mrs. Adel, the lady who lives there, refuse to take the pizza. Oh, boy, does she get steamed up. We can see her arms waving and her yelling "I never ordered a pizza!" We peek through the living room window with the lights off, keeping our heads down, and laugh, thinking it's hysterical. Other times, we call the minimart down in Madison Park and ask if they have Prince Albert in the can. When they say "yes" we tell them to let him out and hang up really fast. That's a good one. They never see it coming. Prank calls are fun and so are Lara and Sandy. We like to watch *Dark Shadows* every afternoon. I'm not afraid of the show anymore. I'm bigger now and understand Barnabas is just an actor with a bad hairdo.

My other new friends live further down the street, past Lara and Sandy's, in a cul-de-sac. I met Kara at the tennis club, and she is my new best friend. Kara has blonde hair and blue eyes, and she looks like a princess.

We like to sit at the snack bar, eat fries and wait for Mrs. Swanson to walk to the pool for Senior Swim at 2:00 pm. Mrs. Swanson is a very elegant lady in her bathing cap and one-piece yellow swimming suit with white shells on it; she wears pantyhose underneath, like she forgot to take them off or she's going to a ball. She's the only lady who swims in her pantyhose. That's what makes her special. Maybe they keep her warm when she's swimming. I'll have to try it when I'm bigger. Mrs. Swanson always carries a screwdriver beverage to the pool. Kara's mom, Alma, says it's because "she likes to get hammered." I'm not sure what that means, but I think she's just thirsty from all the swimming in her pantyhose.

Alma is younger than my mom and really neat. She lets me stay for dinner anytime I want. She has rules for dinner. We can't wear pants and we can't sit down at the dining room table until she does. These are called manners. My mom teaches me manners, like not talking with my mouth full, keeping my lips closed when I chew, not gulping my milk, not putting my hands on the walls; Mean Ned will get yelled at if he puts his feet on the coffee table. But that's nothing like Alma's manners at dinner. See, first, we all stand behind our chair and wait for Alma to sit down, then we pull out our chair and we sit down. She takes her cloth napkin and puts it on her lap, and then we take our cloth napkin and put it on our lap. We all watch, waiting patiently for her to pick up her fork . . . then we pick up our fork. My eyes stay glued on her with mouth-watering suspense, looking for the next move. When she takes a bite, *then* we can eat, no longer having to play Simon Says . . . until next time. It's like having dinner with a queen, which makes sense because Kara looks like a princess, like I told you.

Kara and I will be in fourth grade together at the same school in September. She has two brothers, Mick and Timmy, that are younger, and know how to do the manners thing too. Timmy, the very youngest, is only five years old. I helped him the other day, swimming in the lake, when we were at the club. He's a toe head too. He can swim, but more like a submarine. He used me as his resting place when he got tired, hanging on around my neck as he caught his breath. I didn't mind. Timmy is just a little kid, and I remember needing help when I was his age.

They live by the tee on the eleventh hole. We all love to go play on the golf course at night, running around the fairways, playing tag. It gets dark so late. There are no golfers to yell at us at night. We see bats flying around eating the bugs, and we take the gravel off the golf cart path, throw it in the air and watch the bats chase the pebbles down to the ground. You have to throw it up and away from you, otherwise the bats will buzz you. It can be scary. There are no tarantulas in Seattle. At least, not where I live. Only squirrels and bats.

A lot has changed in the last few months, since we moved to Seattle. I love it here. It's like a dream. It's like a story you read, like Cinderella or Goldilocks, that has a happy ending and they live happily ever after. I think it's going to be wonderful because we're a family again.

We live in the house with my stepbrother, Ron, who is almost seventeen and likes to play football and basketball like Ned and with my stepsister, Jane. She's engaged to be married to a guy who just came back from Vietnam. Lana and Shelly are still in Los Angeles. My mom said that Shelly is moving to Seattle soon and will come live with us too. I can't wait. She's going to go to school to become a dental assistant. That makes me so happy. I've had three cavities already, and she may come in handy.

If I told you what our house looks like in Seattle, you wouldn't believe me. It's beautiful, and it's the biggest house I have ever been in. Ours is bigger than the Pullmans' house on June street because it has two stories and a basement too. We don't have a pool with a fountain in it though, which is fine with me because the tennis club has a big pool where I swim – and a lake too. My room is across from Ned's and Ron's, and I have a door that opens onto the big deck. My stepsister's room opens on the deck too, but she never uses it.

There's something that I am not allowed to talk about in Seattle – that my dad is Jewish. My mom said people won't understand.

"Why won't they understand? What's to understand?" I asked.

"It's just that way up here, Audrey. It's different than California," she told.

"But, Mom, what if I slip and tell?"

"Don't talk about it, Audrey. I know you don't understand. I wish it were different, but, for right now, I'm asking you to keep this secret and not talk about your father being Jewish."

See, we live in a neighborhood that doesn't want Jewish people or black people to live in the houses. It has gates and guards to keep them out. Also, the tennis club I belong to doesn't want Jewish people or black people to belong either. Black people work there, but they can't swim in the pool, or the lake, or play tennis. I don't know why. Clarence works there and is super-duper nice. He looks a little like

196

Edgar, with brown eyes, a short Afro hairdo, and a thin waist. But Clarence doesn't wear a cowboy hat. He wears a tuxedo. He manages the dining room on the second floor at the club. He always smiles at me. Clarence is patient and not bothered by all the kids who charge around the club like a wild herd of gazelles. He should be allowed to swim in the pool. I don't get it.

Something happened the other day when I was walking across the street near the gas station, down by the Arboretum. A woman with browner skin than mine yelled at me. I didn't do anything. When the light changed and I could go in the crosswalk, I said, "Hello," as I walked past her, and she yelled back at me, "Don't talk to me you white honky bitch." It scared me. She called me a bad word. She was really mad at me. I don't understand. I was just trying to be nice. Lula and Mildred never said that to me. Edgar never did either. Clarence, neither. Why would that stranger lady be so mad at me when I was just trying to be polite? I wish I had Edgar to talk to still. He'd tell me why.

Before we came to Seattle, my mom and Beanie finally got married, a little over two months ago. After their wedding in Ojai, we all drove to Los Angeles that afternoon and flew on an airplane to Seattle that same night. It was a long day, I tell you, but also lots of fun – and cake!

It was a really boss ceremony. Shelly, Lana and Thad, Ned, Ron and Jane, and my grandma were there, as well as a few of my mom's friends from Ojai. They got married in the same church as Lana and Thad and had their married party on the terrace at the Ojai Valley Inn, overlooking the golf course. I wore a white dress with a black sash. My mom wore a pretty pink dress, with her legs long slender like a giraffe, and her hair swept off her face. She looked like a movie star. Beanie wore a suit and tie with a flower on his pocket. He looked like the Mystery Date guy that you win the game with. They drank champagne.

The morning of the wedding was really stressful. My mom got a phone call. After she hung up, she told me to ride my bike to my grandma's – my dad was there. My mom did not seem happy at all. I told her I didn't have my bike. The moving van came the day before and took all of the boxes and furniture – and my bike! So, I walked to my grandma's, which only took about ten minutes. I walked down Grand Avenue, which turns into Signal once you go past the oak tree that has its trunk painted white at the bend. Then, I walked a few blocks down to Oak Street. I got there around ten-fifteen in the morning. I came through the door, and my dad was sitting in a chair by the fireplace that never worked. I slowly shut the door, sensing his expression of upset and unhappiness. Hearing the door shut, my grandma, who was in the kitchen, stepped out, wiping her hands on a dish towel.

"Are you hungry?" she asked.

"No. I had some cereal a little while ago," I told her. I did. I had a bowl of *Cocoa Pebbles*, my favorite. I like them better than *Cocoa Puffs*. *Cocoa Puffs* taste weird, like cough syrup.

"Come over here," my dad said. "I have something to tell you."

"Lee . . .," my grandma said. She said his name and nothing else.

I walked toward him. "What's happening, Dad? What are you doing here?"

"Sit on my lap," he said. So, I did. Then he told me, "I'm not going to see you as much."

"Mom says I'm going to fly down every month to see you. Even on weekends." I told him.

"Yes, but it's not going to be the same. I won't see you every weekend."

That's true, I thought. I did see my dad almost every weekend and didn't think about that changing in a way that would make me feel bad. I was excited to move to Seattle. It was a new adventure, but my dad seemed really, really sad. That made me feel bad. I didn't want to see my dad sad. I didn't want my dad to feel alone.

"Don't be sad, Daddy. I'll call you every day, I promise," I told him. "And, I'll see you, and we can go to the movies, and go ride go-carts." I thought that would make him happy.

"That sounds like a good plan," my grandma said. "Lee, she needs to go back now and get ready to go to the hotel."

"Okay, Pop. I love you, and I will see you soon," I told him. I hugged him and he held me tight and kissed me a million times on my face. He began to cry. I didn't know what to do. I just hugged him tighter. As I pulled away to get off his lap, he held onto me.

"Wait. I have one more thing to tell you that you should know," he said.

"What?" I looked at my grandma. She looked worried.

"Before I married your mom and we had you . . . your mom had three children," he said.

"FOR GOD'S SAKE, LEE!" my grandma yelled. "What the hell is wrong with you? Why are you telling her this now?!"

My heart starting to beat faster as my grandma's voice rose in the room. I felt a storm brewing, and I wasn't prepared.

"Because she should know, Angie." That's my grandma's name.

"Not now, she shouldn't," my grandma told him.

"I don't get it, Dad," I said. "What shouldn't I know?"

He set me down on the floor and I stood in front of him, waiting for him to spit the words out. He put his hands on my shoulders and looked straight into my eyes.

"I'm not their father."

"Whose father?" I was confused.

"Lana, Shelly, and Ned's. I'm not their biological father. I'm still their daddy."

I felt like someone pulled a hat over my eyes. My mind went blank. Black. Confusion swirled in my brain for a second. I felt this wave of panic come across my entire body, like when I woke up in the night thinking no one was home. Something was terribly wrong. I moved back, wanting to break free of his grip and run, but my dad was still holding me tight.

"Let me go!" I said.

"Audrey . . . Audrey . . . you haven't done anything wrong," he said.

"They're not my brother and sisters?" I began to cry. I loved Shelly and Lana and even my mean brother. They were my family. I didn't want to lose them.

"Yes! Yes, they are. You all have the same mother. But I adopted them. I'm not their real, real father," he said.

"Yes, you are! You're their real daddy too!"

I remember looking over at my grandma who was looking at my dad with a disgusted face – like she'd sucked on a lemon. She threw her dish towel on the floor in protest and walked out of the room, asking me to follow her into the kitchen. I did what I was told.

"Sit down," she said. I sat in the breakfast nook that looked out onto the oak trees in her backyard and watched her open the refrigerator, grab some milk, and pour the milk into a glass. "Chocolate milk?" she asked me.

"Yes, please," barely getting the words out.

She opened the cabinet, took the Nestle Quik out, measured off a teaspoon, and stirred it into my drink. My grandma always made me good stuff to eat and to drink. She brought my chocolate milk over to the table and set it in front of me. She stroked my head. She was different with me than with my sisters and brother. I think it's because I was the smallest. "You okay, sweetheart?" I didn't know how to answer that.

My dad stood in the doorway. My grandma looked at him and told him his timing was awful.

"I'll drive you home, Audrey," my dad said.

"Don't go near that house, Lee. God only knows what she'll do to you knowing you showed up here right before her day."

"She knows?" my dad asked.

"Of course she does. I called her when I saw you sitting in the driveway, deciding whether you were going to turn around and go home like you should have or come in here and do this. I never should have answered the door – or agreed for her to send Audrey over," she told him.

"Angie, she has a right to know the truth," he said.

"That's what you say. But why today, huh? Because you want to hurt Sophia."

"No, I don't," he said.

"Don't tell me that garbage, Lee. I know you're hurting because she's taking Audrey and Ned to Seattle, but this wasn't the way to make her pay," she told him.

Her pay? Who? My mom? Everything was always happening in front of me, as if I wasn't even there. I wanted to scream, "Stop fighting! Can't you see what it's doing to me?!" But it was like my mouth had been sewn shut. Even if I wanted to say it, I couldn't speak. I was too afraid and kids were to be seen and not heard.

My dad's car idled in front of the house on Grand Avenue. He looked like he did when he'd drop me off on Detroit Street, staring out the front window, lost in his thoughts, not speaking. The radio was playing "Spinning Wheel", which was a song I liked. My mom would play Blood, Sweat & Tears on the record player. One time, we were over at some friends of hers that she knew from high school. Some guy named Roy. He had a huge living room with statues in it and big paintings. The room looked like a museum I once saw. He put on that record, turned up the volume really loud and jumped off some stairs, kicking his heels up. Then he ran and slid across the living room's hardwood floor, like he was a rock and roller on stage or something. I think he was drunk. He was shaking his head and pretending to play the guitar. I remember my mom laughing really hard. I thought it was weird. I wanted to leave.

The song played for a second more before my dad turned the radio off and looked at me. He stroked my face and told me that he was going to miss me. I told him I would miss him too.

"Who loves you?" he asked.

"You do," like I always said.

"How much?"

"The universe, Daddy." He smiled at me.

"Come here," and he patted the seat.

I scooted over to him; he wrapped his arms around me and held me tight. He kissed me all over my face and took one last look at me before telling me I should go inside. I got out of the car and gently shut the door, so I wouldn't get my fingers caught. I could feel him watching me walk every single step up the driveway, up the steps, to the front door. When I got to the door, I turned and waved at him. He waved goodbye. I could see him say, "I love you." I opened the screen door, and I went inside.

I walked into the small hall where mine and my mom's doors were, side by side; I saw my mom in the bathroom, sitting on the toilet.

"What did he say to you?" she asked me. I hesitated, not knowing if I should tell.

"Nothing," I said.

She studied me a moment. I didn't blink.

"You all packed?" she asked. I nodded my head. She flushed the toilet and went to the sink to wash her hands.

"Then, get your suitcase and call Ned. Tell him we're going to be leaving. We'll head over to the country club. Your sisters, Thad, Ron, and Jane have arrived, and we're all having dinner later." Drying her hands on a towel, she took a last look at herself in the mirror.

"Where am I sleeping tonight?" I asked. My bed and dresser were still in my room, but a lot of the furniture in the living room and kitchen had been taken by the movers.

"We're all staying at the country club tonight. You'll stay with Shelly in her hotel room."

"Okay." I was about to go to my room to grab my suitcase. "Mom?"

"Yes?"

"What's going to happen to my bed and dresser and all the other stuff you didn't put on the truck?"

"Well, when we sell the house, then it will be taken away. We don't need any of it in Seattle. You have a new bed and dresser already in your new room. It's a brass bed. You're going to love it. It's going to be a whole new life for you, Audrey. Are you ready for that?" she asked me.

"I guess so, Mom. Do I have a choice?" I knew I didn't.

"So, get your stuff and say goodbye to this little house," she said.

I walked into my room and closed the door. I took a glance at my little space, where my guppies committed suicide and Snowball killed my canary that I had for five minutes; where I'd feel the warm air come through my window on hot summer nights and got dressed every morning for third grade.

"Goodbye, Grand Avenue."

When I said that out loud, I said goodbye to my room, to our little house, to the white knobs on the baby blue kitchen cabinets, to our apricot and walnut trees, to the friends I had made, to Mrs. Rolston, Topa Topa Elementary School, our horse, Lady, the creek where I caught frogs, and to Tarantula Hill. There was more, but my mom told me to hurry up and get the lead out.

Mostly, I said goodbye to that day when I got in the back seat of Gabriel's old car and he did something to me that haunts me like a ghost that has nowhere to live, except inside of your brain where your imagination is. But I didn't imagine it.

20 WEDDING CAKE

I HAD A DREAM A FEW NIGHTS BEFORE I SLEPT IN THE HOTEL ROOM AT THE Ojai Valley Inn, the night before my mom and Beanie were married in the same church as Lana and Thad, the night before the movers came to get our stuff from Grand Avenue and drive it to Seattle where we'd be living like a family again.

In my dream, I was in this big two-story house. I was standing on the stairs looking up at the landing at the top. I could see a woman. She was dressed in a white blouse. Her skirt was hiked just above her knees, and she wore high heels that looked like you could walk in them, without falling. I noticed she wore pearls like I had seen my mom wear (and Mrs. Kennedy when she was on the television). This woman had red hair. I'll never forget that; her hair was red and short like Nanette Fabray's. But it wasn't Nanette Fabray standing there. It was someone I had never seen before.

This woman had her hands on the banister; she was smiling, looking down at me as I stood on the stairs, halfway up. I looked up at her, wondering if I should take one more step. I remember I had my left hand on the wall and my right hand by my side. She didn't say, "Get your hand off the wall," like my mom would. She smiled at me like Mrs. Rolston would when I got an answer right or when I visited her on a Saturday morning and brought her apricots I'd picked from our tree. This red-headed dream lady said, "I hope you enjoy this house." Then I woke up.

Isn't that a funny dream? But nice. I had my hand on the wall. No yelling. I didn't get grounded or told to go to my room. Just some nice lady with red hair that told me she hoped I like my new house.

I finished getting dressed for the wedding and was buckling my Mary Janes. Shelly was in the bathroom, putting on her make-up. I felt really happy to see her because it had been a while. She had a towel wrapped around her body, and I could see her putting shadow on her eyes. I jumped off my bed and walked to the bathroom door to watch.

"Do you think you'll ever move to Seattle?" I asked.

"I don't know. Maybe. Not now, though," she said. "Mom and I get along much better when we're not under the same roof, remember?"

I told her, "Well, Mom said the house in Seattle is going to be bigger, so the roof will be bigger too and it will be easier to be under it with Mom."

"We'll see, Audrey," Shelly said. Then, she opened her tube of mascara and stared in the mirror, combing her lashes with it.

"Can I have some mascara?" I asked.

"Sure. But just a little." She knelt down in front of me. "Open your eyes and look down."

I opened my eyes and looked down, staring at the Jewish star she was wearing around her neck that Joel had given her for her birthday. She gently put the mascara on my eyelashes and not in my eye, because that would hurt.

"You're a good kid, Audrey," she told me.

"You're not mad at me?"

She finished and put the mascara wand thing in the tube and tightened it up. "For what?" she asked me. I hesitated. I didn't want to bring up a sore subject or have her get mad at me, in case she forgot.

"Audrey, you can tell me anything," she said.

"Anything?" I asked.

"Anything, kid," she said.

"And you won't get mad or tell Mom?" I asked.

"Never."

I thought about how I was going to tell her what was bothering me and if I could trust her with my super-secret secret that I was holding inside of me. I let it out like letting go of a long exhale after holding my breath underwater when I'd swim from one end of the pool to the other.

"I . . . I . . . don't want you to be mad at me for wanting to sleep over at Parker's and making Mom mad at you and you running away from home and getting in trouble."

"Audrey," she said. "Listen to me. You did nothing wrong. Nothing. Do you understand?"

"I'm not sure."

"I don't want you blaming yourself for that. None of it was your fault," Shelly told me.

"I hope not," I said.

"Believe me, kiddo. You're too little to be worried about all of that stuff, okay?"

"Do you still love me?" I asked.

"Of course, I do! You're my little sister. I will ALWAYS love you, Audrey," she said.

"Yeah. We're sisters," I said. "Nothing will ever change that."

"Nothing," she told me. I believed her. "Okay, leave me alone. I have to finish getting ready."

"Do I look like you with my mascara?" I asked.

"Exactly like me." She smiled and went back to fixing herself in the mirror, and I left the room to go find Lana and anyone else I could show my mascara to.

The church wasn't nearly as full as when Lana and Thad got married a few months before (and I tried to get Lana to take me on her honeymoon). Only the pews in the front had people sitting in them. Mostly family. My mom and Beanie stood in front of the same pastor. There were no bridesmaids or groomsmen, and Ned didn't pass out like last time, startling the crap out of my grandma and halting the whole wedding.

"You feel okay, Ned?" I kept bugging him. "Huh? Huh? Are you going to pass out? Huh, Ned?"

"Stop asking me that or I'm going to pound you," he said. I couldn't help it. I felt it was my purpose. I love bugging him. It makes me feel like he knows I'm around and won't forget about me, even if he wants to pound me.

I watched my mom tightly hold onto her bouquet of white flowers like I would hang on to my bag of licorice (not wanting anyone to snatch it). Like I said before, she looked like a movie star; she was so beautiful. Her dress looked scrumptious, as pink as cotton candy, and her black hair was done by a beautician – every hair in its place. She wore pearls and a giant smile. I think she put on her own mascara. Her eyes looked like Bambi, big and dark and sweet. I studied her face looking for mine, wondering if I looked like her – like Lana and Shelly did. Lana, mostly, because her hair was the same color as my mom's. But I was the only one with brown eyes. I hoped to grow up to have long legs and dark hair like my mom's too.

Beanie looked like a prince dressed in his grey suit and tie. He got his hair done too. Well, a haircut. He'd definitely shaved though because I didn't see any whiskers. Together, they looked like each side of a heart that made up a whole one. It felt really comfortable and right.

The pastor, who was dressed in a white gown, said, "I pronounce you man and wife." Then, Beanie kissed my mom. It was long and mushy. My mom wrapped her arms around his neck and, when they finished, she smiled at him and then they laughed.

"I now present Mr. and Mrs. Stephen Eugene Thompson."

We all applauded. I yelled out, "Mr. and Mrs. SET!"

My mind went on a scavenger hunt, remembering so many things that happened that last year on Grand Avenue. I tried to figure out my favorite memory. I couldn't decide if it was the day that man brought

Migo home and she ate a can of sardines I gave her, or when my brother was nice to me, taking the yellow jacket stinger out of my foot, or Beanie taking us for pizza and letting me order whatever I wanted, or my dad giving me a dollar for every A I got in school. As I watched my mom and Beanie walk down the aisle toward the front church doors, we all started to follow them. My thoughts landed on that day when, at school, we were playing in the bathroom and my finger slipped into the closing big door and got crushed; I screamed as the kids pushed harder on the other side to keep us in, not knowing my finger was stuck. When they finally stopped, I pulled my finger out, and it was bloody and bent. The nurse called my mom to come get me and take me to the doctor to see if my fourth finger on my right hand was broken. That's the one that got caught. I waited for her in front of school. She left work early to come get me. She drove up along the curb and jumped out of the car, rushing to check on me. "Let me see." She looked worried.

"Are you okay, sweetheart?" she asked me. She studied my expression, making sure she couldn't find any hurt still hiding.

"Yes. Just a little shaken up, Mom. They were pushing really hard on the door, and I thought they'd never stop," I told her.

She looked at my finger and told me that everything would be alright. Then, she kissed it to make it feel better. Even though it didn't work, it was the thought that counted when you were hurting. She helped me into the car, and we went to the doctor. He said I would live, that it wasn't broken just badly bruised. My mom sighed in relief.

Instead of taking me home and going back to work, she asked me if I was hungry. I was. She took me to my favorite spot, the Mighty Bite on Ojai Avenue. It was a tiny hamburger place with a long counter in the arcade across from Libbey park; it had tiny burgers and the best French fries I had ever tasted.

Watching her look at Beanie, the joyful expression on her face as they walked to the church doors starting this new life – she had the same look when she looked at me that day. I remembered sitting at the counter, eating my favorite mighty bite burger, talking about school and laughing about how silly I was to be playing hide and seek in the bathroom, and how I'm lucky I still had ten fingers. I felt at ease. Safe. We laughed and she made me feel better. My finger was throbbing, yet I felt really happy. My mom looked really happy too. And seeing her that way made me happy. I had the same feelings as that morning when she shared her trout with me and no one was awake but us. Mostly, I felt loved. I felt my mom loved me.

The reception took place on the terrace of the Ojai Valley Inn. We were all there, including some of her friends and the tennis pro who she once dated in high school. I know because I took lessons with him a few times; he told me once that he and my mom went to a dance together and did the jitterbug, which wasn't a bug at all, but the dancers acted like they had bugs crawling all over them and wanted to get them off, I think. So, they jittered.

The wedding cake had two layers. It was a lemon cake with white frosting. I like white cake. Lemon cake is my second favorite. On top of the cake were white flowers. My mom and Beanie stood together and held onto a knife with their right hands and cut the cake. Lana and Thad did the same thing. I asked why people did that at wedding parties, and Shelly told me it's symbolic to being a team or something. Usually, there's more people on a team unless it's tennis doubles or ice skating.

The party lasted a little over an hour before we all had to go pack our stuff and head to Los Angeles Airport to board a plane to Seattle. Lana and Thad had driven to our house and put Migo and Snowball in cat carriers and my tortoise, Harvey, in a hatbox. They poked holes in the top so he could breathe. There were lots of tears when we said our goodbyes to Lana, Shelly and Grandma. We were moving to where the bluest skies were and leaving part of our family behind to catch up with us, one day soon, and live there too.

Ron, Jane, Ned, Beanie, my mom, and I all got in a car that Beanie had rented with the two cats and Harvey, and we drove through Oxnard and down the coast on Pacific Coast Highway to the airport.

I remember it was a beautiful day, and the sunshine danced on the waves as we drove along the ocean, making a jewel box of diamonds. We passed Leo Carrillo, and all the memories of camping there whizzed through my mind.

Once we got to the airport, Beanie dropped us on the curb where these men who look like airplane captains (called porters) checked our bags and our cats. I hung onto the hatbox hoping no one would look inside and see Harvey – and just think that it was a hat that needed holes to breathe. The stewardess never asked to see what was in the hatbox sitting on my lap. She just gave me any pop I wanted and a little pack of peanuts. Later, the stewardess served us TV dinners and more pop. I had never been on a plane before. I sat next to the window, next to Jane. We were on Western Airlines, the only way to fly, in first class, which means we were in the front of the plane. It was like being in a flying movie theatre, with rows of seats. The only thing missing was the movie and popcorn.

When we took off, my heart started to pound really fast. I'm not sure if it's because I was excited or I was scared. As we flew over the ocean, I watched as the airport got smaller and was left behind. I could see the marina and boats in the harbor. People were on the beaches – umbrellas too. I saw the P.O.P. pier and the roller coaster. Some girl was in the front holding her hands up in the air, going over the bumps. I could see the Ferris wheel on the Santa Monica pier. It got smaller as the plane went up and past. Stretching, I took one last look over my shoulder at Los Angeles, hoping to see Disneyland. But I couldn't see the Matterhorn. Too much smog, I think.

Right then, I knew my life would never be the same. I had started to understand what my mom was trying to tell me. Seattle would be a do-over.

I've flown back to Los Angeles to see my dad a few times already. I went for a weekend in July and I just came back from two weeks being with him. I saw the same stewardesses on the Western Airline plane. They took really good care of me because I was an unaccompanied minor. I swam in my dad's pool. I saw my Aunt Ru and Uncle Sal. I saw five movies – *Easy Rider, Take the Money and Run, Hello Down There, Staircase,* and *How to Commit Marriage.* They were good. That's what we do, me and my dad. We go to as many movies as I want to. The first thing I say when I get off the plane is, "What's playing, Dad?" – even before I say "Hi" or "I missed you, Dad." He takes me to whichever one I want. It's really nice. I can't wait for *The Computer Wore Tennis Shoes* to come out. I saw the poster for it. I love Kurt Russell. He was so good in *The Horse in the Gray Flannel Suit.* I saw that last year. He's so cute. I want to marry him one day when I'm grown up.

Going to L.A. is fun. It's so different from Seattle. Seattle has a big lake called Lake Washington. You can see big mountains in the east, and there are hills and lots of trees – big redwood trees, like in a forest. There aren't as many people in Seattle as in Los Angeles, but there are more than in Ojai. And it rains a lot, but I don't mind. We still go out and play, or go swim in the lake. Seattle doesn't have a big sandy beach like Los Angeles. I went to the Santa Monica beach and rode the waves on my raft. I had a blast until I got stung by a jellyfish. It hurt like when I got stung by the yellow jacket, except my leg didn't blow up like my foot did. I knew it could happen because jellyfish were spotted in the water. When I felt the electrical burn, like I was dumb enough to stick my finger in a socket, I ran out of the water, back to the beach, and collapsed on the sand in pain. Have you ever been stung by a jellyfish? It hurts! My dad tried to make the pain go away, but you can't. You just have to cry until you stop.

Some kid, who had been bugging me all day about using my raft every time I came in from the surf to rest, came up to me when I was sitting on the sand crying in pain, staring at the three little dots on my leg where the tentacles got me. I thought she felt sorry for me and wanted to see if I was okay. Except, she said, "Can I use your raft now?" I said she could and to watch out for the jellyfish.

After the two weeks in Los Angeles, I flew back to Seattle to finish out summer and start getting ready for the fourth grade (which starts in a few weeks). I will be going to Mcgilvra Elementary School, which only takes five minutes to walk to from my house; you cross the golf course, go through a fenced area, and then through a gate into the schoolyard. It's a big building that has three stories, with all the classrooms inside. I think it's because of all the rain; maybe they don't want you to go outside from classroom to class and get wet and track it inside. The bluest skies may be in Seattle but so is a lot of rain. Mcgilvra is not a school like in Los Angeles, or Canoga Park, or Ojai, where there are many one-story buildings with blue doors and lots of windows. Mcgilvra is a schoolhouse made of brick and stone, and it has a big schoolyard for recess and playing dodge ball.

I'm really looking forward to starting my new school and making more new friends. Kara is excited too. My mom took me shopping, and I have all new clothes, and shoes, and knee highs. I bought some paper and pencils down at Ken Lindley's, the pharmacy in Madison Park where we live. Everything's going to be okay, I think. I think that I'm safe here in Seattle. The people are really nice to me, except Mean Ned. He got in trouble last week for throwing a firecracker at me when I was below his bedroom window in the driveway, playing basketball. It popped by my bad ear that I've had ear infections in, and I told my mom and she yelled at him.

In the meantime, I'm enjoying my new life in Seattle. Besides Ned being a butt sometimes, it's really calm here. I feel a kind of peace I never knew before. I feel like whatever happened to me on Grand Avenue doesn't have to follow me to Seattle. I will always think of Grand Avenue as a grand avenue, still.

21 BACK SEAT

STUFF HAPPENS TO YOU WHEN YOU'RE A KID. IT'S NOT ALL BAD BUT SOME of it is. It can haunt you in your dreams, or make you shake, or sweat, or make your heart beat fast like a card in the spoke of a bike wheel – flipping through fast, the faster you peddle. And you can't speak about it because who are you going to tell? Who wants to tell on themself? Who wants to get grounded for being bad even though you know you didn't do it first. It still eats at you like maggots on a dead bird.

In Seattle, like I said, things seem safer. I don't know why. It's different. I feel protected, except when my mom and Beanie go out to dinner and I stay alone in the house and hear a sound and run across the street to the Robertson's because I'm scared. That's kid stuff, I know, but I'm still a kid. I have this wild imagination from seeing too many movies, thinking the boogie man is going to get me. The boogie man didn't ever come for me at night. He came in the daylight, in front of our house, in an old Ford, in tan work boots stained with grass.

Basements can look different depending on whose house you are in. I'm sometimes afraid to go into the basement of our house. I never had a basement before. They're dark. But I go because in the storage room is a refrigerator and when you open it, it's filled with every kind of soda pop you can think of. Every single one. Orange pop, Coke, cherry Coca Cola, Mountain Dew, Fresca (yuck), ginger ale, something called TAB that my mom and Beanie like to drink (and tastes like aspirin), and my very favorite, root beer.

I was down there the other day, deciding on which pop I wanted to drink. It took me a few minutes because the selection is like an ice cream truck menu. I decided on root beer because there were only a couple left, and I wanted to get one before they were gone. I popped the cap, took a sip, and took a moment, wandering back into the storage room (which is really big). It smells musty, like wet towels under a sink. It isn't decorated like the other room where the television sits. It's dark and has a maroon cement floor. There are skis, golf clubs, lots of boxes, and odds and ends. Some are from when we moved from Ojai that still haven't been unpacked. There was one box that was slightly opened and it had "photographs" written on top of it. The tape that held it closed was splitting, and it took just one tug to unfold the top open. I took a swig of my root beer, set it on another box, and pushed the flaps away to get a better look inside.

I could see lots of photos and piles of little yellow boxes the color of taxi cabs. On the side of one of the yellow boxes, it said, "family movie - 1964." My dad had a movie camera. I remember him shooting family movies, but I wasn't sure which one this could be. At least my mom still had them. My dad thought she had thrown them all away. Yet, there they were in this box, neatly piled on top of each other, hidden in another box like on purpose – like it was a secret meant to be buried like a dead cat.

I rummaged around in the box looking at different photos from when my dad lived with us, remembering picnics at Griffith Park and the zoo, playing in the Chatsworth train tunnel, banging pots and pans on New Year's Eve, hiking in Ojai, and that day when the man with the black and white spotted pony came down Kittridge Street; he took your picture on the pony with you all dressed in a cowboy outfit, chaps, and a cowboy hat. I was five the day that picture was taken. I know that because I can remember – and I'm holding up five fingers. All these pictures were tucked in the box, piled there, from when I had a whole family on Kittridge Street.

I rummaged through the photographs a bit more, digging under the pile, and pulled one out as if it was a deck of cards and a magician was doing a magic trick, asking me to pick a card. It was a big photo of Ned, or so I thought. Looking closer, I realized that it wasn't Ned, but it looked exactly like him. This Ned, or the man in the photo who looked like Ned, was a lot older and looked like Ned's big brother. I turned the photo over and there was some writing in pen: 'Edwin Murphy, Ojai, 1948.' Edwin. He had the same first name as my brother; his real name is Edwin. I flipped it back over and took one last look at the picture: the eyes and nose were so similar; the only difference was that the Ned in the photo had thinning hair, but my brother still had all of his. I tucked the photo back in the box under the pile so no one would know it had been disturbed and closed the box so no one knew I was there.

I picked up my root beer, walked to the door and turned off the light; shutting the storage door, I then headed back upstairs. I decided to never think about that photo again, leaving the memory buried in that box and never speak of it; I wanted to forget the face of that man whose picture lived in a box on Kittridge Street, Detroit Street, Grand Avenue, and all the other streets my mom, Lana, Shelly, and Ned had lived on before. I knew who Edwin Murphy was before I got to the top of our basement stairs. I knew because Ned looked like him, like Lana looks like my mom. I decided to not speak of what I saw at all.

Beanie's brother is named Fred. It rhymes with Ned. In July, we flew to Minneapolis to visit my new uncle and aunt and two cousins. Minneapolis summers are very hot. The city has ten thousand lakes. I saw one. And, there are lots of potholes in the streets. They say it's because it is freezing cold in the winter and super-hot in the summer. The streets don't like the change in temperature. But who really does? I don't like being hot one minute, then cold the next. Mostly, we went to Minneapolis because Beanie was buying a new Cadillac from his brother, and we were driving it back to Seattle. The Cadillac is big like my dad's Thunderbird. But it's black, not blue, with an off-white convertible top and tan seats. It's the most beautiful car I have ever seen, and I've seen a lot of cars. I can't wait to be big and one day drive it when I have my license. I will put the top down and let the wind blow my hair in my face. I bet I will be a good driver and drive that Cadillac like Mario Andretti.

We left Minneapolis early in the morning and drove from Minneapolis to Seattle through Yellowstone Park. It took four days. As we left Minnesota, we drove along a freeway where there were a gazillion frogs crossing the road. My mom said it looked like a locust of frogs. All I could hear was the thumping under the car. They were everywhere. It was terrible. I love frogs, but there was nothing Beanie could do. They had lousy timing, crossing the road. A million frogs in a blender.

The next day we got to Yellowstone. Yellowstone has no stones that are yellow. I didn't see any, and I looked hard. I don't know why they call it that. They should call it Rockstone, or Bedrock, like the Flintstones. That would be funny. Yellowstone Park is the most beautiful place. It's like Yosemite but bigger. It not a park. It's a world and goes on forever, like the universe. We saw Old Faithful, a big geyser, shoot out of the ground. It was boss. We saw moose in the long grass with their big furry horns, and lots of deer. I've seen deer before. Remember when Shelly coaxed the deer into our cabin and my mom got mad?

We were driving on a road and all of these cars were stopped. People were out of their cars taking pictures of two bear cubs sitting in the grass. They were so cute. I asked my mom if we could stop and get out of the car and look.

"No," she said. "It's dangerous. If there are two cubs, Audrey, that means the mama bear is somewhere very close."

"Why is it dangerous if the mama bear is close to her cubs?" I asked. That seemed like it would be a good thing and not bad for a mommy to be close to her babies.

"Because she wants to protect her cubs and will see the people as a threat – she could attack them." My mom looked very serious and concerned.

"That would be very bad, Mom," I said.

"Promise me you will never do anything like that," she said.

"I promise."

Beanie slowly drove by so we could look at the baby bears. I never saw the mama bear. I hope she didn't get mad and hurt any of the people who were taking pictures and movies of her babies. Bears have big claws. I wished that the mama bear just knew that many people aren't mean and didn't want to hurt anything; I hoped she understood that they just thought her babies were cute. That's what I said to myself in my mind. I hope she heard me.

I woke up from a nap in the car and saw my mom was driving. They must have changed when I was conked out because Beanie was sleeping in the front seat. I didn't feel well.

"Mom . . . I don't feel well," I said. I felt chilly.

"Hang on a second. I'm concentrating," she said.

"On what?" I asked.

I could see her tightly gripping the steering wheel and sitting slightly forward, focusing on the road. There was a Mac truck in the right lane, just in front of the Cadillac, and behind the Mac truck was a blue Chevrolet. The man driving looked really mad. He was looking over at our car, and I could see his mouth moving.

"That man looks mad, Mom," I told her.

"Yes, I know. He cut me off about ten minutes ago. Now, I've him boxed in," she said. She was keeping up with the speed of the big truck so the Chevrolet couldn't get out from behind, and pull into our lane. I learned that day that my mom could be very competitive and you never wanted to cross her when she was driving a big car on a highway in the middle of Wyoming. Maybe you never wanted to cross her at all. Maybe that's where my fear hid. It's probably why I sometimes didn't trust that she loved me; I made her mad before and she could box me in and shut me out, like she did that car.

We stopped at a diner to eat and use the bathroom. It was a long drive still and bathroom stops were part of the trip. I went into the bathroom with my mom, and before I could sit on the toilet, she pulled the individual pieces of toilet paper out of the dispenser thing; then, she carefully lined the toilet seat with each square, like she was dealing playing cards. One toilet paper square at a time, in a circle, until the toilet seat was covered. This wasn't the first time. She did that whenever I used a public restroom and she was with me. I asked her why. It seemed like a lot of work.

"I don't want you catching anything from the toilet seat," she told me.

"Like leprosy or a cold?" I wasn't feeling well and that was on my mind.

"Leprosy? What? Where'd you hear that? No. Germs." she said. I knew germs are on the floor because you're not supposed to eat anything once you've dropped it, and I learned that day that germs are on toilet seats in public bathrooms. I have to be honest and say that sometimes I do eat something after I've dropped it on the floor, especially if it's delicious – or candy. The only things you can't eat off the floor once you've dropped them are ice cream and pudding. Everything else you can pretty much wipe off and pretend it never happened.

I figured out what she was talking about. Cooties. She didn't want me to catch any cooties from the toilet seat and get them on her or Beanie. I watched her patiently with crossed legs, holding myself, ready to pee my pants. She put the last piece of toilet paper on the seat, laying each piece over the other like a plate of cold cuts; I pulled down my shorts and underwear and sat down on the toilet paper seat, careful not to knock off a tissue when my bottom touched it – or possibly sneeze and blow them off and have to do this all over again. My mom didn't do this for kicks. The public bathroom was enemy number one and toilet paper on the toilet seat was her secret weapon.

In the diner in Idaho, we sat in a booth near the window that looked out onto a beautiful grassland with mountains peeking out behind. I couldn't eat my food. Not because of the view. I just didn't feel well. I looked at my mom sitting next to Beanie, and they were talking and laughing and they kissed a few times. I felt invisible, to be honest. I felt like I was a ghost. It wasn't the first time on this trip. I just felt like I was in the way. Beanie looked over at me.

"Aren't you hungry, kiddo?" He smiled at me and pointed at my pancakes topped with whipped cream.

"No," I said.

"She's not feeling well," my mom told him. It was true. I still felt chilled. My mom reached across the table, stretching her arm out. "Lean forward. Let me feel your forehead." I leaned as far as I could. She put her hand over my forehead and then the back of her hand against my left cheek.

"You're warm," she said.

I felt my forehead and shivered. "I'm cold," I said.

"I think you have a fever."

My mom handed me her sweater high across the table, over my pancakes, so syrup and whipped cream wouldn't get on it. "Put this on you, Audrey." I wrapped it around my shoulders and held it tight with my hands, feeling too lousy to put my arms through the sleeves. She unsnapped her purse, dug into the bottom and pulled out a bottle of aspirin (I could see the label). She shook two tablets onto her hand and passed them to me.

"Take these," she said. She spilled two round pills into my hand. They were white. Not orange. But I got a sick feeling. Not like feeling sick. Just scared. That scared feeling that can happen in your tummy when you get a bad feeling or watch a monster movie.

"Go ahead, honey. Take them."

I hesitated, then put them in my mouth and picked up my milk. My mom turned to talk to Beanie. But I didn't drink it. I just put it to my lips and pretended to, making a milk mustache – as if I drank it and had swallowed the aspirin. I set my glass down, wiped my mustache off with my napkin like my mom had taught me a hundred million thousand times, and tucked it under my plate of uneaten pancakes.

"I'm going to go wash my hands," I said. She didn't say anything.

I scooted out of the booth and walked into the bathroom, swinging open the door that squeaked like Shorty's screen door at their farm in Northridge. I went over to the small trash can that was filled with paper towels, lifted the paper towels, and spit out the aspirin still in my mouth into the trash. My mouth tasted groady from the melting tablets. I covered the pills with the paper towels, went to the sink, washed my hands, and went back to the table.

I thought my mom was trying to poison me. I'm not sure why I thought that. We were having a good time. The trip was filled with boss scenery, and bears, and rivers, and forests. Along with Yosemite, Yellowstone was the most beautiful place I had ever seen. But my mom felt distant, like she didn't want me there. I felt alone. I thought she looked so happy with Beanie. A kind of happiness I had never seen before – not even with David. I figured I was in the way. She couldn't machine-gun me or throw me in the river with cement shoes like a James Cagney movie – that's against the law. But she could ditch me. I couldn't run that fast. Maybe Beanie wouldn't be in on it or refuse to drive the getaway car. Her only option at that point would be to put poison on the aspirin. I didn't want to die. Christmas was only five months away. So, I spit it out.

Has that ever happened to you? Am I a weirdo for thinking that? I can't imagine why my mom would want to hurt me. I just thought maybe her life would be easier if I wasn't tagging along. I know Mean Ned would like it better if I dropped dead, but my dad would be sad. So would my sisters, I think. I wonder what my mom would say if I told her that I thought she didn't want me around. I'm not going to say anything, just in case I hurt her feelings or she gets sore. Besides, you can still love something and not want it around. Old Yeller was loved by his family, but Travis had to shoot him, and he was his dog. It happens. Maybe in some way I felt like Old Yeller. I meant to be good, but something happened that made me bad. Sometimes, I feel that way, because if I was good, why would certain things have happened to me that made me feel so ashamed?

I'm ready to tell you what happened that day when Gabriel came to clean our yard on Grand Avenue. It was the day I got in the back seat of his old car, climbing onto the grey, ripped fabric that felt like a blanket covering the seat – soft like the hair on a tarantula.

When he showed up at our house that day, I never thought anything of it. I had been around Gabriel so many times before when we lived on Kittridge Street; he would come every week and mow Patrick's yard or bring Mrs. Gabriel's homemade tamales for Patrick's mom. Why would I think he could do that to me? I remember Joanne Meets screaming that time on Kittridge Street, but I never knew why. That day happened two years before, and I had long forgotten about it, I guess.

I remember a knock on the door and answering it. There was Gabriel, standing and staring at me through the screen door.

"Hi, Audrey," he said in his thick accent.

"Hi, Gabriel," I said.

"How are you, Chiquita?" He'd call me that. I'm not sure why he'd call me a banana, but I didn't mind. I like bananas.

"I'm good."

"You get bigger."

"I grew a half inch. My mom measured me." I told him.

"Muy bien. Pretty soon you be a señorita." Then he smiled. His teeth were yellow and one on the bottom was missing.

I called for my mom. "Mom! Gabriel is here!"

My mom met him outside in the front and showed him all the gardening she wanted done. I don't remember her telling him to cut down the orange tree. Maybe he misunderstood.

I followed them as they walked onto the sidewalk by his old car, which was parked in front of our house on the street; my mom explained that she wanted him to clean up the front bed, trimming the plants back. He nodded. Then, she went back in the house, and I went to the creek to catch frogs.

Later that afternoon, I wandered home the long way. I went up and around near where Roseanne lived, past Tarantula Hill, down past Topa Topa onto Grandview, past Mrs. Rolston's house to Grand Avenue – and found Gabriel still working at our house. The driveway was empty. My mom's car wasn't parked; she'd gone somewhere. Ned was at a friend's, or playing basketball, or swimming, or whatever teenagers do who know how to drive. Gabriel was working in the very front, on the sidewalk. I stood and watched him trimming the bushes for a little while. I was bored. I picked up a broom lying by his car and swept dirt on the sidewalk into a pile, being a good helper. I'd helped my dad before when he weeded the grass on Kittridge Street.

"That's good, Chiquita," Gabriel said. "You get the dustpan in my back seat."

"Sure," I said.

I walked over to his car and opened the passenger door. I had to use both of my thumbs to push the round door button in because it was too big for my hand. Pulling the door open, I felt how heavy it was – like opening a barn door. I squeezed my body into the back, between the passenger seat and the door jam; the heavy car door slammed shut on its own. I sat on the seat and looked around for the dustpan. Finding none on the seat, I checked the wheel wells where you put your feet; there was no dustpan, just a small shovel for planting flowers.

I rolled down the back window and poked my head out.

"Gabriel, I don't see the dustpan." I saw him put the rake down and walk toward the car. I sat back in the seat. He came to the window and rested his arms on the side of the car, looking in.

"Over there, Chiquita," he pointed.

I looked. I couldn't see anything in the back seat. It was empty.

"Where?" I asked.

"Justo ahi . . . there." He reached his hand through the window to point.

I was wearing blue jeans and a white, short-sleeved t-shirt covered with some dirt and grass stains from being in the creek. It felt like I sat on a nail. I wasn't sure what was happening at first, until I looked down

222

and saw his arm.

His hand went down the front of my jeans and into my underwear. I could feel his fingernail scraping my inside. It was a pain that I have never felt before, like a burning fire poker left in the coals. I remember looking up at him, and he was smiling at me; it was the kind of evil smile that you see in scary movies. I froze. I didn't know what to do.

He pressed hard inside of me. I whimpered in pain. "Shhhh . . . Chiquita. Relax." I couldn't relax. Something was terribly wrong inside of me. I heard this voice inside my head begging me to tell him to stop. The cat had my tongue, again. Instead, I reached down, grabbed his arm, pulled it out of my pants, and robotically rolled up the window, shutting him out.

My heart was beating fast. I was afraid to move. I felt terrified, like when you scream in a dream and no sound comes out; you're screaming your head off, but no one can hear you. I wasn't sure what had just happened to me, but I knew it was bad. I felt like my insides were broken. I just felt a burn and a painful throbbing that swelled. At that very moment, all I could hear was Joanne Meets screaming in my mind, and I could see her running for her car. I realized that Joanne wasn't running from a bee. She was running from Gabriel.

All I wanted to do was get out of the back seat of Gabriel's car, but I was frozen – too scared to move. He stood outside, staring in. I could see him out of the corner of my eye. I felt like a canary in a cage knowing there was a cat trying to figure out how to get me. I didn't turn my head. I kept looking at the front seat, staying real still, hoping he'd go back to raking. All I could hear was my heart beating in my ears; my breathing sounded like Lady when she loped for a distance through the orange groves.

When is he going to go rake? I didn't want him to climb in the back seat. No. *Please don't let that happen,* I thought.

I saw him move toward the car. I heard the creak of the hinges as he pulled the passenger door open. His right hand moved onto the back of the front seat; his dirty fingernails grabbed the leather. My heart stopped. He pulled the seat forward, his brown grass-stained boot stepping on the door jam. He ducked his head, about to get in. "MOM!" Looking through the front windshield, I saw my mom's car turn onto Grand Avenue. Gabriel looked and stepped back out onto the sidewalk. My mom's car stopped in front of our house, waiting to turn left into the driveway. Gabriel walked away. I jumped up, pushed the front seat forward, scrambled out of the back onto the sidewalk, and ran up to the driveway – waiting for my mom to pull in.

Her car came to a stop and turned off. She got out of the car and looked at me standing there.

"Hi, honey. How are you doing?" she asked.

"Good," I told her. I lied. I felt this burning pain, but that's what you do. You pretend everything is fine. That's what you have to do. You can't be a rat fink on yourself. I shouldn't have gotten in his back seat.

"Gabriel . . . " she said. I followed her eyes, looking beyond me. I turned, and he was standing behind me on the sidewalk. " . . . everything going well?" Frightened, I began to tremble, controlling myself as best I could. Would he say anything?

"Si, si. Ya casi termino," he said. My mom understands Spanish. My grandma and grandpa would speak Italian to my mom and my aunt and uncle; my mom said it sounded a lot like Spanish.

"Okay, let me know when you're done, and I'll give you a check."

She opened the back car door, pulled out a bag of groceries, shut the door, and headed to the porch.

"Can I come help you put the groceries away, Mom?" I asked.

"You sure?" she asked.

"Yeah, I'm sure," I said.

"Come."

I dashed to the porch and went inside, shutting the screen door and locking it. I never looked back to see if Gabriel was still standing there. I never wanted to see him again.

My mom set the groceries on the counter and began putting them away.

"What were you up to?" she asked.

"Nothing. I caught some frogs. Then I swept a little," I told her.

"That was nice of you. I'm sure Gabriel liked your help."

"I guess so."

She handed me some soup cans. "Please put these away." As I got to the cupboard, I went to open the door; I felt something. Wet. Like I peed my pants. I set the cans on the counter.

"Mom, I have to go to the bathroom."

"Okay."

I charged through the living room and went into the bathroom, locked the door and pulled down my jeans. Then, I slipped my underwear down. I stared. There was blood. A rush came over me. I was terrified. At that moment, I thought I was dying.

I yelled, "Mommy!" I grabbed some toilet paper, pressing it between my legs for a moment like you do with a cut to stop the bleeding. I wiped myself a few more times, and the blood wiped away, getting fainter. It finally stopped.

I heard my mom's voice approaching the door. "What's wrong, Audrey?" A knock. Then, I saw the doorknob jiggle. My heart just pounding. "Open the door."

"It's okay, Mom. I'm fine . . . I just thought we were out of toilet paper."

I lied. It wasn't the first time I lied. Remember when I walked into our house on Grand Avenue after seeing my dad at my grandma's house; he told me about my brother and sisters not being his real kids, but that we have the same mom — and my grandma got really upset and threw the dish towel on the floor? Well, when I got home and my mom asked me what happened with my dad and I said "nothing," it wasn't the whole truth. I lied to you. It didn't end there. I didn't walk in my room and get my suitcase or tell Ned we were leaving for the hotel. Not right away. What really, truly happened was my mom asked me what my dad said to me, and when I said "nothing" she said . . . that I better tell her what he said or she'd hit me with a belt.

I think she knew I was lying. I think my grandma may have told her before I got home. I read her face like a comic book and could tell from how dark her eyes looked that she was steaming. She hated my dad. I didn't want her to hate me too. I had to tell her the truth. I lied at first when I said I said nothing because I don't want you to be mad at her for saying that she would hit me with a belt if I didn't tell her.

"What did he say to you?" she asked me. Her voice deepened. There was nothing nice about it. I hesitated, not knowing if I should tell. I was always torn, caught in the middle of hateful things between them, using me like a pawn in a chess game; the pawn is used to protect the king and queen and is usually the first to go. I know. I play chess.

"Tell me, Audrey. I won't be mad."

"That my brother and sisters weren't really my brother and sisters," I said.

"You know that's not true. They are. That will never change," she said.

"I know."

She's not a bad person. She didn't hit me with a belt or even get one out of the closet. I think all of her belts were packed already, so she was just bluffing. She just said she would do it so I would tell her what my dad said. So I did. I told her everything.

Then, like I told you before, I went into my room, got my suitcase and told Ned we were leaving for the Ojai Valley Inn. That's how it happened. Cross my heart. No more secrets.

When the bleeding stopped and I got myself cleaned up, I took my underwear off and hid them in my closet. I waited until Gabriel left to finally go outside again. I walked next door to our neighbor's backyard and stuck my stained underwear in their incinerator, under a pile of destroyed, burnt papers. I looked at my hand, smudged from the soot, and felt as dirty as all those ashes. Later, I took a bath, hoping the pain would go away. The water stung my vagina like that yellow jacket stinger. I sat in the water and thought about Ross, and his pool party . . . and knowing what he did was mean. But Ross never did THAT to me. Gabriel was different. He sprung it on me without even asking me. I had no choice. He terrified and hurt me in a way that when the pain finally went away, the memory of him at the car window never did. And he almost got me in trouble. My mom could have found out. Sitting in the Mr. Bubble suds that went flat, and the water that turned slightly pink, I wondered what I could have done differently. All I could think of – never being born.

I don't feel that way now because I like being born. I just don't feel quite whole yet, like someone took a bite of me and put me back on the plate for someone else to eat. If I'm going to be honest and not keep any more secrets, I still feel a little broken inside. And I'm not sure ice cream or licorice can fix it. I'll just not think about it and let it go away on its own, as if it's a cold. With some rest, chicken soup and cartoons, I'll be better in no time.

22 BROADMOOR DRIVE

THE STREETS IN BROADMOOR HAVE ROUNDED CURBS THAT THE CARS CAN drive over and park on top of. The lawns are perfect. My dad would love Broadmoor, but I guess he's not welcome to live here, or something, because he's a Jew. That's weird. He's no different than anyone else. And the fact that I can't talk about him being Jewish to anyone makes me sad. What is wrong with being Jewish? My Aunt Ru and Uncle Sal are Jewish too, and they are really neato people. Milton Berle is Jewish and he's funny. So is Goldie Hawn from *Laugh-In* and Sammy Davis Jr., who's Jewish AND a black man, like Edgar. I don't understand that at all, being mean to someone because they are not the same as you.

I still like living on Broadmoor Drive. Ned does too. It's clean like Disneyland. Everything looks perfect, in a storybook way. Seattle is so different from Los Angeles or Ojai. I'm not sure how to describe it, exactly. It just feels like a dream. It even smells different. I feel like I am living in someone else's life that I read about it in a book. But it's my life now, and I really like it a lot. I hope I will like it as much as I do right now and nothing will ever make me not want to live here or be afraid.

Shelly arrived in Seattle last night. She came to visit. I am so happy to see her and have her home. I've missed her. I miss Lana too. And my dad. I think Shelly's moving here next summer. I think she wants

228

to be with her family and doesn't want to live in Los Angeles anymore. Like I told you before, my mom said she would like her to be home with us; she can go to school up here to become a dental assistant, working for a dentist. Shelly has really white teeth. She brushes them all the time and made me brush my teeth this morning too. I like that she's here to boss me.

When she came to the house last night, she was wearing a Jewish star around her neck that Joel gave her. My mom told her she needed to take it off, while she was visiting. "Why?" she asked. I was in the kitchen when my mom said that; I told Shelly that Broadmoor doesn't want Jewish people to live here and that she can't talk about dad being Jewish. The tennis club doesn't want Jewish people either, so she has to keep her trap shut about that, too. She had an expression on her face that looked like she had rusted and couldn't move; it was like she needed oiling like the Tin Man. Later, when she was in the sewing room – which also had a single bed where she would sleep – Shelly said that that was "bull . . . crap" about Broadmoor not allowing Jews to live here. She said she wasn't sure she wanted to move here after all. Actually, she used a bad word. I'm not allowed to say it. It rhymes with pit. She took off her necklace, put it in the change purse of her wallet for safekeeping, and snapped it shut. I'm glad my fingers weren't caught in the change purse. She snapped it really hard because she was peeved. I didn't tell her about Broadmoor not wanting black people to live there either. I didn't want her to have a cow and to never want to come home to Seattle again. Maybe that's selfish. I can't help it. I've missed my sister, just like I miss Lana too.

In Broadmoor, a kid doesn't have to worry about playing in the street and getting hit by a car. You still have to look both ways so you don't get out of the habit. I remember when I was almost hit on Detroit Street and I got grounded. My mom still grounds me for that kind of stuff. The other day, we rode the back bumper of the milk truck. You have to sneak on when the milkman isn't looking. I jumped off when it was moving. You can't jump off backward or you'll fall on your face. If you want to jump off a milk truck while it is driving down the street, you have to put your back to the truck and step off the bumper. Just step off. It's easy. Don't be a scaredy-cat. Speaking of milk, I saw my brother sneak through the milk box again, in the cupboard by the back door. It was at almost 7 in the morning, last Sunday. I think he was just getting home. The front door was locked, for some reason; we never lock our doors. After he slipped through, he put his finger over his lips for me to keep a secret. He put everything back in the cupboard that he took out so he was able to slide through without breaking anything. He went up to his room and slept until three o'clock in the afternoon.

I decided I won't tell on him unless I really need to for something – like if he's mean to me. That's how it works. You keep secrets for your mean brother like it's money in your savings account. When you decide that you want to buy something really badly, you use it. I call it my *Big Fink Savings and Loan*. I'm getting rich, I tell you. I'm a snoop and a light sleeper, so I know when he sneaks in the house. Ned better watch his P's & Q's and not throw any more firecrackers or pillows at me – or I'll sink his battleship.

"Sweet Caroline", my favorite song, is playing on the radio. I love its upbeat tempo. It's a cheerful, boss song that captures my summer like you capture a butterfly in a jar; you get to see how beautiful it is and then let it go so some other kid can catch it. "Good times never seemed so good." It's true. Not just for Sweet Caroline and Neal Diamond, but for me too.

The summer has been magical in Seattle. Like I told you . . . a dream. Sunny and warm. It does rain though. Like in Camelot. If it's warm out and if you're already wet from swimming in the lake, it doesn't matter if you get wet from the rain.

I love our neighborhood, Madison Park. They call it a village. It's down the street from Broadmoor, at the end of Madison Avenue, on the lake. It has a hardware store that has candy bars at the counter, the minimart, where you can buy all sorts of candy, and it's where we like to call in pranks (like I told you). "Hey, is your refrigerator running? Well, you better catch it!" I wonder how many times the clerk has heard that one? There's the IGA grocery store, which is another place for buying candy. Also, Ken Lindley's, who lives down the street from our house; he has a pharmacy where I like to go buy toothpaste, or a toy, or candy. I can charge it to a house account because they trust that my mom and Beanie will pay for it. The hardware store and IGA are the same, with charge accounts, because I guess people don't have any cash here in Madison Park and have to charge everything.

I learned to waterski the other day. Beanie has a speedboat, and we all went boating on Lake Washington. When it was my turn, I sat in the water with the lifebelt around my waist and the rope between my two skis. He dragged me slowly for a second to get me just right. When I was ready, I yelled, "HIT IT!" He punched the throttle and pulled me out of the water on two skis. He said I was a really good waterskier, seeing my mom never could get up. Well, she did for a second, then when she fell, she hung onto the rope and looked like a submarine torpedoing through the water. Beanie was yelling, "Let go of the rope! Let go of the rope!" She finally did, climbed back into the boat, exhausted, and said she had enough of waterskiing.

She's a better driver, anyhow. Beanie bought my mom a convertible yellow Datsun 2000 as a wedding present. I think that's the only reason to get married. You get boss stuff. The bummer is that it was wrecked by my uncle's car last week, in the middle of the night. "Welcome to Seattle, Shelly," my mom said. I guess my uncle's Oldsmobile rolled from their house up the street and crashed into my mom's new car, stopping it from going down 'Devil's Dip,' the hill we live on. That's the story. My mom said he was probably drunk and forgot to put it in park or rammed the car himself and ditched it before being discovered. Beanie said he'd get the car fixed so it looks brand new. That's the only real bad excitement that's happened all summer. At least it can be fixed. That's the boss thing about breaking a car. You can fix it, and no one can see the damage.

In a few weeks, I start fourth grade. I am very excited even though I found out they're putting me back in third-grade math. I'm not sure why. My mom told me that they said California's math is different from Seattle's and that they don't want me to get behind. But I'm going into third-grade math when I will be in the fourth grade. That's already behind. Isn't math the same everywhere? Oh well, I don't get it. Kids don't have much say in these matters. "You can't fight city hall," as my mom sometimes says. I'm not sure exactly what that means, or where city hall is, but I'm going to take her word for it.

I was down in the foyer looking for a pencil in the desk. I wasn't being noisy or anything (like I sometimes can be). Rummaging around in the back of the drawer, I found some pictures. I started flipping through them. I saw some pictures of David. Then, I saw our duplex on Detroit Street. It looked like it was a picture of the living room but like it had been turned upside down and shaken. Everything was broken and laying on the floor. The living room looked like Kansas when the tornado came through at Dorothy's Auntie Em's house and blew everything down. I remembered back when my Aunt Ru came to get me at school. Not the day Lana came to get me and we went to the hospital to see David before he died. It was another day, before my mom and dad got divorced and my mom married David.

I remember I had to go straight to Mrs. Porter's house. I think that's why my aunt took me straight there and not home. I think my dad must have been there earlier, and they had to clean up the big mess they made fighting and didn't want me to see it.

I know my mom and dad were very unhappy. They fought too much. They yelled at each other all the time. My dad would leave and not come back for days. When they finally separated and divorced, I was relieved. I was. Because it's no fun being around people who don't get along or who are mean to each other. I am happy my mom found David. I am happy my mom found Beanie. I can tell you that I'm really happy because everyone is calm and has a spring in their step now. Our life is different. It's more quiet, like going from a raging river to a lake early in the morning when there's no breeze and it looks like glass – with nothing disturbing it. Maybe the only person who isn't happy is my dad because he misses me and Ned, and he can't see us all the time like he used to. But it's better this way. It's better not to be in a war zone in your house. Just like all those army men who need to come home to their families so they can be safe again. War solves nothing. War destroys. Especially when the war is in your house and you can't escape.

I'm going to be ten years old in six months. I'm growing up. I'm going to a new school. Again. I think a lot about stuff that happened or could happen. Bad things happen to people every day. You stub your toe on the sidewalk, or your mean brother throws firecrackers at you, or someone calls you a butt, or I see the pictures of war with soldiers who have died and know that their families are crying, or my neighbor's dog gets hit by a car, or you're swallowing your tooth by accident and not getting any money for it from the Tooth fairy. But you know what? Life goes on. You have to just put one foot in foot in front of the other . . . look for the bear necessities. The bear necessities of life. You know that song, don't you?

You have to be Mowgli in *Jungle Book*. Be a bear, not a cub. Sometimes, you get pricked or hurt. You can't let it get you down. You can say, "What a big bummer" or "I'm throwing in the towel." Whatever that means. I know if you fall off your horse, you get right back on. You have to not be afraid. That's what Edgar taught me, when I fell off of Lady once and he told me to get back on and ride like it never happened.

I can try to forget it all, but I can't. My memory has a mind of its own. As a truce, I decided instead to just think about it differently. I know the truth, still. I don't have to always think about it that way. I can write a new story to remember. I can use my imagination.

So, this is how I remember those times that I wish I could change:

It's 1966. I'm at Parker's house with Shelly. My mom and dad show up at the door after being at a cocktail party. They are happy. They come in and ask what we're watching. I tell them, "The Wizard of Oz." My mom thinks that's boss. Then Shelly walks in from outside and tells Paul we're heading out. I tell

Parker I'll see him tomorrow. And we all leave, like a whisper. No yelling. Like cool cats.

My mom is walking down the street with Shelly, with her arm wrapped around her shoulder. They're talking and laughing. I can see them clearly. I'm walking behind with my dad; he's holding my hand, and I'm carrying my Chatty Cathy doll in my other hand. It's a calm, slow stroll down the street on another hot summer night in the Valley. I can hear the crickets. I can hear a dog bark. It's peaceful like the creek when the sun is going down and the frogs have gone back to their lily pads to get some sleep.

We get home and we're in the living room talking about going to Ojai on the weekend. Mean Ned isn't home. But if he was, in this story, he'd be just Ned. He wouldn't be a butt to me or try to kill me with his heavy pillow. He'd let me play his drums. Maybe even teach me a rudiment. That's what drumming stuff is called. Lana would be home and not in Acapulco with another family. She wouldn't want to leave to go to Mexico to be with another family because our own is too fun.

Before heading to bed, my mom hugs Shelly and tells her, "I love you." Then they laugh about something I don't get because I'm too little to understand it. Shelly says, "I love you too, Mom." Shelly is happy. She's safe. She never has a reason to run away from home and be punished.

My dad tells me to go get ready for bed and that he loves me. My mom hugs me tightly, kissing my head; she tells me she loves me to the moon and back. I walk down the hall with Shelly. I take a look back at my mom and dad standing in the living room, and they are holding hands. They are smiling. They are calm. I know I'm going to sleep well because we're all home. There is no reason to run to Georgia's house. I know everybody's home, and there is nothing to fear but fear itself.

That's what I do. I try to think of new things, so to forget about the old stuff that hurt my heart. I don't want to live there in that place of hurt with my brain feeling scrambled if I don't have to. Why should I? I have an imagination. I should imagine, like Mrs. Rolston told me to.

"You have a wonderful imagination, Audrey. Don't be afraid to use it."

See, Gabriel did something bad to me on Grand Avenue that I never saw coming, like a car hitting you when you don't look both ways. But it's still a grand avenue, where my memories grew like the oranges all around and that are still inside of me. Maybe, they were even some of the happiest times of my life; I got straight A's in school, caught frogs in the creek, my mom fell in love with Beanie, they got married, and now we live in Seattle. Another do-over. And I'm going to make a bunch of new memories in Seattle. I already am. They don't have to be the same as before. They won't be, because everything is different. I feel safe so far. I feel like I can pick a pear with my claw. I belong here. In fact, I know I do.

The other day, I asked my mom if I could get some socks because three pairs of my white ones had holes in them, and my mom couldn't see them in my shoes (unless she had x-ray vision). She knelt down, like Lana always did, to make sure I was paying attention. I hoped I wasn't asking for too much, but it's uncomfortable when your toe is sticking out of a sock.

"What kind of socks do you want, sweetheart? I'll buy you any colors."

"Really?" That was a curveball. I scored. I wasn't sure how many colors socks came in, but I was excited. "Can I get white ones and blue ones and orange ones, if they have them?" I like orange again.

"You can get as many colors as they have," she told me.

I must have had a weird look on my face because then she said to me, "Don't look so suspicious, you." I kinda did. I remembered she looked down for a second. I thought maybe she was looking for the hole in my sock. Then she looked up at me again with a very serious face. I thought I might have said something wrong.

"Listen, Audrey, I know things weren't always easy for you kids . . . and that was my fault. Sometimes, us grown-ups make mistakes and can make things worse."

"Like when I put too much chocolate syrup in my milk then I add more milk but it's too much and then I have to add more chocolate syrup and then I add more milk and the glass is too full and it spills over and I have to start over again?" I asked.

"That's exactly the same thing. Almost."

"I understand, Mom."

"I love you, my little püppchen. Don't ever forget that," she told me.

"Do you love Shelly?" I asked.

"I love Shelly very much," she told me.

"And do you love Lana too?"

"Yes. I love Lana too."

I thought a moment.

"What about Mean Ned? Do you love him as much as me?" I wasn't sure she did because he can be a butt.

"I love your brother, Ned, too. I love all of you kids so very much. So, don't worry about that. I want you to stop worrying, Audrey. Everything is going to be okay. Okay?" she told me.

"Okey-dokey, Mom." Then, she hugged me tightly, kissed me on my forehead, and pushed my hair away. She looked at me in a mushy way, and her brown eyes sparkled like the sunshine does on waves in Malibu.

"How about you go put on that pretty flower dress Aunt Ru sent you? We're going downtown to Nordstrom Best to buy you some socks."

I was so happy because I knew right then that my mom loved me and wanted my socks to not have any more holes; I knew things would be different, in a good way.

Remember when I told you that story about the dream I had before we moved from Grand Avenue to Broadmoor Drive that had the lady with red hair in it – standing at the top of the stairs? And she was welcoming me to my new house? I told you I didn't know who she was because she wasn't Nanette Fabray, or Sandy Duncan, or Lucille Ball. She was a lady I had never seen before . . . until today. I was snooping in my brother's and Ron's room. They share a room. It smells like dirty socks and boy sweat because they both throw their clothes on the floor and don't stick them down the laundry chute. They also like to put their dirty dishes under their beds instead of in the kitchen sink where they belong.

I was looking for a pencil. Not really, I wasn't. I was snooping because I like to do that sometimes, looking for loose change or candy. I sometimes go into my mom's purses that she isn't using, looking for loose change so I can buy some licorice or gum.

Bored and feeling that magnet thing that sometimes happens, I decided to snoop in their room and found a photo album on the bookshelf. I thought it was Mean Ned's and wanted to see if he had any pictures of me – and if he scribbled my face out like I do sometimes with his pictures when I'm mad at him. I opened the photo book and saw there were pictures of Ron and Jane when they were smaller. All sorts of photos. In one photo in particular, there was a picture of a woman standing next to Beanie. He had his arm around her. Ron and Jane were standing in front of them. Ron looked more like her than Jane. It was their mom, who had died, like David died.

And her hair was red.

How would I know that she had red hair? I couldn't know. I think she came to me in my dream because she knew I needed to know that I don't need to be afraid anymore – that I'm finally home. I'm somewhere where there is no reason to wake up in the middle of the night and feel alone, or where a war is happening in a faraway garden with palm trees, or in our living room. There's no Big Bad Wolf to blow our new house down, because it's made of brick. I can rest. I can just be a kid. Do-overs are not repeats and I can make up my own story if I use my imagination.

Everything is going to be okay. My mom said so.

And you know what?

I have this boss feeling she's right.

The End.

ACKNOWLEDGEMENTS

This book is a love letter to myself . . . and to my sister, Charmaine, and my brother, Chuck, because we have come so far from places that only seem like they were dreamt. We shared in the shadows of growing pains etched by beautiful and painful memories. Complicated, like most families. Yet, purposeful in their teaching. My family shaped me in all ways that root me today, no matter whatever joy or sorrow we endured . . . my siblings, including my sweet sister Melissa, my beautiful mother and endearing father and my stepfather Wonderful Warren – as they four look over me – and equally blessed me with this life for which I will be forever grateful. I couldn't have chosen a better family to guide me through this journey of twists and turns and plot lines, no matter what was dealt to us. We are survivors because of all of it. We are better because of each other.

I wish to thank my editor, Adam Strange, and Strange Media, with whom this book would not be possible; a kismet collaboration, who sparked to my words and believed in its story telling as it was written and trusted that it should be told by a nine-year-old girl, because it was important to me that Audrey tell HER story and her voice not be diminished. You agreed. And for your tempered ease and guidance that made this process so hopeful and joyful. I am also grateful to you and for you.

To my dear friend Wendy Holden who lead me to Adam – in the middle of a night writing course for me, UK time – and who has been an inspiration to me over the years through her illustrious career as an author, her beautiful books and poignant storytelling, and her kind, kindred friendship.

And, I give thanks to my English and Creative writing teachers, from middle school through high school – Sister Marcia O'Dea, Mary Moeschler and Mary Anne Callaghan Buerge who taught me at Forest Ridge School. I was paying attention. And using my imagination, like Mrs Rolston instilled in me.

Finally, I wish to acknowledge Jim Kiehl who was my freshman creative writing teacher at Skidmore College and who was the very first person to tell me that I was a writer. It took me 40 years to believe him. I am grateful for his words, his encouragement and I will never forget them, nor, him.

I present this book with no regrets or shame. In the words of Anne Lamott, words that ring in my head like a bell of freedom and that I use as a daily mantra: 'You own everything that happened to you. Tell your stories. If people wanted you to write warmly about them, they should have behaved better.'

ABOUT THE AUTHOR

Mandy Goodwin has been in the entertainment industry for nearly 40 years.

She secretly always wanted to be a novelist.

The secret is out.

She resides in the PNW.

CPSIA information can be obtained
at www.ICGtesting.com
Printed in the USA
LVHW010307200721
693160LV00006B/951